SHADE

SHADE

ALL THEY HAD TO DO
WAS CATCH HIM

CHAD NICHOLAS

This book is dedicated to Nami,
the best German shepherd in the world.

"You either die a hero,
or live long enough to see yourself
become the villain."

–*Harvey Dent*

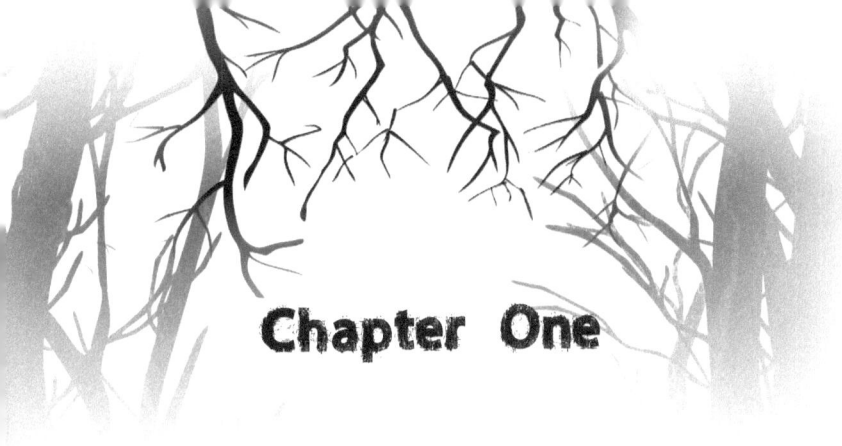

Chapter One

The six agents stood at the edge of the forest, guns shaking in their hands. The night was deathly quiet, and so dark and lifeless it almost appeared empty, with only the sound of their own breathing to remind them they were still awake, still alive. So far. To combat the all-consuming darkness, they clicked on the lights attached underneath the barrels of their weapons, each one projecting little glimpses of light within the trees, illuminating bark, leaves, and a trail leading into the heart of the forest.

A trail of blood.

One agent looked back, taking a final glance at the house behind him. Light shone through its white curtains, revealing the house within–the house they had been called to investigate. The house they had found empty.

As he turned back to the forest, his eyes once again stayed focused on the blood. He knew what it meant: something was waiting for them inside the

forest, within the trees. Something they wouldn't be able to escape from.

Deep down, they all knew.

Which was why they continued to stand on the edge, outside of the trees, outside of the danger-trained agents acting like children afraid of their own closets, for fear of the unknown horror that hid within.

Bulletproof vests draped over their chests, enveloping them in a shield of safety, and large black riot gear helmets mounted their heads, making them appear larger, more imposing than they actually were, just like a defenseless animal who tries to make itself look threatening so that maybe, just maybe, the bear won't devour it.

Defenseless, however, they were not. Armed to the teeth, each agent had a pistol holstered to their side as a backup, and either a Benelli shotgun or an AR-15 rifle rested in their hands; each weapon was equipped with a tactical flashlight as well as a green laser sight, and they carried enough ammo to fend off a small army.

But it wouldn't be enough. Not if they found what they were expecting in there. Not if they found him.

"Eyes up." The words came from the agent in charge—code-named Alpha—who tried to force himself to sound calm. "We don't know for sure

what's in there, so no one shoot until we have confirmation." He wanted that part to be clear at least. They didn't know what was in there. They knew who, and they thought they knew why, but they had to be sure. 'Maybe we're wrong,' the agent thought. 'Maybe the blood doesn't mean what it appears to. It's possible. Sure, we could be wrong.'

He prayed they were.

"Let's go," he finally said, taking his first cautious step forward. The rest followed, and soon, they had entered the dark forest, their boots crunching the brittle leaves beneath them. Hollow trees seemed to stretch on forever, surrounding them like vultures ready to witness a slaughter and take the carcasses for themselves.

They followed the trail of blood as best they could, but it was scarce. More distance was growing between every crimson-painted leaf, and the trees seemingly began inching closer together, as if the forest itself was trying to suffocate them, keep them from progressing, from moving farther into its heart.

Alpha drew a deep breath. If they continued at this rate, they wouldn't find anything until morning, and if they were right about what was in there, it would be too late by then.

If it wasn't already.

"Split up," he said. "Groups of two. Delta, take Echo, sweep right." Delta was a big guy, practically a giant, highly trained and fearless. Alpha tried to hope that it would make a difference. "Charlie, you're with Foxtrot." He pointed left, knowing it was unlikely that the blood would lead that way, hoping they would find nothing. Charlie was tough, rugged, not easily put down, whereas Foxtrot had the quickest draw time Alpha had ever seen, almost as if he was a gunslinger pulled straight from the old west. But they were also young, inexperienced. If they found what they were looking for, it would be a massacre.

The agents turned to look at him, trying to hide the fear in their eyes behind the black visors of their helmets. But he saw it nonetheless.

He didn't blame them. He heard it too, the voice in his head telling him to run while he still could. But he also knew it wasn't a choice they could make. They had to find him before something worse happened. Before he did what they thought he had come here to do.

Bravely, he took one step forward, signaling to the agent on his left, Bravo, to follow him. "Stay on coms. Check in every minute. If you find blood, say something, and we will move to your location. And if you see him, don't engage. No matter what, don't engage."

His voice managed to come out strong; years in the field had granted him at least a calm voice in the midst of terror. But the same didn't apply to his hands. He fought hard to control them, but they were shaking so badly it was causing the light to flare back and forth, distorting their path even further.

"Sir?" Bravo asked, concerned.

"I'm fine," he lied, keeping his eyes on the ground as they progressed further, looking for any hint of blood, anything to lead them to him. Because it wasn't just about finding him. It was about finding him before he did it—what they thought he had come here to do. Because maybe, if the line hadn't yet been crossed, they would be okay. Maybe then they could talk him down. But if not?

If not, he didn't think they would be leaving the woods.

Jagged pieces of bark sliced at his shoulders, trying to grab him in the darkness as he moved between the trees. Suddenly, there was a noise to his left. The faint crackling of a branch. From the low volume of the noise, he knew it was just a small animal, most likely a squirrel, but his adrenaline was racing, borderline spiking, as was that of the agent beside him. They both swung around, training their guns on the perpetrator, seeing that their instincts were right. It was just a squirrel, bent over a fallen branch, unaware of the carnage that was about to ensue.

"Sir," Delta's voice whispered over the speaker, "I found something."

"What?"

"Blood, sir. It's everywhere."

The two agents stared at the blood, their feet frozen in place.

"Stay where you are," Alpha instructed over the coms, and they would have been happy to oblige had it not been for the breathing they heard in front of them.

Slow and methodical, it almost sounded like wind twisting through the trees, calling to them. They looked at each other and slowly nodded their heads in agreement. They wouldn't go far, just enough to investigate the breathing. Truth be told, they thought it was in their imagination.

It wasn't.

Both carrying shotguns, they kept the barrels up, watching as the combination of light and lasers crept through the forest, crawling over the trees. They progressed slowly, both fighting the urge to run back, out of the woods, away from whatever they would find in front of them.

The further they progressed, the louder it got, until finally they saw the trees in front of them. Light gray bark appeared almost white in the light of their

flashlights, contrasting sharply with the red stains spattered across it. They knew the smart thing to do would be to wait, to tell their commanding officer what was on the trees and wait for their backup. But if the breathing was loud enough for them to hear, he was close. Close enough to hear them if they spoke, and help would never arrive in time.

So they had no choice. They each took a deep breath and continued on, catching only glimpses of what lay beyond the trees. As fleeting as the glimpses were, they were enough. They saw him.

They stepped forward, their guns trained on his back as they entered the small clearing, barely fifteen feet wide, seemingly disconnected from the rest of the forest. That was probably why he was there, kneeling in the dirt, hunched over something they couldn't see, not even acknowledging their presence.

The agents stared at his back, unable to speak for a moment. They couldn't see his face, but they knew it was him. Their lasers remained trained on his head, limiting the flashlights to revealing only the top few feet of him, leaving everything below his shoulders shrouded in darkness.

Finally, Delta found the strength to speak. "Agent Shade?"

No answer came. He just stayed there, like a wolf guarding its kill, his head twitching slightly. The

two agents started to move, walking on opposite ends of an imaginary circle as they made their way around him. Slowly, as they moved forward, their flashlights revealed more, bringing the grisly picture before them into focus.

They could see his face now. It was bruised and covered in blood, but there was no mistaking it. It was him. Shade.

In his hands was a knife, so soaked in blood that the silver glint of the blade couldn't be seen. His black coat was also stained red, and torn to shreds. Someone had fought back.

And even now, with the flashlight in his eyes, Shade didn't acknowledge their presence. Instead, his eyes moved back and forth wildly, following a seemingly random pattern, as if he was staring at monsters that only he could see.

"Agent Shade, where is she?" Delta asked, but still no answer came. Shade just continued to look into the distance, and the agents came to a horrifying realization, one that either fear or hope had hidden from them. The blood that covered him. It wasn't his own.

Delta nodded to his partner to keep his gun trained on Shade's head while he himself lowered his, the flashlight creeping down Shade's body, revealing what had been shrouded in darkness only a moment ago.

Seeing it almost caused him to drop his gun. What was lying in front of Shade, what he was hunched over, was a woman.

Dark red hair appeared to climb up from the mud and onto her head, surrounded by pale skin. Her navy-blue T-shirt now appeared purple, and her blue eyes stared up at the moon, unblinking, lifeless. Her throat was slit, and her stomach was opened, with so many stab wounds the agent couldn't find a single piece of remaining skin.

No longer realizing what he was doing, Delta stepped forward. "What did you do?" he asked as he moved his gun back up toward Shade's head. "What did you do?!"

In his shock, he took one step too many.

A bloodcurdling shriek echoed through the woods. "Delta?" Alpha frantically asked over the coms. "Delta, Echo, what happened?"

No answer came.

His feet began running, despite his mind telling him to turn around. He knew by the time they got there it would be too late, but he ran anyway, as did the agent beside him—through the forest, through the trees, over the footprints heading in the opposite direction.

"Delta!" he screamed as he passed the trees stained in blood and emerged on the other side. He swung his gun around, searching through the darkness for the bodies, until finally, he found them.

The two agents lay in the dirt by the edge of the trees, their limp bodies about ten feet apart. Despite knowing they wouldn't answer, he called out to them. No reply. Desperate, he ran to them, checking for a pulse, praying he would find one.

He did.

They were still alive. Unconscious and bleeding, but still alive. For a single moment, Alpha allowed himself to hope. If they were still alive, maybe the line hadn't been crossed yet.

That was until he heard the nervous voice behind him. "Sir?"

"What?" he asked, turning around to see his fellow agent, Bravo, a man who had seen countless horrors just like he had, who was now so white with fear he could almost be mistaken for a ghost. "What is it?" After receiving no reply, he was forced to follow Bravo's hollow gaze down to the dirt, where the horror he had feared was finally revealed.

Staring at the woman's mangled body, he fought the urge to vomit. He'd seen countless crime scenes in person, countless more in photographs, but this

was the most horrific corpse he had ever laid eyes on. Except for–

Behind the body, something moved in the trees. A dark figure, too large to be an animal. He tried to follow it with his gun, but in an instant, it was gone. Knowing he still had two agents left out there, he issued a single warning over the coms.

"He's here."

Fifty yards to his left, Charlie and Foxtrot walked back to back, their guns shaking as they held them up in front of them. They walked slowly, in tandem with one another, making their way to the sound of the shriek, trying not to let their imaginations get the best of them, when suddenly, Charlie saw something shimmer between the trees, too far away to see clearly, but close enough to instill fear. He moved his laser to it, watching as the light reflected back off into the forest, askew at first, until whatever it was began to turn, forcing the laser's reflection to creep back across the trees, until finally it stopped, right on Charlie's chest. For a breath, the object remained still, and in his terror, he thought it looked like a claw.

The knife flew through the air, impaling his chest via a razor-thin opening within the lining of his vest. Blood crept out of his mouth as he

dropped to his knees, his gun falling to the ground, sinking down into the mud below it.

Foxtrot felt him fall away from his back. "Are you okay?" he asked, not daring to turn around. He told himself that it was because he had to continue to watch his side, and that his partner had merely stepped away–anything to justify not turning around and facing reality. But when he heard the sound of his partner's body colliding with the ground, he knew he had no choice.

As he spun, his gun turned with him, the light piercing through the darkness like a bolt of lightning, revealing the figure standing only inches in front of him.

Gunshots rang through the forest. The thick wall of trees hid their flashes from his sight, but Alpha knew where they had come from. "Report in," he pleaded desperately over his coms, waiting a moment for an answer he knew he wouldn't receive. He turned to Bravo, whose face had finally regained color. "It's just us now. Keep your gun up."

They both readied their weapons and began walking back into the thick of the forest, leaving what was left of the body behind them. Whereas before, the agents had heard nothing but silence

from the forest, now they could hear every branch that cracked, every leaf that scraped against the rough bark of a tree as it fell, every gust of wind that blew through the night air, whispering to them softly. And with every new noise, they pointed their guns toward it, until soon their flashlights were moving so quickly, desperate to reveal something, anything, that they ended up revealing nothing.

Finally, Bravo saw a figure standing in the darkness, watching them. He started to fire his weapon when the flash went off. A flash that didn't come from his own rifle.

Almost as quickly as the bullet had torn a hole in his stomach, his legs gave way beneath him.

Hearing the shot, Alpha turned to fire his weapon, but the figure in the woods had vanished. All that was left was his fellow agent, lying on the ground, the blood from his stomach mixing with the mud below.

He moved Bravo's hand aside, seeing his stomach, trying to find the entry wound.

The bullet had hit right below the vest, in a place that would cause enough blood loss to incapacitate him, but maybe not kill—not if he got medical attention in time.

As Bravo grunted, beginning to lose consciousness, Alpha picked up his gun once again and

started spinning it wildly, looking for the figure in the woods, the monster who had done this. The light went back and forth across the trees, searching for something. For someone.

"Where are you!"

Something pulled against his throat from behind. Instinctively he tried to bring his gun up to fire, shifting the barrel so it rested on his shoulder, pointing backwards, but it was knocked from his hand as the thing gripping his throat began to cut off the oxygen to his lungs. In a last-ditch effort, he gathered all the strength he had left and began trying to pry it off, to remove the hold on his neck.

But he couldn't.

His feet left trails in the leaves as he was dragged backward by a force he couldn't see. His eyes began to lose their sight, and the sound in his ears grew fuzzy and distorted. Finally, he allowed his body to go limp; it was no use fighting against the force. They had lost. Now all he could do was hope the figure allowed him to live. As the world began fading from his vision, he managed to speak a single question.

"Why are you doing this?"

He received no answer as his world turned to black.

Chapter Two

"Help me!"

Trembling, Sara woke from the nightmare. She closed her eyes, trying to stop the tears, like she'd done so many other mornings. This time, she was successful. Usually she wasn't.

She remained in the bed, sitting cross-legged on the sheets, trying not to remember. Deep down she knew she could never truly forget it—she'd tried and failed many times—but that didn't mean she had to remember it every day, every second of her life. But the sound in her head was deafening.

"Help me!"

On the nightstand beside her rested her necklace—a long silver chain with a clasp at the back and dog tags hanging down from it. She placed it around her neck, inspecting the tags as she did. She didn't know why she wore them anymore. She certainly didn't need the reminder. But she'd worn them for so long they had almost become a part

of her, a part she couldn't let go of, even after everything that had happened.

Eventually, she moved from the bed to her closet, trying to pick out clothes without looking up at what had been stored on the shelf above. A med kit, the same one she had used in the Army. The same one she had carried with her that fateful day.

She didn't know why she had put it on the shelf, rather than just throwing it away. She supposed she could move it now, but that would mean she would have to get it down herself. Look at it. Feel it in her hands. Remember.

So instead, her eyes remained down as she grabbed clothes for the day. Blue jeans, a white T-shirt, and a brown leather jacket. Clothes she picked for a reason she didn't dare admit to herself. Clothes she would want to be found in, just in case today was the day it happened.

Later that morning, she sat on her couch, sipping coffee. Her feet were propped up on the glass coffee table in front of her, but her eyes were focused on the drawer in the corner of her room. The voice in her head grew louder as she began to fight the memories once again, burying her head in her hands.

"Help me!"

The words echoed in her mind, causing her to stand in a helpless attempt to escape. But even while pacing the floor, every now and then, she caught a glimpse of herself in the mirror as she passed it. On the surface she saw what she always did, bright blue eyes and blond hair. But beyond the surface, beyond what anyone else could see, was the reflection of someone she had come to hate.

Suddenly, the urge arose to rip the mirror from the wall and throw it to the ground, shattering her reflection into a thousand little pieces, creating a distorted image that couldn't haunt her anymore. But what was the point? Eventually she was just going to see her reflection again somewhere else. Unless today was finally the day.

Once again, the drawer crawled its way into her thoughts. It had been so long since she had opened it; part of her wondered if what was hidden inside would still be there. It helped to think of it that way, as if maybe, when she finally made the decision to open it, she would find the drawer empty, the choice taken out of her hands. But inside, she knew it was still there, right where she had left it.

Without realizing it, she had been brought closer to the drawer, betrayed by her nervous pacing.

She tried to talk herself out of it, just as she had so many other days. But as always, she found herself defenseless. Sure, she could think of what a stranger might say, that her life had meaning,

that there were people who would miss her. But that was a lie she couldn't bear to consider.

She didn't have any family who would miss her, didn't have any friends, at least none that had made it back. She wasn't anything to anyone; she was just hiding out in her apartment, alone, trying to forget the world. Bottom line: she should have died a long time ago anyway.

As usual, Sara's eyes soon caught the picture that she had placed above the drawer, the picture of herself, in full military gear, smiling. Standing next to Her.

She had family, Sara told herself. There were people that missed Her, people that wondered why She hadn't come home. People that wouldn't have been able to look Sara in the eyes if they knew.

She opened the drawer.

Inside, she saw an unloaded silver revolver, and a box of ammo beside it. The revolver's metal was cold to the touch as she began spinning its barrel slowly beside her ear, listening to the clicks; she had always liked that sound. She then reached out and loaded a single shell into the cylinder before running the chamber across the length of her arm, listening to it spin as it went. She wasn't sure which chamber it landed on. That made it easier.

Seconds turned into minutes as she stood there silently, staring at the picture of herself and the friend that hadn't come home. Because of what Sara had, or rather hadn't, done.

In that moment, the decision was made. She deserved this.

A cold tear streaked down Sara's cheek as the barrel crept slowly up to her chin. Motionless, she stood for what felt like forever, until finally her grip tightened on the trigger. The hammer was inching backwards now. Only a few more centimeters until–

Someone knocked on her door.

She sighed. 'Guess today's not the day after all.'

She placed the gun back in the drawer and walked over to the door, wiping the tear from her face. She didn't bother asking who it was. After what she had almost done, she didn't really care.

As the door swung open, she was greeted by a man roughly her own age, wearing a very dark blue suit, with brown hair. He met her with a smile.

"Sara Michaels?"

"That's me," she said, forcing a smile in return.

The man held up a badge. "I'm Special Agent Jack Diamond. I work for the FBI. We need to talk."

Chapter Three

It had been over five hours since the body was reported, and the abandoned warehouse was teeming with local police. It was old; the metal on the side had rusted over years ago, and the roof looked on the verge of caving in. Yellow crime scene tape sealed the entrances, like the web of a spider, desperate to keep its prey all for itself.

'Why is it always the creepy warehouses?' Jack wondered to himself.

He flashed his badge to the cop at the door, who nodded his approval. As he raised the tape above his head, he got a glimpse of what lay within. Inside, CSIs were everywhere, examining the multiple pools of blood left on the ground. In the distance sat a small metal desk, almost resembling an operating table, with a sheet covering whatever was on it. A few more pools of blood lay beside it, and, as if to complete the grisly puzzle, chains hung from the ceiling.

The sight of the crime scene made Jack's skin crawl, not out of horror or disgust, but out of anger. The metal table, the chains, the pools of blood—he had seen it before. Serial killers were always doing crap like that, making the crime scene appear creepier than it actually was, cheap theatrics to satisfy some sick need to feel important.

The mere thought of it caused him to grind his teeth. He could already picture the man who had done this—out there looking for another victim, probably thinking about how he was doing this for some higher purpose. As Jack took another glance toward the sheet, he sighed to himself.

The guy who had done this didn't have some higher purpose, wasn't more enlightened than everyone else. He was just another piece of trash who needed to feel special.

For a brief moment, Jack smiled as he imagined how special the killer would feel once he was rotting in a cell—one that Jack had put him in.

Before he had time to walk over to inspect the sheet, he was met by a cop wearing a brown overcoat, with glasses resting on top of his head, the skin below his eyes wrinkled and dark. "Special Agent Diamond, I presume?" he asked, reaching out his hand.

He shook the officer's hand. "I prefer Jack."

"Very well, Jack. I'm Detective Washington. I was told you'd have a partner with you."

"He's on his way," Jack said offhandedly, his eyes focused elsewhere, noticing the expression on all the cops' faces: pale and ghostlike. Outside, he thought he heard someone vomiting. Never mind, make that several people vomiting.

"What's wrong with them?"

"You'll see."

"That sounds ominous," Jack replied, half-serious. "What are we looking at?"

"Homicide," Washington said. "This morning, some kids came down to play in this warehouse and found the body."

"Were the kids questioned?"

"Yes, but they didn't seem to know anything."

"Any chance they could be involved?"

"No. They found the body but had alibis for the estimated time of death. And frankly, they just didn't seem like the type."

"They never do," Jack said. "Tell me about the victim."

"Her name was Betty Grant. She grew up here and was currently living in a dorm at the local college. Her roommate reported her missing four days ago."

"Her roommate—"

The detective held up his hand, anticipating Jack's question. "We already contacted her. She appears to have a strong alibi, no motive, and can't think of anyone else at the school who would want to do this."

"You've been working fast. Do we know anything else?"

"Not much. There's the specifics of the victim— black hair, green eyes, twenty-one years old." Washington started leading Jack through the crime scene, past the chains, past the blood, past all the other meaningless objects of the killer's self-indulgence, and towards the only thing that actually mattered. The body.

"Have there been any other victims recently with that profile?"

"No, she's the first."

The sound of rattling chains echoed through the warehouse, causing Jack to flinch slightly as he heard it, a reflex he had never forgotten. He turned to see a CSI pushing on the hanging chains, probably out of boredom.

"Don't do that," Jack told him, his tone deadly serious, as if he was instructing a child. The CSI looked at him for a moment, seemingly trying to gauge whether or not he should take the instruction. Finally, he stepped away, leaving Jack and the detective alone.

Jack thought for a moment longer before his tone returned to normal. "Why did you call the FBI?"

Washington raised an eyebrow. "What do you mean?"

Jack shrugged. "It's just that typically local cops don't like it when the FBI takes over their case, and with only one victim, it doesn't seem serious enough to warrant calling us in so soon. Why not just handle it yourself?"

The old detective looked at him for a moment, considering the question. He then sighed as they reached the body. "See for yourself."

Below him was the metal desk he had seen earlier. Only now he realized it didn't just look like an operating table; it was an operating table. Beside it stood a small square tray, the kind used to hold a doctor's tools as they worked on a patient. The same kind of tools that lay on the one in front of him: two scalpels, a few needles, and a surgical saw, covered with so much blood it spilled over the tray and onto the floor.

'More theatrics,' Jack thought. It was unlikely the killer had actually used the tools, especially while the victim was still alive. Even so, he couldn't help looking away from it, so he shifted his gaze back to the operating table. Covered with a white sheet, which was checkered with bloodstains soaking through from whatever was below, it stood as still as a tombstone, waiting for the rotten contents lying within to be revealed. As Jack lifted the sheet, the body of the girl stared back at him. Suddenly, he understood the expressions on the faces of the cops around him.

He held a hand up, covering his mouth, fighting the urge to vomit as he looked down at the body. He had seen crime scenes before, and while he never liked looking at them, this was different. This wasn't brutal or sadistic—those he could handle. No, this was something else, something calculated. The girl's entire chest was opened up, and to Jack's horror, he noticed something was missing.

Even after he had replaced the sheet, he could still see the image, already engrained in his mind. For a long time, he stood in silence, trying to remain calm. 'It's just another crime scene,' he told himself. But it made no difference. In that moment, he knew that no matter what he did for the rest of his life, he would never get that image out of his head.

In an attempt to still do his job, he lifted the sheet back up. "The cuts look precise," he said, talking more to himself than the detective beside him, who was looking to the side, avoiding the sight of the body. "The—" Jack choked on the word. "The—" It wouldn't come out. He couldn't say it. "What was done to her looks like it was done well. The killer has experience. He's definitely a doctor, most likely a surgeon of some kind, and from the looks of it, a good one."

Jack took a moment to gather himself, trying to avoid gagging, and then continued. "She has abrasions on her arms, and blood underneath her fingernails, indicating she fought back." With those words, Jack lowered the sheet back over her and turned his attention back to Washington.

"Have you found any drugs in her system?"

"We're running toxicology tests on her blood now and will do a full analysis as soon as we move the body, but the forensics officer doesn't think it looks like she'd been drugged."

'Demented jackal,' Jack thought, anger forcing his neck to tilt slightly. No drugs meant no anesthesia. That psychopath had done this to her while she was still conscious.

"What are you thinking?" Washington asked.

"I need a list of every surgeon in the city with a criminal history, anything from aggravated assault to a parking ticket, so we can start a database of suspects. Focus on those that worked in whatever hospitals she frequented, and those who've lost their medical license."

"We're already working on it. But it's a big city, that's going to be hundreds of names."

"I don't care," Jack said. "We have to find this guy before he finds his next victim. Which will be soon."

"You're sure there will be a next victim? Isn't there at least a slight possibility that the killer just wanted to do it this one time?" Not even the detective believed the words as they left his mouth, but in moments like this, hope was something to be held on to.

Jack looked at the sheet, checkered with blood. "Whoever did this probably told himself it would be just this one time. That he could scratch the itch and then it would go away, and he could go back to his life the way it was. Most serial killers think that. But it's never just one time. No one ever crosses that line and then comes back from it. Not after something like this." Jack's eyes met the detective's. "He's going to kill as many as he can until we find him."

"Okay. We'll start looking into the doctors." Washington looked at Jack, curious. "If you don't mind me asking, how many cases have you worked on?"

"Dozens."

"Have you ever not solved one?"

"No," Jack said. Truth be told, he had never even had a case get to three victims before. But even then, he knew. Somehow, deep within himself, he knew: this case was going to change that.

"Well, then, I'm glad I called the FBI."

Jack nodded as he began to walk away from the body to get a look at the rest of the warehouse. Cheap or not, sometimes the theatrics hid clues. But suddenly a thought occurred to him, and he turned around once more to face the detective. "When my partner gets here, don't show him the body."

"Why?"

Jack sighed. "Just don't. Please."

"Very well."

As Jack walked around the warehouse, he couldn't keep the feelings of unease from returning. In his bones, he could feel it: this case was different from the rest. And once again, he found himself closing his eyes, unable to forget the image of the girl, lying on the operating table, covered in blood.

Missing her heart.

Chapter Four

"May I come in?" Jack asked.

Sara feigned a frown. "Is this serious enough for an in-house visit?"

Jack smirked back at her. "Afraid so."

"Well, then," Sara said, waving her hand toward the inside of her apartment, "come on in."

She noticed him give a subtle, more genuine grin as he walked past her. She knew why. It probably wasn't every day that he introduced himself as FBI without getting a door slammed in his face.

"Nice place."

"Thanks," she answered, walking over to the couch and slumping down on the cushions. "Care to have a seat?"

"I would actually prefer to stand, if that's alright."

Jack was still smiling, but just then, Sara noticed something else in his voice. He sounded nervous. Not in the *is this lady going to slam the door in my face?* way, but genuinely nervous. He even seemed to be shifting uncomfortably where he stood, as if he needed to be ready to move at any moment.

"Suit yourself," she said as she leaned back on it, her arm draped over the armrest.

He first pointed to the picture of her above the drawer and then glanced to the dog tags still hanging from her neck. "You're former military?"

She smiled to herself. It was cute, the way he tried to act like he hadn't done a background check on her before he'd shown up. She decided to go with it. "Yep, served four years."

"Army?"

"Marines, actually," she said, just to see the reaction on his face.

"Really?" he asked, clearly shocked by the answer.

"No," Sara said. "I was an Army medic." A rare grin spread across her face as she watched him. "But then again, my background check already told you that, right?"

Realizing he'd been caught, he laughed slightly. "Yes, I guess it did. Why medic and not something else?"

Why had she chosen that? She used to tell herself it was so she could help people, save them. But after what had happened, she didn't know anymore. So she simply shrugged. "They needed more medical personnel, and I was trained in that

field. Plus, my blood type is O negative, so I could give blood to anyone, if the need arose."

"Well, if I'm ever bleeding out, I'll make sure to call you."

"Are you trying to get my number, Agent Diamond?" Sara asked, playing with him. She wasn't sure why. Probably just an attempt to get her mind off what had almost happened before he'd knocked on the door. What she had been about to do.

"It's Jack," he said, grinning. "And I already have your number. Background check, remember?"

"Oh," Sara said. "I see." She leaned forward on the couch, now resting her elbows on her knees. "Well, not that this conversation isn't entertaining, but do you mind sharing what this visit is actually about?"

The jokes seemed to have calmed whatever nerves Jack had as he began speaking. "Well, I have"–he paused for a moment, seemingly searching for the right words–"unfortunate news."

Sara leaned back on the couch again, sensing his hesitation. "You don't have to sugarcoat it. I'm a big girl."

"Okay," Jack said, moving his hands to his pockets and pulling out a small blue pen, clicking it once. "The FBI has reason to believe that you're being targeted by a serial killer."

Sara's eyes grew wide as she recoiled slightly in shock. "Not the answer I was expecting."

"I know," he said, nodding.

She saw his nod. An attempt to act sympathetic, so that she would trust him. It had been tried on her before, but something about this nod felt genuine, like he really didn't want to have to be here, telling her this.

"Am I the first, or have there been other victims?" she asked, her first question chosen from a vast ocean of others that had all entered her head in an instant.

"You're the second," he replied. "A woman was killed in the forest behind her house, roughly eight months ago."

"Eight months? Why would the killer wait so long for another victim?"

"It's complicated," Jack said, clearly not wanting to elaborate further.

"Okay," Sara said, standing up from the couch. "Why me?"

"We aren't sure that it's you—it's just a possibility."

"Still, it's a big city, and with only one victim, how could you possibly have narrowed it down just to me?"

Jack took a step closer to her as he spoke. "The last victim had red hair and blue eyes. That's a one-in-a-million combination. You have—"

"A greater chance of being struck by lightning than running into someone who has both," Sara said, finishing his thought. She'd heard it before.

Jack smiled. "Well," he said, taking another step closer, "you have blue eyes, and I'm guessing that you're not a natural blonde."

"Easy there, Detective, you're getting a little personal."

Jack smirked.

"But how would he know?" Sara asked, shifting the lighthearted tone back to serious. "It's not like my hair color is listed in the phone book. How could this killer possibly find me in a city this big if that's his only pattern?"

"We found you," Jack countered.

"Yeah, but you're the FBI."

"Uh-huh."

Sara waited for him to elaborate further, but after a few moments it became apparent that he thought that was a sufficient explanation, as if the killer would have no more issue finding her than the whole of the FBI. It made her uneasy to think what that might imply.

"Well, in any case," Jack continued, "we're not sure the next victim will follow that pattern, but just in case, we've been monitoring the very few women in the city with red hair and blue eyes, and

in the past few days, security cam footage outside your house has shown someone walking by on multiple different nights. Their face is obscured, so we're not sure that it's him, but it's not worth the risk of waiting if it is."

"Why would he have walked by on multiple days?" Sara asked, confused. "Why not just come up to my room, break in, and kill me on day one? Why waste time?"

"He was probably trying to talk himself out of it."

"What kind of serial killer tries to talk himself out of killing people?"

Jack's tone suddenly grew serious. "One who doesn't want to."

She noticed him stepping closer and saw the uneasiness creep back into his eyes. "Well," she said, looking for an opportunity to end the conversation, "you've done your civic duty and alerted me. I'll be sure to lock my doors."

"If it's all the same to you, I'd rather take you back to headquarters to keep an eye on you for a while."

From the tone of his voice, she knew this was serious. Honestly, she should probably be at least a little worried herself. But then her mind went back to the gun, and she realized something. Serial killers are only scary if you care about living, and she wasn't sure that she did anymore.

"Thanks, but that won't be necessary. I can take care of myself. Former military, remember?"

Jack's eyes lost the last bit of remaining color in them, and suddenly she realized just how much he didn't want to be here.

Someone knocked on the door.

Jack spun around in an instant, already having his gun pointed at the door; the reaction was so fast, she wasn't sure how he had even had time to draw it. He was practically sweating as he watched the door, looking nothing like the calm, collected Jack that had greeted her just a few minutes earlier.

Whoever this killer was, it must be serious.

Like a character in a horror movie, Jack walked to the door slowly, as if expecting a masked monster to be hiding on the other side, waiting to reveal itself before killing them both. Sara moved silently through the living room and into the kitchen, pulling a pistol from the kitchen cabinet, this one a black 1911 with a brown grip. Just in case.

As he crept toward the door, Jack looked back and saw the gun, nodding his approval.

"Sara Michaels?" a voice called from outside the door.

Jack's expression changed, and he lowered his gun, motioning for her to do the same. He must have recognized the voice, Sara thought. But even

now, the look of fear hadn't left his face completely; it only seemed to have shifted from sheer terror to intense anxiety.

But even after she'd prepared herself, what was on the other side of the door still shocked her. At least a dozen men, all in what looked like riot gear, holding either semiautomatic rifles or some variation of a shotgun.

"What are you doing here?" Jack asked the one in front, sounding to Sara like he was both irritated and nervous at the same time.

"Williams told us you thought you'd found the next victim, so he sent us here to escort her back to base."

"I was doing that alone," Jack said, still irritated. "So I could do it without him noticing. If Shade sees you here—" Jack stopped speaking and once again checked the room, as if still waiting for the monster to make his appearance.

Sara thought his reaction was strange at first, until she looked more closely at the men outside her doorway. All armed, all wearing body armor, but still looking back and forth like Jack, tapping their feet, their guns shaking in their hands.

They were all terrified.

Before Sara could ask who Shade was, Jack took hold of her arm and led her through the

door, into the middle of the agents, not giving her time to protest. "Let's go," he ordered them, and they crowded around her, breathing as though they might drop dead at any moment. Even in the military, she had never seen anyone this scared.

Soon, they were outside, and she was escorted to the back seat of a car, which took off down the street the moment the door was closed, and the other agents piled into a van that followed closely behind.

Still in shock, Sara looked over at Jack, seated beside her, who had managed to calm down somewhat. The other agent in the front seat, however, was still gripping his weapon close to his chest.

At first, she sat quietly, trying to take in everything that had just happened. The 1911 still rested in her hands, and in that moment, she found herself grateful that she had brought it, that she had a way to defend herself against whatever was happening. Because, as she knew all too well, at the end of the day, you can't rely on anyone else to save you. If you do, you'll end up dead, bleeding out into the dirt, wondering why your savior never came; why they never cared.

When she finally started to calm down, she looked into Jack's eyes, searching for an answer. "Who is Shade?"

For a moment, he just sighed, his eyes displaying a look of regret that she recognized all too well.

"He was my partner."

Chapter Five

"What are you thinking?" Jack asked. They stood in his office, looking at the photos of the crime scene, which were sprawled out over the desk.

Shade was trying to control his breathing. Remain calm. He'd known the crime scene photos would be bad, but they were even worse than he'd expected. Just looking at them, he already knew—this case would be worse than the others. But he couldn't let it get to him. Just like in the military, he had to stay calm, had to stay focused. Or else bad things happened.

"It's definitely a serial killer," Shade responded, forcing his breathing to become steady. "No one does something like this and just stops."

Jack nodded in agreement. "Okay, so let's go over this one more time. What do we know?"

"We know that two weeks ago, Betty Grant's body was found in an abandoned warehouse. All of her immediate family and friends have alibis, so they can be ruled out. The local police also ran toxicology screens, and her body was completely clear of drugs. Nothing was used to knock her out, either in the original abduction or during the surgery that followed."

Jack continued from there. "We also know that, due to the nature of the wounds inflicted, the person who did this must've had some form of surgical training. We have the local police looking at the names of every surgeon that the victim could have come into contact with, and every hospital they've been to. However, according to her family, she had never had surgery of any kind and had only visited the hospital one time, two years ago."

Examining the photos more closely now, Shade responded, "Which means that the killer most likely didn't know her. Which explains the defensive wounds on her arms."

Jack walked over to the chair on the other side of his desk and sat down, tilting his head back in frustration. "So basically, we know absolutely nothing about the killer."

"What about the victim?"

"What do you mean?"

Shade picked up a photo of the girl, one the family had provided. "We don't have enough information to find the killer, but it's possible we can predict who his next victim is going to be. Even if the killer doesn't know the victims, they will still most likely follow a similar pattern."

Jack nodded his head. "Okay, so what do we know about the victim?"

"She was twenty-one years old, had black hair and green eyes. She was in college, majoring in biology, and had been reported missing by her roommate a few days before the body was found."

"So," Jack said, leaning forward in his chair to look at the picture of her that Shade had set back down, "none of that really narrows down the victim list."

"No," Shade said. "No, it doesn't."

Jack ran his hand over his eyes, visibly nauseated at the sight of the crime scene photos. He then looked up at Shade, his eyes focusing on the dog tags hanging around his neck. "Be honest. In your time in the military, did you ever see anything like this?"

Shade didn't answer him, instead closing his eyes, trying to keep the memories from entering his head. Trying to keep the voices at bay. He took another deep breath, forcing himself to calm down.

Noticing the haunted look in his eyes, Jack stood up and walked over to him, placing a hand on his shoulder. "Are you sure you're up for this case? I mean, I know it hasn't happened since you were discharged, but—"

"I'll be fine."

"Okay, just let me know if you start having..." Jack hesitated. "You know."

"Really, Jack," Shade said, "I'm fine." But deep down he knew he wasn't. He knew there was something different about this case. He could already feel it crawling into his head, making him remember.

The phone rang. Jack picked it up. The expression on his face told Shade what had happened before he even said it.

"They found another body."

This time, it wasn't an abandoned warehouse; rather, the body was found in a room in an old apartment building. But while the location might have been different, the grisly scene within remained the same.

"The neighbors noticed she hadn't come out of her apartment for several days, which was unlike her," Detective Washington informed them as they walked through the building, making their way to her apartment. "They knocked on her door to make sure she was alright, and when she didn't answer, they used a spare key she had given one of them and went inside to check on her."

"And that's when they found the body," Jack said as they approached the door to her apartment: open, but sealed off with police tape.

"After you," the detective said, raising the tape for Shade and Jack to walk under it. Once inside, he walked them both across the living room, passing pools of blood just like before, to the silver operating table that rested at the far end of the room—once again covered in a white sheet, once again sitting beside a tray of operating equipment.

Shade could feel his muscles tense up just from walking closer to it. Once they reached it, he felt his lungs grow heavy and his eyes start to twitch slightly. He wasn't sure if he could handle seeing the body, but he had no choice. This was his job, and he couldn't just ignore it.

"Maybe you shouldn't," Jack started to say, but the look on Shade's face told him it was pointless.

"Okay," Jack said as he lifted up the sheet, again greeted by the same gruesome scene as before. A girl, lying on a table, an operation having been performed.

Shade shut his eyes immediately. He shouldn't have looked at it. His heart began racing in his chest as he tried desperately to stop from shivering. He tried to control his breathing. As long as he could do that, he would be okay. Even after opening his eyes, though, he kept his vision trained on the ground. He was afraid to look up. Afraid of what he might see.

"So," Jack said, forcing the words out. "Same deal as before. Victim was operated on and has defensive wounds on her arms and cracked fingernails, indicating she was awake long enough to fight back. This victim has blond hair and brown eyes, suggesting the killer doesn't have a type when it comes to the look of his victims. What about college?" he asked the detective. "Did she attend the same one as the first victim, or at least have the same major?"

"No. This one didn't attend college at all. In fact, she dropped out of high school her senior year and has been living here ever since."

"What about doctors? Did she go to the same hospital as Betty? Did she have any surgeries done?"

Washington sighed. "We're still looking into which hospital she currently went to, if any, but according to her parents, she never mentioned having surgery of any kind."

"Great," Jack said as he paced a few steps back and forth. "That still leaves us with nothing."

Finally, Shade spoke. "How old was she?"

With a solemn expression, Washington looked to the body, now covered with the sheet again. "She turned twenty a few weeks ago."

Shade and Jack looked at each other, not saying anything for a moment.

Finally, Jack took a deep breath. "I hope that's just a coincidence."

Later that night, Shade stood in his own home. The room was dark, and he paced the floor, trying to get the image of the girl's body out of his head. He felt the dog tags pulling down on his neck, like an anchor dragging him down into the cold, unforgiving depths, drowning him from within, forcing him to remember.

His hands were shaking. He tried to stop them, but he couldn't. So instead, he focused on trying to control his breathing, control his thoughts. Not let the horrors in. But he could feel them crawling their way into his head.

Immediately after he had seen the body, he had known he needed to excuse himself from the case. It was too much—it would cause them to come back, and he wasn't sure he could handle it. Not again.

But he also knew he couldn't let the case go. Whether he could handle it or not, that wouldn't change the fact that girls were dying, that there was a serial killer out there, murdering them. If he didn't stay on the case, he couldn't help save them. What happened to him didn't matter, as long as he could save the victims. That was all he could focus on now— saving the next victim's life, helping someone else survive, like he had. Like so many he knew hadn't.

The memory of gunfire rang in his head. The screams of his fellow soldiers.

Shade felt the pull of the gun around his waist. It was too dangerous. Couldn't trust himself. He went to a lockbox hidden in the room and placed his gun, still in its holster, into it before locking it again. He might not be able to walk away from the case, but maybe he could remove the gun from the equation. Just in case it happened again.

Suddenly, Shade heard something behind him. He turned around to see a girl standing in the corner of the room, perfectly still, her eyes glassed over, blood pouring from her chest, repeating the same words to him over and over.

"Why didn't you save me?"

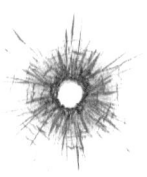

Chapter Six

"So," Sara said, "he wants to kill me because he thinks it will get rid of his hallucinations?"

Jack nodded.

He had told her everything: who Shade was, the last case they had worked together, the hallucinations, and the six agents who Shade had put in critical condition in the forest. They now stood in Jack's office, him leaning against the closed door, her leaning against his desk.

"But if killing the woman in the forest didn't make them go away, why would he think killing me would?"

Jack sighed, crossing his arms and holding a blue pen in his hands. "I'm sure killing her did make them go away, at least at first. But it's been eight months. They must've come back."

Sara twisted her neck, popping it. She could barely believe everything he'd told her. But she also felt like he had left something out. Not something

he'd lied about, but something he just couldn't bring himself to talk about. At least not to her. Not yet.

Still, she couldn't believe someone could resort to killing someone just to make hallucinations go away. Part of her thought that it was just his excuse. That he had always wanted to see what it felt like to kill innocent people; he'd just needed a justification.

"The hallucinations must've been pretty bad for him to do something like that," she prodded, hoping to watch Jack's face as he responded, to see if he believed this was Shade's only reason.

"They were bad enough to get him discharged from the Army," Jack said, knowing what she was thinking and not giving an inch.

"Still, to kill someone just to make them go away," she said, still pushing him. But from the look on his face, it was clear he believed wholeheartedly that Shade was only doing this because he saw no other option.

"I was there when it started happening again," Jack said. "Shade was the kind of person who'd barely flinch if a bomb went off beside him. But when he was hallucinating, it was different. You could just see the fear in his eyes." As he spoke, Sara could tell he knew what she was thinking. That it was still just an excuse for killing. "Have you ever had a nightmare?" he continued. "I mean a really vivid nightmare, the kind that leaves a chill running down the back of your spine even after you've woken up?"

She had those kinds of nightmares every night.

"Help me!"

But she couldn't tell him that. She had never told anyone that. Telling someone would make it real, make what she had done inescapable. "Yeah," she said, trying to sound like she was shrugging it off. "I've had them before."

"Well," Jack said, his voice firm, "it's like that, only he never gets to wake up."

She could tell how hard he was trying to defend Shade. They must've been close partners, maybe even friends.

"Yes, we were friends," Jack said, seemingly reading her mind.

"This must be tough for you, then, with him turning out to be a serial killer." She misspoke intentionally, still trying to see if she could pry more information out of him and figure out what it was that he had left out.

"He didn't turn out to be a serial killer," Jack said, knowing she'd said it on purpose but correcting her nonetheless. "You don't know him, don't understand everything he's been through. He's a good person, which is partially why the hallucinations happened

in the first place. He couldn't take the fact that anyone was dying because of him. I tried to help, but I think he finally just got pushed a little too far."

There it was. That was what he had left out.

"What was it that pushed him over the edge?" Sara asked.

Jack rubbed the back of his neck and clicked his pen, clearly uneasy at the question. "You're just full of questions, aren't you?"

"I'm just trying to get a better understanding of why someone wants to kill me, that's all," she said, standing her ground. "Plus, before I was a medic, I did some training in military investigations. Old habits die hard, I guess."

"I guess they do," Jack said, trying to figure out what to say. She clearly wasn't going to leave it alone, but he also wasn't ready to talk about it. To say that name again. It had been so long since he had. "Let's just say that something happened, something bad, and he couldn't take it."

"Sounds like maybe you couldn't either," she said, trying to sound sympathetic. Clearly, whatever it was, it was bad, so she didn't press any further.

The room sat in silence for a moment as Sara looked around Jack's office, noticing the crime scene photos he had taped up on the walls. So many dead bodies. So many victims.

"I don't know how you look at these every day."

Jack stood up from leaning on the door and walked to the wall they were stuck on, examining them. "You get used to it."

"I bet," she said, walking over next to him. "Have you had any major cases since...?" She couldn't bring herself to say it. "You know."

Jack nodded. "I've been assigned to three different cases in the last eight months."

"Solved any?"

"Two," Jack answered. "Both before they could kill more than two victims."

"What about the third?" Sara asked.

Jack pointed to a crime scene photo of a woman with a noose wrapped around her neck, hanging from a lamppost. "The newspapers call him the Hangman. He showed up a few months ago, and so far we haven't been able to find any real leads."

"How many—" Sara started to ask before stopping herself. She wasn't sure if she wanted to know the answer, but she found out regardless.

"He killed his third victim four days ago."

"I'm sorry," she said. She wasn't sure why she said that, but she got the sense that Jack was the type to take the cases to heart.

"We'll catch him before he takes his next victim," Jack said, sounding like he didn't have a shred of doubt.

Sara guessed you'd have to always be sure that you could save the next one, or else this job would drive you crazy. Like it evidently had Shade.

"One thing I don't understand," she said as she resumed leaning on the desk.

"What's that?"

"Well, you told me that Shade was an agent, and that he was former military, but that doesn't explain why everyone here is so afraid of him. I mean, half the guards we passed on the way here looked like they might have a heart attack on the spot, just seeing me."

"They know that you being here means he'll come for you."

"Exactly. Why is that so scary? I mean, this is an FBI field office for crying out loud."

Jack smiled at her. She had no idea. "Well, like I said, Shade was former military. Since he was discharged because the hallucinations made him unstable in combat zones, Director Williams always tried to keep Shade on cases that didn't involve any chance of physical confrontation. That's why he was paired with me in the first place."

Jack paused for a moment and pointed to a picture on his wall of a slightly older man, with very broad shoulders and a sense of power in his eyes. "This is Frank Burrows. He's currently the biggest crime boss in the country. Money laundering, drugs, guns—you name it, he runs it."

Sara wrinkled her brow, slightly confused. "If you know all that, then why isn't he already in jail?"

"Because he has people everywhere, including the FBI. Every time we get a piece of evidence, it goes missing before we can tie it back to him. Except for one time," Jack said, holding one finger up. "Another division had gotten a tip, found one of his drug warehouses. Supposedly it had so much evidence inside that if we collected it, it couldn't possibly go missing. The director sent everybody, including us, to make sure it went smoothly. He instructed Shade to wait outside and only go in if it was absolutely necessary. He didn't want Shade to lose it in the middle of the bust."

"What happened?"

"When we went inside, we found nothing. It was just an empty warehouse. Our informant had given us the wrong location. Or at least we thought that, until we were ambushed by more people than we

could count. Within two minutes, most of the agents had been gunned down, and the ones that weren't, including me, had been disarmed and knocked out, presumably for a recorded execution. Send a message to the rest of the FBI that Burrows was off-limits."

Jack's eyes began to glaze over as he spoke, clearly reliving the events as he described them. "When we were knocked out, we all thought for sure we'd never be waking up again. But then we did. We looked around the warehouse, not sure at first what had happened. Everything was still too foggy—until our eyes finally adjusted, and we saw it. Blood everywhere, more bodies than we could count, and Shade, covered in blood, sitting on the floor in front of us, leaning against the wall."

Sara knew she should have felt chills down her spine, knowing this person Jack was speaking about was coming for her. But still she wasn't afraid. Not because she doubted Shade could get to her, but because even if he did, she wasn't sure she cared what the outcome was. If anything, she wondered if deep down, she didn't hope he did make it to her, save her the trouble of going back home, looking at that gun, probably doing it herself.

"Help me!"

As she was trying to fight the memory back down, Jack walked over to his desk and opened the

bottom drawer. He pulled out a black holster for a 1911 pistol and tossed it to her. "Here."

"Thanks." She put it on and placed her pistol inside it, then practiced drawing her weapon a few times, an old military habit. Always test your gear before your life depends on it. The holster had a black latch that needed to be pressed to pull the gun out, and it was sticky, causing the gun draw to be delayed, so she reached down and snapped the piece off.

"Hey," Jack protested.

"Sorry." She tried pulling the gun again. It was quicker this time.

"It's fine," he said, moving his arm and wincing slightly. "It's old anyway."

Sara noticed him rolling his shoulder. "You okay?"

"What?" he said before realizing what she meant. "Oh yeah, I'm fine. Just an old shoulder injury. It acts up sometimes."

She nodded and ran her fingers across the wall, inching over the cracks of a thin dent, about waist level.

Jack answered her question before she asked it. "Chair."

The answer confused her even more than the dent itself. "How?"

"I may or may not have thrown it in anger. But that's a story for another day."

"Okay," she said, rolling her eyes sarcastically before looking over to the corner of Jack's office and noticing a folded-up cot with sheets on top of it.

"Do you sleep here?"

"Occasionally."

She frowned to herself. It was sad. Jack probably barely had a life outside of this, instead spending all his time trying to catch the bad guys and save the next victim. Time he was now wasting on her. She looked around at the photos of the Hangman's victims. Limp bodies strung up from lampposts, nooses around their necks. Soon there would be another one, if Jack didn't catch him. And how could he, when he was wasting his time trying to save her? Someone who didn't deserve to be saved.

She also thought of the agents outside. Jack had said that Shade wouldn't kill them, just like he hadn't killed the agents in the forest, because it wouldn't make the visions go away. But the agents didn't know that for sure, and they were clearly terrified. Still they stood out there, willing to die to possibly save someone else's life. Her life. A tear fell down her cheek, which she quickly wiped away before he could see.

"I don't think I'm worth this," she said, accidentally out loud.

Jack looked at her strangely. "What?"

Suddenly, the lights went out. Jack opened his office door, seeing that they were out in the whole building. Someone had cut them off. He turned back to face Sara in a panic.

"He's here."

Chapter Seven

Breathless, they looked down at the corpse of the third victim.

This one had been found in a hotel room. From the appearance of the body, it must have been there quite a while, a few days at the least. She was a brunette and did not bear even a passing resemblance to either of the previous two girls, adding to the evidence that the killings were not based upon the physical appearance of the victims.

The state of the corpse, however, was exactly the same as before. Scratch marks on the victim's arms and hands, her chest cut open, and something missing.

Jack lowered the sheet. "What do we know?"

"The hotel was paid for in advance," the detective answered. "The name used was John Buck, but for obvious reasons we don't think it's the killer's actual name. The room was reserved a few weeks ago, paid for in cash, and no one in the hotel ever saw him or the victim come in or leave. Victim's name is Susan Doyle."

"What about hotel cameras?"

"In this neighborhood?" Washington let out a soft chuckle. "We're lucky the doors even had locks on them."

"The desk clerk," Jack continued, still fishing for whatever evidence he could get. "He should have seen the guy when he reserved the room."

"Agreed," Washington said, "but we already checked with him, and not only did he not remember what the guy looked like, he also both failed a drug test and appeared intoxicated when we showed up. I'd be surprised if he even remembers us tomorrow."

"Who found the body?" Jack asked, shifting his weight. The name used irritated him. John Buck. The killer clearly thought he was clever. Probably the type to think he was doing the girls a favor by gracing them with the honor of getting operated on by him. Jack wasn't sure he had ever hated someone he hadn't met so completely before.

"The room had been reserved for two days. When the time was over and the guest still hadn't left or responded to their calls to the room, security unlocked the door to escort them out."

"And then they found her," Jack said finishing the thought and glancing back down at the body now covered with the sheet, once white but now stained in red. "What about friends, parents? Anyone report her missing?"

"She had just started college, so her parents didn't know she was missing. Her friends were being interviewed while you were on your way here. They said that they noticed she wasn't there, but that she had already been ditching classes, so they didn't think to report it."

"How old?" Shade asked, his gaze never leaving the body, whether it was covered in the sheet or not.

"Nineteen."

Shade and Jack looked at each other in horror, both finding themselves unable to speak.

"What is it?"

After a few moments, Jack found the strength to answer the question. "The first victim was twenty-one, the second turned twenty a few weeks ago, and now she," he said, pointing to the body, "is nineteen. The killer's counting down."

"Maybe it's just a coincidence," Washington said, not really believing the words himself.

"It's not," Shade said, his eyes meeting the detective's for the first time. He didn't elaborate. He didn't have to.

Jack rubbed his forehead, squinting as if it would make the revelation go away. But he knew it wouldn't. Three victims, each younger than the last. Which meant the longer it took to catch this guy, the worse it would get. But they would catch this monster before the next victim, Jack told himself. They would catch him.

They had to.

"What about medical history? Has she had surgery of any kind?"

"Actually, yes," Washington said. "We just pulled her files before you arrived, and it shows that she was involved in a kidney transplant two years ago. She was the donor."

"Who performed it?" Shade asked.

"The surgery was performed by a Dr. Kevin Urich."

"Has he been questioned yet?" Jack asked, excitement creeping into his voice. He knew this wasn't proof, or even a true lead. More than likely it would turn out to be nothing, but maybe it wouldn't. Maybe this would be the guy. Maybe it would finally be over.

Jack wanted it to be over.

"Not yet. I thought you two might want to be the ones to question him."

"You thought right," Jack responded. "Where is he now?"

"At the hospital, working. We haven't approached him yet."

"Don't," Jack said, looking around the room, trying to get the image of the victim out of his head. "Let it be a surprise. We might catch him off guard."

"Okay," the detective said. "Remember, we've kept the nature of these crimes out of the news so far, so if he knows anything at all about what happened to her—"

"This isn't our first rodeo," Jack said, shaking the cop's hand and starting towards the door, until he noticed Shade wasn't beside him. When he turned back, Shade was still standing there, looking at the body covered in the sheet, his eye twitching rapidly.

"Shade?"

No response came; it was as if Shade hadn't heard him at all. Moving closer, Jack studied how he looked at the corpse, until he was sure of what was happening. Shade wasn't really looking at a corpse. He was looking at something else. And now his head started to shake, as if he was trying to block something out. Some image or sound creeping in.

"Shade, are you okay?"

That evening, Shade and Jack stood in the hallway of the hospital where Dr. Kevin Urich worked, waiting for him to get out of surgery. Occasionally hospital staff would walk by, looking at them but not bothering to ask them anything.

"You want to tell me what happened back there?" Jack asked, despite knowing exactly what had happened back there.

Shade said nothing as he looked past Jack into the distance.

"Sure, Jack. It was nothing, Jack. No reason to be concerned, Jack," he mocked, trying to pry something out of him.

Still Shade said nothing.

Jack grew more serious. "I know the hallucinations are back." That at least got Shade to look at him. "And, no, I'm not going to tell Director Williams and have you removed from this case. I just need to know that you're not going to lose it on me. You're not going to, right?"

Shade nodded.

"Good," Jack said. "Because I need you. We have to catch this guy, and we have to do it fast. Because this only gets worse from here."

What felt like an hour passed as they waited for the doctor. Jack stood with his arms crossed, leaning against the wall, uncomfortable. He couldn't place it, but there was something wrong with this hospital. It didn't look strange—the floors were clean, the paint wasn't cracked or faded—but something didn't feel right. He couldn't explain it, but he felt more uncomfortable now than he had at the crime scenes. It almost felt like the hospital itself was sick. Like all the cleaning, all the white paint and shiny tile were just bandages, covering the bleeding heart hiding underneath the surface.

A heart waiting to burst.

"So how do you want to play this?" Shade asked.

Shaking off the uneasy feeling, Jack responded, "Figure we just come right out with it, ask him if he has an alibi for the time of death, ask him what he knows about the victim." He looked over at Shade, who was once again staring at nothing. At least nothing that anyone else could see. "I'll do most of the talking, of course," Jack said, trying to distract Shade from whatever he was looking at. "You can be bad cop, brooding silently in the background."

Shade said nothing, but Jack knew he could hear him.

"Obviously you can't be good cop. I mean, look at you," Jack said, pointing at Shade. "You're terrifying. Spiders crawl away from you."

At that, Shade glared up at Jack, who held his hands up.

"I've seen it happen."

The door to the operating room finally opened.

"Excuse me, Dr. Urich?" Jack said, raising to signal for the doctor.

"Yes?" one of the doctors exiting the room said as he split away from the rest and walked over to them. "Can I help you?"

"Hopefully." Jack pulled out his notebook. He didn't really need it to remember his notes, but writing down what people said as they said it made them uncomfortable, more likely to slip up. He also flashed his badge. "I'm Special Agent Jack Diamond, with the FBI. This is my partner, Special Agent Shade. We'd just like to ask you a few questions."

"Certainly," the doctor said. "My office is just down the hall if—"

"Actually, we'd rather do it here," Jack said. The doctor's office would be a place where he felt safe—his domain, so to speak. Jack didn't want that. He needed him to feel out of place, and while the hallway surely wouldn't feel completely foreign to the doctor, it was better than nothing. Whoever this killer was, he was good, and Jack didn't want to give him any further advantage, just in case it happened to be the man standing in front of him now. "It'll only take a moment."

"Okay," the doctor said. "What is this regarding?"

They both examined Urich. He looked around seventy, with graying hair and small glasses that rested on his nose. He was also overweight, but just slightly. Nothing about him screamed suspicious to Jack, but then again, neither does the appearance of most killers. True insanity isn't what everyone thinks it is. It's not the mental patient growling in the corner of a room, or the psychopath singing opera while dismembering a victim. The truth is, most killers appear the same as everyone else, sometimes even more so, because they have spent so much time faking it, so much time hiding their true nature, sometimes even from themselves. So, as Jack had learned a long time ago, you can't judge a suspect based on whether or not they look unstable. If you do, you're likely to be wrong and let the real killer escape your vision.

Jack shifted his weight and tilted his head slightly, ready to gauge the man's reaction to the question. "Do you remember a patient of yours by the name of Susan Doyle?"

The doctor furrowed his brow, trying, or at least pretending to try, to remember. Finally, he spoke. "Not offhand. I have a lot of patients. Do you know what surgery she had done?"

"She donated a kidney," Jack answered. "Two years back."

Urich thought for a moment, and then a look of realization covered his face. "Oh, yes. Teenager, right?" he asked, looking for clarification. If this was an act, it was a good one. "Brown hair?"

"That's her," Jack said.

"Okay, yes, I do remember her. I believe she came in to donate a kidney to her younger sister. I forget her name." The doctor paused for a moment. "Is Ms. Doyle okay?"

Jack hoped Shade would respond. His voice would scare the doctor more than his own would. And right on cue—

"She had an open-heart surgery performed."

"I'm sorry to hear that," Urich said, now looking at Shade. "I hope all—"

"Unwillingly," Shade added.

The shock was clear from the doctor's eyes as he covered his mouth with his hands and shivered. "What?"

"Where were you two days ago?" Jack fired back, not giving him time to process what he had just been told. He would be more likely to slip up that way.

The doctor started to answer but then took a second to consider the question and realized what they were really asking him. "Here," he finally said. His reaction showed no hint of nervousness, as if two FBI agents asking him for an alibi wasn't anything to worry about. Jack didn't know whether that was a good sign or a bad one.

"The whole day?"

"Yes," Urich said, nodding. "I got here at seven in the morning, same time I always do, and I stayed late for an overnight surgery."

"Heart transplant?" Jack asked, trying the abrupt approach, thinking it might put him off his game if this was an act.

"No, it was a coronary artery bypass. Why?"

"No reason," Jack said, brushing it off. "What about yesterday?"

"Here," Urich said again. "I showed up a little bit early for a staff meeting and had another overnight surgery."

"Can you prove you were here both days?"

"Certainly. There are files that I signed for the surgeries. Plus"—he waved up at a camera in the corner of the hallway—"they record everything here."

"We'll need to see the footage," Jack said, although he didn't get the feeling that the doctor was lying to him. "No offense."

"None taken," he said, his light tone making it seem like he was genuinely trying to help. "They keep all of the recordings in the security room down the hall."

"Show me," Jack said. He motioned for Shade to stay behind and look for anyone else that seemed nervous about two FBI agents being there.

The security room was small, with only one chair and a few monitors. As Dr. Urich explained the situation to the guard monitoring the cameras, Jack looked around. On the walls were posters, most either notices explaining hospital policy or ads for some kind of new medication. Jack noticed one of them was the security guards' schedule.

"I'm sorry," the guard said, "but I can't show you the security footage. It's against hospital policy."

"Certainly it's not that strict of a rule," Dr. Urich replied.

"I'm sorry," the guard said, looking up at Jack. "A few years ago, someone at the hospital showed a cop security footage of a patient, and then when the patient found out, they sued the hospital to kingdom come. So now, we don't show footage to anyone." The guard turned slightly to look directly at Urich. "You knew that, Doctor."

Jack cut his eyes over at the good doctor. Maybe that was why he had been so open about his alibi; he knew they couldn't follow up. The thought irritated him, but he remained calm and looked back at the security guard.

"Three girls are dead," he said. "And you're telling me you can't let me look at security footage of one of the suspects, because you're afraid of getting sued?"

"If you come back with a warrant, I can show you whatever you want."

Jack ground his teeth. This was idiotic. "By the time I get a warrant, another girl might be dead. Do you understand that?"

"I'm sorry," the guard said. "I really am. But I can't show you the footage. It's against hospital policy."

Policy. The word irritated Jack. How many times had he heard someone tell him that—that they couldn't arrest someone because of policy? That they couldn't inspect a known murderer's house because of some rule that someone who didn't understand the consequences had made up? Someone who didn't know what it felt like to be helpless, left alone with a monster.

Jack flinched as he remembered the chains.

"Why did you become a doctor?" he finally said. He needed to know whether or not Urich was worth what he was considering.

The doctor looked shocked by the question but answered it nonetheless. "I never particularly wanted to become a doctor. But I believe that some people are placed on this earth with a certain gift, a gift meant to help the less fortunate. You, for instance, were clearly meant to be a detective, a hunter of evil. I, however, was meant to heal, to try and help mend the broken things in this world. To deny your calling would be a greater transgression than never having one in the first place."

Jack smirked. It was a nice speech. It was also quite possibly the most suspicious thing any suspect had ever told him.

"Okay," Jack said finally, having made up his mind as he glanced over at the schedule posted on the wall. He smiled at the guard. "I'll be back with a warrant."

Later that day, after it had gotten dark and most of the hospital staff had left, Jack walked through the hallways toward the security room. The schedule had revealed that the guard's shift ended at nine, with the new guard getting there early enough to create an overlap. However, considering that the night shift guard would want to do a sweep around the hospital before he locked himself in a room all night, and given the vast size of the hospital, Jack estimated that he had about a five-minute window.

As he approached the door, he reconsidered whether he was really going to do this. It felt wrong, but at the same time, he knew if he didn't, he'd probably never see the footage. They didn't have enough evidence on Urich yet to get a warrant, and even if they did, it would take too long. If it wasn't him, they needed to know so they could move on to other suspects, and if it was him, then he would probably kill someone else before they could prove it.

Jack imagined what the girls must've felt like, knowing what was about to happen to them. The fear that must've coursed through them. Then he imagined what the killer must've felt like. He'd probably felt proud—like killing them was his purpose in life. Like dying by his hands was the best thing the girls could have ever accomplished.

Jack's blood boiled as he made up his mind. He had to get the footage, so he could know for sure. So that if it was Urich, if killing was what he thought he was called to do, then Jack could stop him before anyone else died because of his sickness.

He reached the door and tried the handle. Locked. Jack rolled his eyes and then broke the small glass window in the door with his elbow before reaching in and unlocking it from the inside.

Once inside, it didn't take him long to find the footage. It was an old system, its recordings still stored on tapes. He hid them in his jacket before erasing the last ten minutes of footage from the cameras, removing any evidence of him breaking in. Had his life gone a different way, he could have made an excellent thief.

As he walked out of the hospital, a rush of guilt came over him. He had broken into a room like a common criminal. But it was what he had to do, to save other potential victims, and to stop the monster who was killing them.

He pulled the tapes out of his jacket and looked down at them. If it was Urich, he would know soon, and then he could stop him. He imagined the cops rushing into Urich's house, the look of surprise on his face. Killers always had that—a look of surprise. As if they thought they were too smart to ever get caught.

The feeling of guilt left him. If he hadn't taken the tapes, he would just have been allowing more girls to die because of what he wouldn't do, and he refused to be the reason that the serial killer took their lives. He would find him before he hurt anyone else.

Whatever it took.

Chapter Eight

"Run."

Jack opened the door to his office, pistol in hand. Outside, a dozen agents stood bewildered, not yet realizing what was happening.

"Why?" Sara asked. "Shouldn't we stay here?"

"No," Jack said, already out of the door, motioning for her to follow him. "If Shade cut off the lights, that means he's at the south entrance. There's barely one room between there and here, but if we can get to the director's office at the north end of the building, he'll have to get through ten rooms, all filled with armed agents."

"Okay." Sara drew her pistol out of its holster, trying to ignore the voice in her head telling her it wasn't worth it. Telling her she should just stay there and let him find her. Kill her. That was the only way to make the memory go away.

'No,' she told herself. The memory would go away eventually. It had to.

She moved behind Jack. "Let's go."

The guard to the south entrance held his gun up, trying to breathe as quietly as possible. Save for the small circle of light projecting from his gun's light, the room was pitch black, and in the darkness, he found himself afraid. Afraid of the unknown, afraid of what was coming.

He knew what the lights being cut off meant. He knew that he was here now. Shade. Out of desperation, he tried to quiet down his breathing and listen for anything, any sign that Shade was close to him. But he heard nothing. In the darkness, he felt completely alone.

He wasn't.

The guard kept his gun up, slowly moving it back and forth across the room. He kept his back to the wall, ensuring nothing could get him from behind. As long as he kept scanning the room, he would be fine, he told himself. Although even he knew that was only a fantasy. The lights were completely off, meaning Shade had both cut the power and disabled the backup generator, most likely placing him somewhere outside the south entrance. The guard knew that if Shade attacked, odds were he would be the first one to see him coming. He was wrong.

He never even saw him.

"Are you there?" Jack pleaded over the coms. "Please respond." The only answer he received was silence, which in a way was an answer itself. He looked back to Sara, who kept pace jogging behind him, gun still in hand. She was former military after all. She could probably raise the gun and fire in a split second. Probably faster than he could.

"He's not answering. Shade's already through the south entrance."

"Why wasn't there security guarding the power?" Sara asked, frustrated as she ran behind him in the dark.

"There was."

Outside of Jack's office were three agents, each armed with pistols. They stood perfectly still at opposite ends of the hallway, with one knelt down in the middle. Their pistols lacked flashlights, causing them to stand in complete darkness, not even able to see the weapons in their hands as they waited, silently praying he wouldn't come.

They heard a door creak open. Instinctively, one agent almost fired, but he stopped himself. In the darkness, there was no way to verify that it wasn't another agent, and they couldn't ask; that would give away their position. So instead, all three

agents stood silently, pointing their guns randomly, waiting for something to happen.

One of them screamed.

The others pointed their guns at the sound and fired out of panic, regretting it the moment they did, praying they hadn't hit their fellow agent. The flash illuminated the hallway for a split second, revealing a figure standing over their partner's body.

Before they could take aim, the light faded away. They fired a second time, once again illuminating the room, but it was now empty. There was nothing in front of them.

Just as one of them breathed a sigh of relief, something pulled him from behind. "Help," he tried to scream, but the words couldn't leave his mouth. The grip on his throat was too tight, and he began to black out.

The other agent still standing turned but didn't fire, at least not at first. In the darkness, he had no way to know he wouldn't be shooting his partner. So instead, he pointed his gun at the ceiling, firing a single round, which once again lit up his surroundings, as well as the figure now standing directly in front of him. As he tried to lower the gun, something caught his arm and ripped the weapon from his hands.

As he stood, alone in the suffocating darkness, now without a weapon to defend himself, he did the only thing he could think of.

He screamed.

Something struck him.

He collapsed backwards onto the floor as his entire head erupted in pain from the impact, feeling almost like a spike had been driven into his skull. Dazed and confused, he found the courage he had lacked just a moment ago. Gathering what little strength he had left, he stood back up.

The figure in the darkness knocked him down again.

The strike was so violent his body crumpled. With broken teeth and blood seeping out of his mouth, he now lay on the floor. He couldn't fight anymore. Could barely move. But still he tried. Tried to reach for his com, alert everyone else where he was. He had almost reached it when his eyes finally adjusted to the darkness, and he saw the horrific figure standing above him.

After that, everything went black.

Sara continued to follow Jack through the building. Suddenly, figures appeared in the darkness in front of them. Taking a second glance, she tightened her grip on her weapon. There were four of them.

Finally, her eyes fully adjusted to the dark, revealing four agents decked out in black riot gear, holding shotguns. One of them raised his hand, motioning for Jack to stop. "Director Williams said to tell you to get to his office. He has agents guarding the entire hallway leading up to it. Get there and she'll be safe."

"What about you?" Jack asked.

"We're here to slow him down, give you enough time to get there."

Jack looked at the agent, who was clearly terrified. "Are you sure?"

The agent nodded. "Go."

In the room past the one where the three agents had been incapacitated, five more stood. Each of them kept their aim on a different section, their lights illuminating almost the entire room.

Almost.

From a dark corner, a silver blade flew into the chest of one of the agents. As he fell, his gun twisted, flashing a light across the room. The other agents all turned to their fallen partner, not seeing the brief glimpse of a man in the corner that the twisting light revealed.

Another knife flew, pushing itself into one of their backs, an inch away from the spine. As the agent fell forward in pain, gasping for air as the knife stole it from him, the others turned their guns to the center of the room.

The one in the corner turned his gun the quickest, but it was caught as it swung. He fought against the force, but the gun wouldn't budge. Whatever was in the darkness had too strong of a hold on it.

The rest turned their aim to him, their lights revealing a man dressed in a black cloak, holding the other agent's gun in one hand and presumably his own in the other. It was pointed at them.

Before they could fire, they heard the crack of bullets flying through their knees, dropping them to the floor. They could do nothing as the man in the darkness turned back to their partner, whose gun he was holding. First, he twisted the gun, breaking it away from the agent's grip and letting it fall before grabbing the agent's throat and slamming him back against the wall.

As the gun hit the floor, it landed on its stock, spinning as it tipped over, its light illuminating the man standing in front of the agent one last time.

"Why are you doing this?"

The agent heard nothing as he was pulled from the wall and then shoved backwards again, the wall cracking as his head collided with it, rendering him unconscious.

Sara approached the hallway that led to the director's office. It appeared at least fifty feet long and had agents on either side of it, all wearing body armor, holding rifles, shotguns, or something similar. Some of them had lights, some didn't. Jack led her past them and through the door on the other side.

Two agents, neither one field operatives, stood in a small room—barely ten feet in either direction, now the only room in the entire building with actual light, thanks to battery-powered lanterns that one of the agents had left in his desk, just in case something like this ever happened. His partner had called him paranoid. The agent guessed that the joke was on him, but at the moment, as they stared at the door, waiting for something, someone, to appear, nothing seemed very funny.

The light coming off the lanterns was dim, but it was enough to illuminate the room to a decent degree. The two agents could barely make out the ends of their weapons as they stood side by side. The same agent who had brought the lanterns had a bulletproof vest on. He never took it off, even before the lights had gone out. Maybe he was paranoid.

Suddenly, the door they were both looking at slammed open, colliding with the wall behind it. Something slid into the room. The paranoid agent felt a blade pierce through the bone of his ankle, causing him to trip. The other agent fired suddenly out of fear, but his partner with the newly bleeding ankle fell in front of him, the vest taking the shot, but at this range it still knocked him out.

"No!" the agent who'd fired screamed before he heard another gunshot and felt the bone in his leg shatter. As he fell forward in pain, something grabbed him and slipped a knife into his side before letting go and allowing gravity to take his body once again.

In his last conscious moment, he cried out in pain, seeing the man above him, fully visible in the light of the lantern.

Jack and Sara rushed into the director's office, locking the door behind them. Inside, an older man with gray hair, wearing a faded blue suit, stood from behind his desk to greet her.

"Sara Michaels, I presume?"

She nodded.

"I'm Director Williams. You already saw the men outside this door, and we have more covering the rest of the rooms in between here and where we think he is. We also have a team outside, working to get the backup generators running so we can have light. You'll be completely safe here."

His overexplanation of her safety made her question whether she believed it. The look on Jack's face told her that he certainly didn't. But there wasn't anything else they could do now. This might have been the safest room in the building, but they had also backed themselves into a corner with no way out. If Shade managed to get there, there would be nowhere to run. No escape.

Part of her felt relieved, but she couldn't dare admit that to herself. She had to believe that it would get better. That eventually, the nightmares would go away. Eventually the voice would stop screaming in her head. Then it would be okay. Then she would be able to look at herself in the mirror again. Then she wouldn't find herself like she did now, secretly wishing she'd died long ago.

"Help me!"

'They'll go away,' she repeated silently to herself, over and over again until it seemed like a broken record, played so many times it was now hard to hear and covered with scratches, making the sound a hollow shell of what it had once been. But that didn't mean it wasn't true, right? Eventually, they had to go away.

"Hello," the director asked, leaning over the coms system on his desk. "Hello, can you read me?"

They all went quiet and listened for a response. None came.

"Maybe the coms are down too," Sara suggested. "Like the rest of the power."

"No, the coms run off their own power, a precaution in case something like this ever happened." The director looked down, solemn. "The agent who suggested it is who I now can't get ahold of."

"Shade won't kill him," Jack said.

"How do you know that?" the director said. "After what he did to those agents in the forest–"

"Those agents survived," Jack countered. "They were hurt, some badly, but he didn't kill them. Shade is sick, disturbed even, and might be trying to kill Sara to make the visions stop, but he isn't just going to murder innocent agents. That's not who he is."

"That's not who he was," the director countered. "Even the strongest wills can be broken, if you get desperate enough."

Sara could tell by both the look in Jack's eyes and his clenched jaw that he was about to say

more. It shocked her. Defending Shade to her was one thing, but in her experience, arguing with a commanding officer was never truly worth it, and they were wasting time with this pointless debate.

"Do we know how close he is?" Sara asked.

"If he's where the agent was," the director said, "that means he has six more rooms to go before he gets to the hallway outside."

"Wait," Jack said, eyes suddenly wide. "Be quiet, do you hear that?"

As they held their breath and listened, they heard it too. Breathing.

Jack stepped closer to the com unit's microphone, dread creeping into his voice. "Is that you?"

He received no answer.

"Shade," Jack said, leaning down to talk directly into the coms. "If that is you, please don't do this. I know what you're doing, and I know why. But this isn't going to change anything. This isn't going to make them go away." Jack's voice was completely breaking now as he pleaded with his former friend. "So please just stop. No one else has to get hurt."

The com disconnected.

Shade stood over the now-unconscious bodies of the two agents. He looked down at his hand, which

was spattered with blood. A lot of blood; more than he remembered getting on it. Deep down he already knew what that meant, but he tried to ignore it. Not now. It couldn't be happening now.

Cracking his neck, he lifted up a lantern from the floor. His eyes had now adjusted to the dark, and he was betting the same was true for the agents in the next room. The light would hurt.

He kicked open the door and threw the lantern, counting six agents scattered around the room, all of whom followed the light moving across the floor.

Shade moved to the agent closest to him, shoving his head into the wall, leaving a dent. The other agents turned to see him, but staring at the light had caused their eyes to readjust, and now they only saw an empty black space.

A knife slipped into the shoulder of one of the agents, and then his stomach.

'Can't let him scream,' Shade thought as he covered the agent's mouth, holding him against the wall as he slid down it.

Another agent found Shade in the darkness and was flipped over Shade's back, his head smashing into the floor, knocking him unconscious immediately.

Someone fired into the darkness at the origin of the sound but hit nothing. The flash, however, had

revealed Shade kneeling over their fellow agent. The sound of four gunshots echoed throughout the room as all four agents dropped their guns slowly, falling to the floor and clutching their bleeding stomachs.

Shade stood up and reloaded his pistol.

Even in the dark, he saw more blood on his hand. Too much blood. He shook his head side to side, trying to make it go away. 'Not now,' he begged. 'Please not now. Not when I'm this close.' But his pleading availed him nothing. He heard the squeak of a small operating table rolling behind him but didn't turn to look. It wasn't real, he reminded himself. It couldn't be real.

Five rooms to go.

Two agents stood in the center of the room, each wearing a bulletproof vest. Shade put a bullet in the first one's knee and knocked the gun from the second's hand, proceeding to choke him from behind, using his vest to block the gunfire of a third agent hiding in the corner. As a rifle blast hit the vest, Shade dropped the man, whose ribs were now most likely fractured, and fired on the agent in the corner.

With two agents now on the ground and one kneeling with a broken knee, Shade stepped over and picked up the rifle. 'He'll try to draw,' Shade thought, and a moment later the kneeling agent lifted his pistol.

The butt of the rifle broke his nose.

Shade checked the rifle's magazine. Only three rounds left. Blood was now trickling down his entire arm. Familiar blood. Her blood.

He squinted his eyes, trying to unsee it. But it wouldn't go away. He looked down and saw the bodies of the three agents, who now appeared as the first three victims. Eyes rolled back in their heads, limbs jutting out from their bodies at unnatural angles. Their mouths moved slowly, speaking to Shade.

"Why didn't you save us. Why did you let us die?"

Shade tried to ignore them. It wasn't real. It couldn't be real. He replaced the mag and chambered a round. 'Just keep moving,' he told himself. He couldn't let them distract him. Not now. Not when he was this close to finally ending it.

Four rooms left.

Within the next room, four bodies stood waiting for him, four corpses of those he hadn't saved. Those he had let die. Or were they agents?

The first agent shot at him, the bullet passing through his left shoulder, causing an adrenaline spike that for a moment returned his clarity to him. Raising the rifle, he put bullets into the first three before throwing the rifle at the last agent, knocking his gun from his hands.

The agent pulled a knife from his back pocket.

Shade blocked the agent's first swipe and was about to throw him against the wall when suddenly the agent turned back into one of the corpses. The corpse of the fourth victim. Blond hair stained red, green eyes that had now turned into empty black holes, and arms that were currently holding her bleeding chest together, keeping everything inside. At least what had been left inside.

Shade hesitated. He knew it wasn't real, but he couldn't do it. Couldn't strike her. Not when she was looking into his eyes, begging him to save her. Asking why he didn't.

She then raised a knife and brought it into Shade's chest, just below his clavicle. The pain tore through his body, returning his vision for just a moment—a moment he used to pull the knife from his own chest and shove it into the agent's, dropping him to the floor.

The visions came back. The sound of the operating table squeaking as it rolled past the surgical tools that now lay on the floor. Scalpels, needles, a spinning saw.

"It's not real, it's not real," Shade said to himself. He threw his fist into the wall beside him, trying to make it go away. "It's not real!"

Three rooms.

Hallucinating so badly that he could barely tell where he was, he stepped into the next room. In reality there were only two agents in the room, neither one holding weapons, but he saw four people standing there, the rotting corpses of four girls, begging him to save them. He closed his eyes for a moment, not being able to fight if he looked, and threw a knife at the first one. It passed through her, sticking into the wall on the other side. The other three walking corpses charged him. He closed his eyes again and moved at one, but he hit air.

Before he could turn, another of the corpses struck him in the back of the head. Shade was brought to the floor but kicked his leg backwards, tripping the corpse behind him, causing her to fall as well. Without looking, he shoved her head into the floor, knocking her out.

The remaining corpse lunged at him. He closed his eyes, not looking at her, as he caught her arm and threw her across the room, her back colliding with the hilt of the knife still stuck to the wall.

A fifth corpse lunged at him unexpectedly. In shock, he dropped to the floor and crawled backwards, the corpse crawling after him like a spider with broken legs.

"Why didn't you save me?"

"I'm sorry," he said, as he found himself unable to move.

"You let me die!" she screamed, lunging after him. *"You let all of us die!"*

"I'm sorry," he repeated, his back against the wall. He was too paralyzed to move. All he could think about was the corpse in front of him. Why it haunted him. Who he hadn't saved. What he would give to make it go away.

Sara.

Shade remembered why he was here. She was so close. Just a little longer and it would be over. For a brief moment, just long enough to stand up, he regained clarity.

Two rooms.

With five rounds left in his pistol, Shade opened the door to the next room, containing the four agents armed in riot gear, holding shotguns. With their body armor, five rounds from a pistol wouldn't put them down. At least so long as they weren't headshots, but he couldn't do that. They weren't who he was here to kill.

Before the agents could react, Shade had fired four rounds, each on the edge of their riot helmet's visor, cracking it. It wouldn't take them out but would impair their vision, causing them to see dozens of Shades reflected in the cracks of their visor.

One, younger than the rest, probably barely out of training, still fired his shotgun, but he missed by a mile, aiming at the wrong reflection. The real Shade fired his last pistol round into the agent's hand, causing him to drop the shotgun. Catching it midair, he turned it to the others, putting two rounds in each of the first two agents' vests. At this range it was enough to knock them out.

The remaining agent fired his shotgun. He missed, but the muzzle was within inches of Shade's head, causing everything to go temporarily quiet in Shade's ear. Everything except the voices.

"You let us die."

Shade grabbed for the shotgun's barrel, pointing it at the floor, towards the agent's own foot. The agent fired again instinctively, not realizing what had happened until it was too late. As he fell over forward, Shade rammed the butt of his own shotgun into the helmet, cracking it and rendering the agent underneath it unconscious.

Shade turned back to the young agent whose gun he had stolen, who had now drawn a pistol, pointing it at his head. Shade cursed himself under his breath. He should've seen the pistol.

In an instant, Shade had the shotgun pointing at the agent's head, causing a standoff.

"Put it down, kid."

The young agent said nothing.

"Don't make me do this," Shade pleaded. But he knew the kid wasn't going to put it down. In the circumstances, he wouldn't have either. But he had to get to the next room, and he couldn't kill the kid for no reason.

'His hands are shaking,' Shade thought to himself. Maybe just enough to cause him to miss the first shot. He took the chance, spinning his weapon and slamming the butt across the young agent's face.

The kid had enough time to fire, but the bullet barely missed Shade's stomach, instead tearing through the wall behind him.

One room left.

Shade knew what was on the other side of the door. If Director Williams was smart, and he was, he probably had every agent left camped outside of the door, in single file, to remove any chance of being taken by surprise. Shade loaded the remaining ammunition into the shotgun. Six shells. Not enough to take everyone down, but maybe enough to cause panic. He also removed all the lights from the agents' guns, a total of four. Clicking them a few times, so they would flash rapidly, he took a deep breath and felt the hallucinations start to come back.

'Just a little bit longer,' he pleaded with the voices in his head. 'Just have to make it a little

further.' But he could already hear the operating table squeaking behind him, and he knew he didn't have much time before he completely lost it. He had to go now.

He twisted the doorknob and hid to the side of it, letting the door creak open itself as all of the agents' flashlights moved to the doorway. Shade looked in front of him one last time, seeing the corpse he had hoped he wouldn't. The last victim. The one that had caused everything that came after. The breakdown, the killing in the forest, all of it.

'No more time,' he thought as he threw the flashlights into the room, their wild flashing disorienting the agents just long enough for him to enter without being shot. Immediately he found the agents who held weapons with lights. Five of them. He shot each one in the chest, the force of the blast knocking them off their feet. One shell left, and he used it to shoot the rifle out of the hand of another agent who was only seconds away from pulling the trigger.

As the guns with lights fell to the ground and agents in the middle frantically stopped the other lights from flashing, the room was filled with absolute darkness.

The hallucinations returned.

In the director's office, Jack and Sara stood with their guns trained on the door, trying not to listen to the horrific screaming coming from the other side.

Shade stabbed someone in the arm. He wasn't sure who. Wasn't even sure if this was real anymore. Someone tackled him to the floor, but he shoved them off into the wall beside him. As his eyes started to adjust to the dark, he saw figures standing straight up, dozens of them in every direction. They were light brown, almost white, but covered in red blood, standing upright like ghosts, watching him. He recognized them. The trees from the forest.

"No, not now," he mumbled to himself as he started to feel himself slipping. He couldn't lose it now. Not when Sara was in the other room. Not when she was this close.

Something attacked him from the right. He kicked low, finding it in the darkness. Something cracked, and whatever it was began to scream.

To his right, he saw all the victims slither between the trees, their heads tilted too far sideways to be connected to their necks. Shade backed up, running into someone, who he brought to the floor without thinking. He turned to run from the walking ghosts, but they were behind him too. They were everywhere.

He couldn't escape.

"You did this to us!"

Shade turned wildly, trying not to look at them but unable to look away. "No, I didn't," he pleaded. "I didn't, I-I-I tried to save you."

"What about me?"

Shade looked into the distance, beyond all the trees, and saw the woman from the forest, her stomach filled with so many knife wounds that no skin was left.

Shade fell to his knees. "I didn't—I'm sorry."

The woman continued to walk towards him as Shade lost all bearing on reality.

The screaming suddenly stopped. Sara stood with her gun trained on the door for what felt like hours, even though it was only thirty seconds.

Jack grew restless. "If Shade was going to come in here, he would have done it by now."

The director glared at him, knowing what he meant. "Under no circumstances are you to open that door."

"If they'd killed Shade, they would be answering their coms, and if Shade was still stable, he would've busted through the door and killed us by now. But if he is out there, hallucinating like I think he is, we may have a shot to take him down." He turned his gaze to Sara. "But it won't last long."

Sara nodded, and Jack opened the door, both of them greeted by a long, dark hallway. They stood at the edge, their guns aimed out into the dark abyss, when Director Williams called out from behind them, repeating a message heard over the coms. "The power is almost back up."

Jack and Sara remained still, keeping their guns up, looking into the vast darkness, when the lights switched back on, revealing a white room covered almost entirely in crimson, at least a dozen agents lying scattered across the floor, unresponsive, and Shade sitting in the corner, shaking violently.

Sara moved her gun to him and stepped closer. Jack did the same.

Shade didn't acknowledge their presence, his eyes seemingly looking at nothing as he cried, pleading with someone who wasn't there.

"I'm sorry," he said quietly, his voice breaking. "I'm sorry."

In his eyes, Sara saw the same thing she did every time she looked in the mirror. The look of remembering horrors of the past. The look of wanting to do anything to forget, to be free of the

memories. In that instant, Sara realized it wasn't an excuse.

But there was something else too. Looking at him, she realized she had lied, trying to talk herself out of using the gun in her drawer, telling herself the memories would go away. But now, standing here, looking at Shade, she realized that his never did, and so hers never would either.

As Jack hit Shade with the barrel of his pistol, knocking him out, she stood motionless, having lost all hope of moving on, reliving a nightmare from her own past.

"Help me!"

Chapter Nine

Shade knelt down, covering his face in his hands, trying to get the image out of his head.

It had been a week since the last killing. They'd watched the footage Jack had stolen from the hospital, but it had only confirmed their fears. Dr. Kevin Urich, their only suspect, had been at the hospital at the time of the murders, just like he'd said. Which meant they were back to no suspects, no leads, and seemingly no end in sight.

The warehouse was crawling with cops. Yellow police tape guarded the entrances, keeping out the reporters, who were almost breaking their necks to get a picture inside. CSIs had collected evidence from everywhere they could find it, and Jack and Shade had just been shown the body of the fourth victim, Angela Carter. She was eighteen years old.

Shade continued to take deep breaths, trying to stay calm, not let the images in. But it was no use. Every time he closed his eyes, he saw the bodies of the victims, lying on the table, blood dripping from them. But that wasn't what scared Shade. It was the times when he didn't close his eyes. When he saw the horror around him, the ghosts of the girls he couldn't save.

He shuddered as he realized what was happening. The hallucinations were coming back, just like they had in the military. Only this time, he wouldn't be discharged. The choice was in his hands now, and he knew he couldn't walk away. Because if he did, more girls would die. And then it would be on him.

But what if he stayed on the case and the hallucinations made him lose control again, like he had in the military? That outcome would be far worse than if he just walked away now.

"What do we know?" Jack asked.

Detective Washington shook his head, the wrinkles on his face showcasing a tired, experienced officer who'd handled enough cases to know when one was beginning to slip away. "Not much. She was eighteen, blond hair, green eyes. She had just graduated from high school, with a scholarship in track and field. In other words, not at all similar to any of the other victims, apart from being female, and relatively young."

"Was she reported missing?" Shade asked, arms crossed and head down, trying to remain stable.

"Her parents filed a missing persons report two days ago."

"Any prior medical history?"

"Not that we've found so far, but it's still early. We only found the body an hour ago."

"Has anyone interviewed the parents yet?" Jack asked.

"Not yet. I was about to head over there once the CSI guys finish up here."

"Let us do it."

Washington thought about it for a moment. "Okay, go ahead."

"Thank you."

As they began to walk away, Shade saw the body of the girl again, but this time she was standing upright, on the other end of the warehouse. Her skin was pale, almost ghostlike, and her eyes were rolled back in her head. She raised up her hand, rotting and covered in blood, and began writing on the wall. Shade stood frozen in place for a moment, watching her add letter after letter to her message, until finally she stopped and turned back to face him.

Shade's eyes flinched as he saw the message written in blood.

They stood outside the parents' house, Jack leaning on a wooden column, Shade standing in front of him.

"You ever think maybe this isn't a real serial killer?" Jack asked.

"What do you mean?"

Jack ran his hand over his neck. "It's just, the crime scene, the way he's killing the girls, it just seems a little"–he paused, looking for the right word–"overdone."

"Overdone?"

"Yeah. Like, what was the first thing we both said when we saw the crime scene?"

Shade considered the question. "That it was a serial killer."

"Exactly. Normally we only realize it's a serial killer when there are a few victims with the same manner of death. But this guy went out of his way to make the crime scene as gruesome as possible. Maybe that's because he wanted us to assume exactly what we did. That he's a serial killer."

"Okay. But how does that give him an advantage?"

"Because," Jack said, motioning with his hands as he spoke, "if it's a serial killer, we look into possible motives for the killer to kill every victim. But what if this guy, whoever he is, only wanted to kill one person? One girl that he wanted dead. And this whole charade is just a cheap parlor trick to hide his real motives, so that when he finally gets his desired kill, no one will suspect him."

Shade thought it over. It was a good theory, one that he couldn't necessarily find any holes in. But there was one aspect of it that made him nervous—one aspect that made the theory dangerous.

"Makes sense," Shade said. "But are you saying that because you really believe it, or because it means that eventually he'll kill his target, and then this will be over, whether we catch him or not?"

Jack hesitated to answer, and Shade saw in his eyes what he had feared. Jack wanted it to be over, just like Shade did. But once you start focusing on that, you start making mistakes—mistakes that are costly.

But Shade couldn't dismiss the theory entirely, mostly because he needed to believe it himself. "Just don't lose it on me, okay? After all, you're supposed to be the stable one."

"Well, then, we really are screwed," Jack said, causing a brief moment of levity as they both grinned for the first time in weeks. But soon, the moment passed.

"So," Shade said. "We're not going to tell the parents the specifics, right? They shouldn't have to know."

"Agreed. We only mention what we absolutely have to."

They stood in silence for a moment longer, trying to work up the nerve to knock on the door. It was hard, meeting the parents of the kid you couldn't save in time.

A few moments after they knocked, the door opened, and a woman stood behind it, eyes red from crying. "Who are you?"

Jack flashed his badge. "We're with the FBI. Can we come in and speak to you about your daughter?"

Inside, the mother led them through the house. On their way to the living room, they passed a dark green door that probably led to the basement; the paint was starting to chip off, the wood beneath was anything but smooth, and there was something else about it that felt off. Jack purposely ducked his eyes, removing it from his sight. It was an almost imperceptible movement, but Shade caught it all the same, if only because he had known it was coming. Everyone had their own memories to hide from, and he supposed that was Jack's. Shade himself avoided glancing at the picture frames hanging on the wall, containing photos of Angela Carter smiling, unaware of the fate that would eventually befall her.

But despite the sudden barrage of unflinching images, soon Jack and Shade sat on a plain white couch, facing the parents of the fourth victim. They looked to be in their mid-forties. The father was tall, but broad enough he didn't look like it, with ruffled brown hair and a small brown beard to match. His eyes looked tired, and his face looked rough.

The mom, however, was the spitting image of her daughter.

They sat side by side, each appearing to have done their fair share of crying since the police had informed them of what had happened earlier that morning. Which was good, Jack knew; they would be more likely to remember details now that the initial shock was gone.

"What can you tell me about your daughter?" Jack asked.

The mother spoke first, having to force the words out. "She was happy. She was a happy kid. She—" The mom started crying. "I'm sorry," she sobbed.

"That's okay," Jack said. "I know this is a hard time for both of you. Maybe we should do this later?"

"It's fine," the father said. "You can ask your questions."

"Okay," Jack said. "When was the last time you saw your daughter?"

The father answered. "Five days ago."

Jack wrinkled his forehead. "I thought you only filed the missing persons report two days ago?"

"We did," the father said, his voice cracking.

"But why wait three days to file the report?"

The father shifted in his chair. "I had gotten into an argument with her, and she stormed out. At first, we thought she was staying at her friend's place. She had done that before, so we figured we'd let her cool off, but after the first few days passed, we called to check and realized she wasn't there."

"What was the argument about?"

"It doesn't matter anymore," the father said, shaking his head as tears fell from his eyes.

"It does matter," Jack said. "Time of death was yesterday, so we need to know where she could've gone before that."

"Okay. We had an argument about the college she wanted to go to. I thought it was too far out of state. I mentioned that to her, and it just snowballed from there." His voice rose slightly as though he was scolding himself. "Just stupid stuff we shouldn't have even been arguing about."

"Any idea where she could've gone when she left your house? Any place she went to a lot, aside from her friend's house?"

The mother continued to cry, but the father held himself together enough to answer. "Not really. I mean, she mostly would just spend the night at *friends' places, but we already called all of them, and none of them have seen her since—" He fought back the tears. "Since she left."*

"Before," Shade said suddenly.

"What?"

Shade looked up directly at him. "You said she had gone to her friend's house before. Did you argue a lot?"

The father looked confused. "Occasionally, I guess. Why?"

"No reason," Shade said, staring at the father. Something seemed off.

The room was quiet for a moment before Jack asked another question. "Can you think of anyone at all who might want to hurt your daughter? Did she ever complain about anyone watching her or, you know, anything like that?"

The father thought for a minute. "Not really. As far as I know, everyone at school liked her."

"Anyone like her too much?"

The father shook his head. "Not that I know of."

They sat in silence for a moment, and then Shade saw a girl standing in the corner of the room. The same girl from the warehouse. Angela Carter. She was standing next to a picture of herself hanging from the wall, both faces looking directly at Shade; one of them a captured image of a happy moment, the other a ghostly shadow of the grisly reality. Neither one breathing, neither one really alive, both twisted reflections of a girl whose life had been stolen from her by an unseen horror, which so far refused to reveal itself, leaving only the victims to tell the story.

It caught his eye for a moment, but then he looked away. He couldn't break down, not here. As he moved his gaze back, he noticed the father had seen him look away. They stared at each other for a moment, the father seemingly trying to figure out what he had looked at, when Jack pulled photos from his jacket, laying them on the coffee table in front of him.

They were photos of the doctors that had tended to the previous victims. Only one, Dr. Kevin Urich, was actually a surgeon, and his alibi had checked out. But still, it never hurt to check.

"Do you recognize any of these men?"

The mother answered first. "No, I don't think so."

The father picked up one of the photos, specifically the photo of Dr. Urich. "He looks familiar. I think I used to work with him, before I was transferred to another hospital."

Jack and Shade looked at each other for a moment in shock. Finally, Jack turned his gaze back to the father. "I'm sorry, did you say hospital?"

"Yes," he said, noticing their strange expressions. "I'm a doctor."

"You trained in surgery?" Jack asked, barely giving him time to finish his sentence. Shade could tell from Jack's voice that he was excited that they finally might have a lead.

"It's not my main field, but I have some experience in it. Why?"

"Where have you been for the past few days?" Jack asked.

The father's tone completely changed as he realized what they were saying. "I didn't murder my daughter."

"Didn't say you did," Jack said. "Just asked for an alibi."

The father stood up quickly, causing Jack and Shade to do the same. "I was at the hospital every day, doing double shifts. For—for the few hours I was off, I was here, right here," he said, pointing to the floor violently as his voice grew irritated, seeing the look of disbelief in Jack's eyes. "What, you think I would kill my own daughter because of some stupid argument?"

Jack didn't answer him, instead looking to the wife. "Is that true?"

"Yes," the wife said plainly. "He was doing double shifts, and he was here every hour in between." She saw the look in Jack's eyes, knowing that he thought she might be lying. "She's my daughter. If he wasn't here on those days, I would tell you."

Shade looked over at Jack. He could tell from his eyes that he was thinking the same thing. Something was definitely off about the father, but the mother didn't appear to be lying to them. And even if she was, they could check with the hospital to verify his story. Which meant there was no reason to stay.

"Okay," Jack said, picking the photos back up and putting them in his jacket pocket. "We've taken up enough of your time. Call us if you remember anything else." He walked to the door, along with Shade, when the father spoke.

"Why was it important that I was a doctor?"

Shade answered immediately. "It wasn't."

"No," the father said, stepping closer. "You showed me a picture of a doctor and then only accused me after you found out I was one. You asked me if I was a surgeon. Why?"

Jack answered this time, seeing he wasn't going to let it go. "There were details about the case that suggested the killer might be a surgeon. That's all." He squinted; he shouldn't have told them that.

The father stepped closer, tears falling from his face, his voice almost a growl. "What kind of details? What was done to my daughter?"

Jack and Shade kept silent, not knowing what to say.

The father erupted, grabbing Shade, the closest to him, by the collar and backing him to the wall. "What was done to my daughter?!" he screamed as he held Shade there, his voice breaking up as he pleaded through tears. "What was done to her?"

Jack moved his hand over his weapon instinctively as he watched the man holding Shade against the wall, but he knew he wouldn't need to draw it. He just had to wait.

"What was done to my daughter?" the man asked, finally breaking down completely and falling to the floor, sobbing. "What'd they do to my daughter?"

"Why didn't you save me?" the girl whispered to Shade.

He was in his own office. His light was turned on, but all he could see was darkness. Everything except the most recent victim: wet rotted skin, soaked in blood, and missing her heart.

'It's not real,' Shade told himself. But it was getting harder to tell. And it wasn't just the new hallucinations. It was the old ones too, coming back to haunt him. The screaming, the gunfire.

"Why did you let me die?" the corpse growled.

He had let her die. He hadn't been able to save her. If he had done his job like he was supposed to, she would still be alive. They all would. But instead, he had been worthless, hallucinating in his room instead of catching the guy who had done it. The guy who would kill again. The guy he couldn't catch.

It was his fault. All of it.

He couldn't bear to look at the corpse of the girl in front of him, instead sitting on the floor, burying his eyes in his hands. Why couldn't he save her? Why couldn't he save any of them?

Why did everyone he was supposed to protect die?

Eyes lit up in the darkness behind the corpse. White, rolled-back eyes, three pairs. Watching Shade. Judging him for not saving them. The eyes moved closer, the bodies they belonged to coming into focus.

"You let us die!"

"I know," Shade said, shaking on the floor. "I'm sorry."

As they moved closer to him, his shaking grew worse. "Go away," he pleaded. "Please just go away."

One of them, the original victim, stopped and leaned down, whispering into his ear, "You know what you have to do to make us go away."

Later that day, as the sun began to set in the sky, wind blew through the cemetery, carrying leaves with it, dancing over the graves, both old and new. In the middle of the cemetery, Shade knelt, looking at the tombstones in front of him. Dozens of them—gray marble slabs, sitting in the grass, each with a name he knew carved into it. He reached his hand out and ran it across the one closest to him. In that moment, it wasn't the girls' voices he heard, the victims of the new serial killer. It was the sound of gunshots, ringing in his ear. Memories of what had happened, what he had wanted to forget.

As he knelt there, contemplating what to do, a leaf crunched behind him.

"Thought I might find you here," Jack said.

Shade acknowledged his presence with a slight nod but didn't respond.

"Are you okay?"

Shade sighed for a moment as he looked at the tombstones. "You know," he said finally, "no one ever truly knows what they're capable of until they're pushed too far. Until the horror, the desperation sets in, and then they realize that, in order to survive, they have to become something they don't even recognize."

Shade took a deep breath, finding the words, before he continued. "First combat mission I ever ran,

I was on a team of forty. We had all been trained together and thought we knew what we were getting into. Until the shooting started. Within minutes, half my team was dead. Before long, more followed. In that moment, I realized what I had to do to survive. It was almost an instinct, like something inside of me had been bottled up, just waiting to be set free. And it was."

Shade looked at the ground, almost ashamed of the words that were coming out of his mouth. "Afterwards, the ones that were left called me a hero. But I couldn't get the faces of my teammates, my friends, the ones who didn't make it, out of my head. Soon, I got put on more dangerous ops, practically suicide missions. But every time, I came back. And every time, fewer men came back with me."

Shade squinted. "Eventually, the team was down to five. Everyone else had died," he said, his voice cracking. "But not me. Of all those who could have survived, who they couldn't kill, it was me. Not the ones who had kids at home, or the ones who never should have been drafted for these missions in the first place. That's when I realized, what's the point of being able to survive if no one else survives with you? What's the point of taking so many lives, seeing so much horror, if the only person you can end up saving is yourself?

"That's when it started. It was just nightmares at first, but soon I began seeing their faces even when I was awake. Their rotting corpses asking me why I couldn't save them, why I could fight hard enough to save myself, but not them."

His eyes watered. "Then one day, those of us who were left were sent on another mission. I thought I would be okay, but then the gunfire started, worse than it had ever been before, and I snapped. I started hallucinating in the middle of combat." He shut his eyes, trying to hide from the memories as he spoke them. "By the time I realized what was real again, everyone was dead, including my team. And I was hallucinating so bad, I can't—" Tears fell from his face. "I can't remember if I'm the one who killed them."

They both sat quietly for a moment before Shade spoke again.

"I can't do this. I can't keep going. I'm already beginning to see things, corpses that aren't real. Before long I'll just be getting in the way, making mistakes." Shade's eyes cut back up to the tombstones in front of him. "I can't let myself lose control again. I'm sorry."

Jack looked at the field full of graves for a moment and then turned back to Shade. "Remember when we first became partners, and I asked you why you joined the FBI? Why, after everything that happened, everything you saw, you didn't get out of this life completely? Find something to do where you didn't have to wake up every day and see reminders of just how messed up the world really is? Where you could just forget about everything you saw and move on? I'll never forget what you said to me. Do you remember?"

His question went unanswered.

"You told me that ignoring the horrors doesn't make them go away." Jack knelt down beside him. "You didn't know it then, but I had been about to quit. I couldn't take it anymore—all the rules, all the other agents who didn't care. Who didn't understand what was actually at stake, what the monsters of the world will really do to someone, how completely they can break you, how alone they can make you feel." Jack smiled. "But then I met you, and I saw someone else who understood. Someone like me, who couldn't see past the victims, who knew how dangerous the monsters really were.

"So," Jack said finally, "if you want to quit, quit. I'm not going to stop you. Maybe if you do, the hallucinations won't come back. Maybe you'll be able to forget about them." Jack pointed at the tombstones. "But the girls' graves are going to be filled whether you ignore it or not, and I can't catch him without you. The cops, the other agents, they don't care the same way we do. But maybe if you stay, maybe if you face it, we can save the next victim."

For a moment, the cemetery was quiet as Jack placed his hand on Shade's shoulder, joining him in looking out over all the good people the ground now contained, lost from the world, but not forgotten. Finally, Shade rose from the ground. "The next victim," he said, resolve now firmly back in his voice.

"What?"

"You said we save the next victim. If we can find one of the next victims, we can protect her."

"Right," Jack said, nodding. "But we don't know how the killer is choosing the victims, so we can't predict the next one."

"But the third victim. Dr. Urich said she donated a kidney. He said she gave it to–"

"Her younger sister," Jack finished, his voice growing excited. "And if the killer is choosing his victims based on a pattern, even if we don't know what it is, it's a good bet she'll follow whatever pattern her sister did, making her a target. And if we find her–"

"We can protect her."

Jack reached out his hand. "We'll save them," he said. "I promise you, whatever it takes, we will save the next victim."

Shade hesitated, remembering what Jack had said. He was right. Ignoring the horrors wouldn't save the girls' lives. "Whatever it takes," Shade repeated as he shook Jack's hand.

For the first time in weeks, they felt hope.

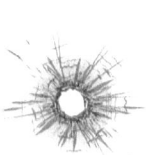

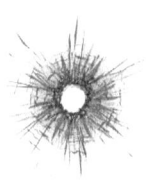

Chapter Ten

Sara stood in front of a two-way mirror. Beyond it, Shade was sitting on a small metal chair behind a desk, wrapped in a white straitjacket that was bolted to the wall behind him, making it impossible for him to move any farther forward than he already was.

Before he had regained consciousness, they had moved him to this facility. Evidently it was a prison, designed to hold the FBI's more dangerous inmates. The interrogation room in the center, the one Shade now sat in, was designed to ensure that, even before questioning, the prisoner couldn't escape.

Had she not been following Jack, she would have gotten lost trying to find her way through it. From what he had explained, it was designed like a maze, each hallway leading endlessly to others, with only two exits, two ways of escape. Because of this, all the guards typically stationed outside of prison were standing guard in the hallways instead,

since in the history of the prison, the farthest anyone had ever made it was two hallways. Outside guards simply weren't necessary, so they crowded the hallways instead, like lines of soldiers waiting for a war that would never come.

Sara noticed Jack staring in at Shade. He looked so depressed. It must've hurt to see his friend like this. Locked up, being watched like an animal. Broken.

Her train of thought was interrupted by Director Williams. "I don't like this. We should've just put him in a cell."

"He's in a straitjacket, bolted to the wall, in a small locked room. He's not going anywhere."

"Yes, I know," the director said, shaking his head. "But this just seems pointless."

"Let me at least try to talk to him," Jack said. "I know what he's done, I know he's never getting out of here, but maybe I can still help him. Help the hallucinations go away. We owe him at least that."

They continued to argue, but Sara stopped listening to them—she saw something familiar on Shade's face. In his eyes, in the way his head shifted back and forth slightly, trying to block out the noise, the memories of his past, the ones for which he was willing to kill in order to escape. In his eyes, she recognized her own reflection, her own look of anguish, of running from a memory you couldn't forget. A choice you couldn't take back.

"Help me."

Telling herself that one day it would stop was the only thing that had kept her going. The only thing that had kept her from using the revolver in her drawer the second she had gotten back from the war. The thought that maybe one day, she would close her eyes and not see her friend's bleeding face staring back at her.

But now she realized that was a fantasy. It was never going to go away. The voice in her head would never stop begging her for help; instead, it would only get worse. Truth be told, it already had, but she had just denied the signs. Told herself it had to get worse before it got better. Shade had probably told himself the same thing, until one day he couldn't take it anymore. One day when he'd just found himself willing to do whatever it took to make them stop. Make the hauntings go away.

The same day that Sara now felt had come for her.

"Let me talk to him," she said, interrupting their argument.

"What?" Jack said, turning to face her.

"Let me talk to him," she repeated.

"Under no circumstances can that happen," the director stated, looking toward Jack, expecting him to back him up. "Certainly you can't think this is a good idea."

Jack ignored him for a moment, instead looking directly into Sara's eyes. She could tell he was trying to figure out what she was thinking. Why she wanted to go in there. Finally, it looked as though he had reached a conclusion, before asking for clarification. "Why do you want to do this?"

"Maybe I can get him to talk, to tell me why he's doing all this," she lied. "Maybe it can help him move on."

"Are you sure?" Jack asked, still visibly trying to read her, trying to see if she was telling the truth.

Sara nodded.

Jack thought for a moment longer before clicking the pen in his hand once. "She's right, this could help him. And she'll be careful. She'll stay behind the desk at all times." He turned to her for confirmation, and she gave it.

The director shook his head, still not convinced.

"If anything happens to her, it's on me," Jack added.

Williams sighed. "Fine. But if she moves even an inch past the desk, or Shade does anything unexpected at all, we pull her out."

"Deal," Jack said, looking to Sara now. "Are you sure you're ready?"

She nodded.

Shade was still shaking slightly when Sara opened the door to the interrogation room and walked inside. It was a small room, thick walls on every side, with only one small door behind her, making her feel uneasy, as though she were trapped inside of a coffin buried six feet underground, with no way to dig herself back up, no way to run. But then again, she wasn't planning to try.

She glanced at her reflection in the two-way mirror but instantly looked away. It was just another reminder that she had lived, and she didn't want any more reminders than she already had in her head.

The table in the center was rectangular, putting about five feet of distance between them as she took her seat opposite him.

At first, she didn't speak, instead just studying how his eyes twitched and trying to imagine what he must be seeing. Even now, he still hadn't acknowledged her presence in the room. She wondered if he even knew she was there.

She was surprised by what he looked like. She had expected him to look somewhat like Jack:

brown hair, strong jaw, trusting smile, exactly what you'd expect an FBI agent to look like. But the man in front of her now made her feel nervous just looking at him. She didn't know how to describe it, but there was something about him that felt... not threatening, but intimidating. Pitch-black hair, eyes that would have been unsettling even if they hadn't been twitching back and forth. It was like looking at a rabid dog itching to get off its leash.

She also noticed the dog tags hanging from his neck. The prison guards had wanted to take them off him, but Jack wouldn't allow it. She appreciated that. Her fingers crept up, running over the engravings in her own tags. It would have felt strange without them, not feeling the slight pull on the back of her neck, the chain digging gently into the skin. But as she looked at Shade's, hanging down in front of his straitjacket, she noticed something she hadn't before. They were covered in blood.

At first, she assumed it was from the agents he had just taken down at the FBI headquarters, but after looking closer, she realized the blood wasn't just resting on them, it was stained on—a brand that would never go away.

"So, Jack tells me you're former military," she finally said. "I guess we have that in common."

She had hoped he would give her some sort of a response, something to tell her that he could at least hear her. But he didn't.

"I was a medic. Did it for my whole tour. I take it you were something else."

Still no response.

She kept talking, lying to herself that it was to get a response from him, but deep down she knew she was just stalling, trying to buy enough time to talk herself out of it. Sometimes, she'd found, if your true intentions are terrifying enough, the only thing you can do is talk: tell stories, make idle conversation, anything to delay the inevitable tragedy for a few mere moments, if only to savor the last few breaths before the horrific reality struck, and your life was changed forever.

"So, after the military you decided to join the FBI. That seems like an odd choice. Care to tell me why?" She spoke without pausing, not really expecting an answer at this point. "Jack says you were good, though, and despite the director's mean exterior, I think he likes you too."

Still, he said nothing, eyes twitching back and forth, trying to block the visions out.

Sara watched him, regretting what she had thought earlier about it just being an excuse. Now, sitting here looking at him, she honestly couldn't

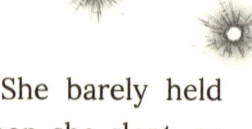

believe he hadn't lost it sooner. She barely held on herself, and she only saw it when she slept, or occasionally heard it during the day. From the look of him, he never escaped it, never had a moment where he wasn't reminded of it. Or, as Jack put it, never got to wake up from his nightmare.

And yet still, unlike her, he hadn't given up. He had lasted months, trying to work the case with Jack, trying to find the psycho who was killing girls, trying to save the next victim, until finally, something had happened that had made him lose it. The thing that Jack hadn't told her about.

Her tone grew sympathetic. "What exactly do you see?"

He didn't respond, but she got the feeling that he knew she was there. That he could hear her, even over the voices in his own head. "What do they say to you?"

She hesitated, trying to stop herself from saying it, because she knew as soon as she started, she wouldn't be able to stop. But part of that also made her feel calm. It would finally be over.

"You know, I hear voices too."

A small weight was lifted off her chest as she finally said those words out loud. Finally admitted it to someone. It also caused Shade to stop flinching for a moment. It was almost imperceptible, but she caught it. He was listening.

Just like water after a dam breaks, the rest began to pour out of her. "When I was in the military, a few months after being put in the field, I was on a rescue detail. Some of our soldiers had been gunned down by an enemy convoy, and we were sent to get them out. But when we got there, we realized they were hurt worse than we thought. We tried to patch them up as best we could in the field, but not all of them made it. Then, after we loaded up the survivors into our convoy and drove off, we hit an IED. It flipped us, and the blast gave away our position. Enemy soldiers showed up not long after, not many, but we were all already in the dirt, our heads too dizzy from the explosion to see anything clearly, even before the shooting started."

She took a deep breath, for once not fighting the memories as they came back to her. "After they killed everyone else, I felt a gun press against my head. I was too out of it to run, and even if I wasn't, my leg had been broken from the explosion. But then all of a sudden, the guy holding the gun fell. And then so did all the others." She smiled. "And then I saw her. A Marine in the area who just happened to be on a recon mission when she heard the blast and thought someone might need help. She put her arm around my shoulder and walked me over five miles back to base."

Sara adjusted herself in the chair as she continued talking, knowing Shade was hearing her despite his nonresponsiveness.

"After that, we became friends. We were stationed at the same base, and we would train together, laugh, talk about what we would do when we got out." Sara laughed. "She was like the sister I never had."

In an instant, her smile began to fade. "Then one day, she was assigned a detail. It was just reconnaissance, basically a stakeout from a small house out in the middle of nowhere. It was just going to be her, her commanding officer, two other Marines and one medical officer. Another medic had already been assigned, but she somehow talked her commander into assigning me instead. Told me she couldn't imagine spending a week cooped up in a small house with anyone else.

"We were there three days," Sara went on, her voice cracking as she struggled to get the words out, "talking about the same stuff we always did, when all of a sudden, the commanding officer fell. Then so did the other Marines. A breath later we heard the gunshots. Sniper."

Sara began to choke on the words as she spoke them, now on the verge of tears. "A row of bullet holes lined the wall, one for each soldier that fell. I ducked and hid underneath the table without

being hit. She dropped to the floor, but it was too late. One of the bullet holes in the wall belonged to her. The sniper had hit her in the chest. She didn't die immediately, though. The wound itself wouldn't kill her, but the blood loss would, unless someone stopped the bleeding. Someone like me."

Sara began sobbing, trying to wipe the tears from her face as they fell. "But I didn't. She called out, begging me to help her, but I couldn't move. I couldn't bring myself to come out from under the table. I was too scared of what might happen to me.

"The doctors who looked at me afterwards said I was in shock, but it doesn't matter. All that matters is that I watched my best friend, one who had risked her own life to save me, bleed out into the dirt, begging for help."

Sara closed her eyes, momentarily stopping the tears from falling out of them. "I'll never forget the look on her face when she realized I wasn't going to save her."

After that, Sara cried silently for a moment, taking in everything she had just said. Remembering every detail of that day, even the ones she had tried so hard to forget. If she hadn't been sure what she was about to do before, she was now. She looked back up to Shade, who was now looking at her for the first time.

"So, I know what you feel," she said. "I know how much you want the visions to go away, how much you want the voices to stop." She looked at the mirror, taking in one last look at herself and standing up. "Jack wants to save me from you," she said. "But I don't deserve saving."

Jack watched her from behind the window. "What's she doing?"

She took a step toward Shade, tears still crawling down her cheek. "So if killing me will make the voices stop"—she was almost within his range now—"just do it."

Jack rushed for the door.

Sara stepped even closer, now pleading with him. "Please, just kill me."

Shade didn't move as he stared up at her, looking sane for the first time. She saw the same sadness in his eyes she saw in her own. "Please just end it."

Jack ran through the door, grabbing her arm from behind and pulling her backwards. She fought his grip, still trying to move forward.

"No," she cried as he managed to move her back. "No, please." She took a final pleading glance at Shade as Jack dragged her to the door. "Please!"

Jack managed to get her to the door and pushed her through it before closing it behind her.

She continued to cry on the other side, trying and almost succeeding in fighting off the agents holding her. But eventually, she gave up and dropped to the floor, weeping, as the voice of her dead friend returned.

"Help me."

Jack remained in the room, looking at Shade—still sitting down, wrapped in the straitjacket. Shade didn't appear to be hallucinating, at least not at the moment, but he still wasn't looking at Jack, instead looking down at the table.

"Why are you doing this?" Jack said with pain in his voice, pleading with the man who had once been his partner, now locked up in a prison he would probably never get out of. Jack wondered how they had let it come this far.

"What you're doing, it won't make the hallucinations go away. Please, just let me help you."

Shade said nothing.

Jack sighed. It was no use. Shade wouldn't listen to him. He was too far gone. So he turned back to the door, but as he reached it, he heard Shade's voice behind him.

"Do you even remember her?"

Jack walked out of the room. There was nothing to say.

Chapter Eleven

Shade stood, staring at the photos hanging up on Jack's wall.

They were photos of every possible suspect in the case, even the ones with no motives, or with rock-solid alibis. Jack had thought it'd be a good idea to run back over them in case they had missed something. On the desk sat the crime scene photos, and Jack sat in his chair, looking at the same photographs as Shade.

"Let's do this backwards," Jack said. "We assume that they're guilty, and then we try to prove that they're innocent."

"Okay," Shade said, pointing to the first photo, a picture of a twenty-two-year-old brown-haired girl with a very small frame. "Amber Collins, the first victim's roommate."

"Motive," Jack said. "She was jealous of her roommate, they got in a fight, she accidentally killed her, and the rest of this is just to cover it up." He sighed. "Not the best motive ever, but let's just go with it. Can we prove that she's innocent?"

"Well," Shade said, still staring at the photo, "for one thing, she doesn't have the medical knowledge to do something like this. For another, she has an alibi for her roommate's time of death."

"And even if she didn't," Jack continued, "every victim has defensive wounds, and most of them are bigger than she is. There's no way she could have overpowered them."

Shade took down her picture and threw it on the floor. He then went to the next picture. "Dr. Kevin Urich. His motive, he wanted to kill Susan Doyle, a girl we have proof he operated on two years ago. He has the medical experience and vaguely matches the profile of a serial killer who believes he has a higher purpose."

"More than vaguely," Jack said. "He straight up said he felt 'called' to be a doctor, and that everyone had a purpose to fulfill. I swear I felt like he was giving me his big villain speech right then and there."

"So, why's he innocent?"

"Because," Jack said, sighing and rubbing his forehead, "he has an alibi for the two nights that Susan Doyle was being abducted and killed, and we have video proof of that alibi, as well as staff *testimony that he never left the hospital. It's impossible that he killed her."*

Shade took his picture off the wall and let it fall to the floor. They moved on to the next photo, a picture of a doctor that they discovered had once treated the second victim.

"Dr. Reynolds," Jack said. "Old, retired, and doesn't even live in the state anymore." The picture fell.

Next, the kids who had found the first body. "No," Shade said. "Too young to pull this off, too many of them to do it without someone talking. Plus none of them have the medical expertise to do this." Another picture fell.

Next, three pictures of the nurses who had assisted with the operation on Susan Doyle.

"Alibi, alibi, and out of town," Jack said, putting his elbows on his desk and resting his head in his hands.

Three more pictures fell.

Shade pointed to another. The neighbors who had found the second victim's body. "No alibi, but also no motive, and no medical experience."

Two more pictures fell.

Shade moved to look at the next picture but then stopped. "Why is he on here?" he said, pointing to a picture of Detective Washington. "Is he a suspect?"

"No."

Shade looked at him, confused. "Then why–"

"I had a picture of him, figured it wouldn't hurt to put it up there, look into him. Thought maybe the killer turning out to be the 'mild-mannered cop' trying to find the killer would make a cool twist or something." Jack shrugged. "I don't know, man, I'm desperate."

"Okay. But, for the record?"

"I looked into him," Jack said, nodding. "He's clean."

Another picture fell. Only two remained. The first was a picture of the best friend of the fourth victim, Angela Carter, the one whose house the parents thought their daughter had stayed at after her "fight" with her father.

Shade spoke first. "She has no motive, no medical experience, and we can piece together enough of her week to know she didn't have enough time to kill anyone."

Another picture fell. Another suspect gone. A single photograph remained on the wall.

"That just leaves the fourth victim's father, Benjamin Carter."

"Dr. Benjamin Carter," Jack corrected.

"Fine, Dr. Benjamin Carter."

Jack stood up from his chair and joined Shade in looking at the photograph. "Our best suspect.

He admitted he was a doctor with experience in surgery, so he would be capable of performing the operations. He has a personal connection to at least one of the victims, and he has a motive. He had just been in a fight with his daughter and admitted they had fought on other occasions. He could have killed the first three victims at random, to avoid suspicion when his own daughter died. Honestly, it feels like we should already have him in custody."

"Except this theory is based solely on his daughter being his target, and so far, his daughter is the one victim he has a rock-solid alibi for; he was doing double shifts at work, and his wife accounted for the rest of the time. And if we can't pin him to his daughter, his entire motive falls apart."

"Maybe his wife is lying," Jack said, knowing that he was grasping at straws but doing so anyway, trying to force the case to make sense out of desperation.

"Even if she was, I checked out the distance from the hospital to where the body was found. No way he could have gotten there in time. Plus, the daughter has defensive wounds on her arms, implying she fought back immediately—"

"Which means she didn't know her killer," Jack finished before taking a long angry breath and ripping the picture off the wall, throwing it to the floor.

The wall now rested completely empty. Not a single suspect remained, not a single lead to go on.

Jack sank back in his chair, defeated. "We have nothing. Four dead, and we have nothing!" He slammed his fist down on the table. "What are we doing wrong? Why can't we find this guy?"

"I don't know."

The question kept ringing in Jack's head. Why couldn't they find him? They had dealt with serial killers before and had never let it get this far. Why was this time different? Why couldn't he find this guy and put an end to this madness? Was he not doing enough?

Deep down, though, he knew the answer. Just like Shade, he had gotten too close. He was having trouble looking at the case objectively. Every time he tried, he would get angry with the killer—for doing this, for being the monster that he was. Then he would get angry at himself for letting it get this far.

He was so focused on why he couldn't catch the killer that he didn't notice Shade hallucinating beside him.

"Shut up," Shade said suddenly.

"I'm not even talking," Jack said, annoyed, from behind his desk before looking at Shade and realizing what was happening. "Oh, sorry."

"It's okay," Shade said, shaking his head, trying to make the voices go away.

"What do they say to you?"

Twitching, Shade answered, "They want me to do something. Something to make them go away."

Jack tilted his head, growing uneasy. "What do they want you to do?"

Someone knocked on the door.

Jack took one last suspicious glance at Shade before turning to the door. "Come in." An agent opened the door and leaned his head inside.

"Susan Doyle's parents are here to see you."

Jack sighed and looked back at Shade. "Well, maybe we can at least save one."

"Mr. and Mrs. Doyle," Jack said, shaking their hands, "I'm Special Agent Jack Diamond." He pointed to Shade, who shook their hands as well. "This is my partner, Special Agent Shade. We're the agents assigned to your daughter's case."

"It's nice to meet you," Mr. Doyle said, trying to be polite, but it was obvious he was having trouble getting the words out without crying.

"So," Mrs. Doyle said, "why are we here?"

Jack got right to the point. "I'm sure you've already been told that your daughter was the victim of a serial killer. He has killed four victims, and we don't currently have any strong leads."

"You're going to catch him, though, right? You're going to catch the man that took our daughter from us?"

"Yes," Jack said, trying to sound as reassuring as possible. "We are going to catch him. But in the meantime, we've been trying to figure out how he has selected his victims so that we can protect those he may be after next. We think whoever is doing this has a connection to either doctors or hospitals in some way." He didn't dare elaborate further, not after what had happened with the fourth victim's father. "And since Susan donated a kidney to her sister, it's possible her sister might be a target as well."

"So what do we need to do?" Mrs. Doyle asked. "Can you put us in protective custody or something?"

Jack shook his head. "If we had any actual proof that she was a target, we could. But for now, it's just a hunch."

"So what, then?"

"Well, you can either take your daughter home and keep her at the house with you at all times. I don't think the killer would risk attacking all of you for one victim, but anything's possible."

"What's the other option?" Mr. Doyle asked, his eyes tired, full of fear. He was old, especially to have daughters as young as these. His eyes showed clearly that he didn't think he could protect her.

"We keep her here," Jack said. "We can't give her witness protection or anything, but we can keep her here, in this building, by us, at all times."

"How long?" the mother asked. "How long would she have to stay here?"

"Until we catch the guy," Jack said, not letting his voice waver. "Hopefully no more than a few days, a week at the most." He wasn't sure he believed the words as he spoke them.

"How do we know that she'll be safe here? What if the killer breaks in and gets to her?"

"If the killer did manage to get in here—which is impossible, but if he did—your daughter would still be with Special Agent Shade, which is the safest place she could be."

Mr. Doyle's gaze left Jack and went to Shade, looking him directly in his eyes. "Is that true? Can you protect my daughter?"

Shade started to respond before hesitating. Jack knew he was thinking about the cemetery, the graves of all the other people Shade couldn't protect, all the ones he couldn't save. But eventually, Shade found the words.

"Yes. I can protect her."

The father looked at him for a moment, not sure if he believed it. But finally, he spoke. "Okay," he said. "She'll stay here with you."

Ready to protest, his wife turned to him. "You can't leave her here; she needs to be with us. We can keep her safe."

"No, we can't," he answered, crying with her. "But these men can."

She looked up at them. "Promise me," she said through her tears. "Promise me you'll save her."

Jack nodded, and Shade followed suit.

Shade watched as the parents spoke to their child across the room. "We can protect her, right?"

"Yes," Jack said. "We can protect her. We have to."

Eventually, the parents waved goodbye, walking out of the room crying, leaving their daughter behind with strangers. Jack could only imagine how helpless they must have felt, to lose one daughter and then have no control over the other's fate.

In the parents' distress, however, they had failed to introduce them to the girl. So instead, the girl walked over to them, alone.

She was small and had brown hair, just like her older sister. She had wet streaks coming down her chin, presumably from crying, but she wiped them off before she reached them.

Once she got there, Jack knelt down in an effort to be eye level with her. Before he introduced himself, he asked, "What did your parents tell you?"

"That the man who killed Susie wants to kill me too, and that I have to stay here so that I'm safe."

Jack was relieved. He didn't have to explain the situation to her. "Well, you can call me Jack"–he pointed behind himself–"and my terrifying friend back there is Shade."

"Hi," she said simply, trying to be polite, just like her father.

"What's your name?"

"Nora."

"Well, Nora," Jack said, smiling at her, "it's nice to meet you."

Nora sat in Jack's chair as they all stood in his office, looking at the suspect photographs now scattered across the floor. Jack had put the crime scene photos back in his drawer before she'd walked in. She didn't need to see those.

"How old are you, Nora?" Jack asked. He already knew the answer from her file, but he wanted to try to break the awkward silence filling the room.

"Thirteen and a half," she answered.

His eyes flinched. Thirteen. That was how old he had been. Suddenly, the sound of chains entered his head, ringing in his ears. The feeling of helplessness crawled over him, causing him to shudder. He couldn't let the same thing happen to Nora. He had to stop this monster before it got that far, before scars formed that would never be healed.

"Why do you wear those?" she asked Shade, pointing to his dog tags.

"They're dog tags," Shade answered, running his fingers against them. "You get them in the military, so that in case you get hit, it has a record of your information."

"I know that," Nora said. "But why do you wear them?"

"I don't know. I guess as a reminder."

"Of what?" she asked.

Shade shrugged as Jack saw him remember his own demons. "I don't know."

Nora added, seemingly at random, "I like them."

Shade smiled. "I'm glad."

No one said anything for a few moments, until a tear fell down Nora's cheek.

Jack noticed and knelt down beside her. "It's okay. We're not going to let anyone hurt you, okay. I promise we'll keep you safe." He waited, hoping she would stop crying, but she didn't. Desperate, he then looked at Shade, wondering what to do, why she didn't feel safe, but as he saw Shade's eyes, he realized *that underneath the rough, terrifying exterior, he somehow understood better than Jack ever would.*

"She's not crying for herself," Shade said. "She's crying for her sister."

After a few somber moments, a phone call broke the silence. Jack answered it, and within seconds, he gave Shade a glance that told him what the call was about without having to say it. They had found another one.

"Where?" Jack asked, pulling out his notepad and writing down a location. "Okay, we're on our way." He was about to hang up when the man on the other line said something else, igniting Jack's temper. "What do you mean the reporters got there first?"

Jack slammed the phone down and started out the door, Shade following him to a room containing a TV. As he flipped to a news station, Nora tried to step out of his office, but he motioned her back, not sure of what the TV might show.

The reporter spoke. "We are now learning that this is the fifth victim in a killing spree that the police department has been trying to keep under wraps due to the severe nature of the murders. This fifth victim was found just minutes ago, lying on an operating table, with numerous surgical wounds–"

Shade and Jack looked over at each other. Another victim they couldn't save–a fifth girl who had died for nothing.

"Reports indicate that the other murders were carried out in a similar fashion, and it looks to be the work of a serial killer."

'Don't give him a name,' Jack said internally. Killers loved the attention of a name, loved how it immortalized them as something grander, like a monster from folklore whose legend is passed around the campfire at night. Sick freaks like that didn't deserve the satisfaction.

"Reporters on the scene are calling him—"

'Please don't give him a name.'

"—the Surgeon."

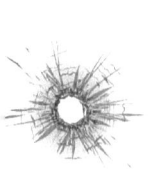
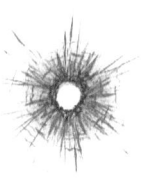

Chapter Twelve

"We are going to talk about what just happened," Jack scolded as they stood outside the now-empty interrogation room. The inside had been gassed, and Shade, now unconscious, was being transported to a secure cell.

"Later," Sara said, although she didn't plan on discussing it later either. "Where are you taking him?"

Jack groaned. "If I tell you, do you promise not to go there and try that again?"

"Oh, please," Sara said, rolling her eyes. She really didn't want to get into that right now. "Just tell me."

Jack hesitated at first before finally relenting. "We're taking him to a cell in the east wing of the prison. We already have guards stationed there waiting for him when he gets there and wakes up."

"Are you sure it's a good idea? To have him in the same prison as—"

"They're in entirely separate wings. They'll never see each other."

That was good. Shade shouldn't ever have to see him again. She still couldn't help feeling sorry for him, even knowing everything he'd done, the woman he had killed in the forest. "Is he ever going to get out?"

Jack shook his head solemnly. "No. No, he's not."

The guards kept their guns trained on him as they rolled him down the hallway. He was still in a straitjacket, strapped upright to a special gurney. It was vertical, with the top slanting backwards just a hair and wheels at the bottom. Attached to it were straps, which covered his arms, legs, and chest and all met on a lock in the center. So long as it wasn't tampered with, Shade could barely move.

"What if he wakes up?" one guard asked nervously.

"He won't," another answered. "They gassed him with enough tranquilizer to knock out a horse. It'd take a shot of adrenaline for him to even open his eyes."

"But what do we do if he does?" the guard asked again, trying to take deep breaths.

"Simple. He's in a straitjacket, strapped to a gurney. We just knock him back out," the second

guard said as he pretended to hit Shade in the head with the butt of his gun. "What are you so nervous for anyway?"

"Why aren't you?"

"He's new," the guard in charge replied.

A table squeaked as it rolled across the floor. The entire room was black, except for the small glint of silver light reflecting off the table itself. "Where am I?" Shade asked, his voice echoing within the walls of the small room.

In the darkness, a figure emerged, wearing a white surgeon's gown.

"No," Shade said, trying and failing to move. "This isn't real. You can't be here."

The sound of a surgical saw spinning its blade drowned out Shade's protests as the surgeon picked up a scalpel and put a medical mask over his face.

"No," Shade said, still trying to move, to somehow stop him. But he couldn't.

The surgeon looked up towards Shade, staring him right in the eyes for a moment before turning back to the table, and the girl that was now on it. The girl Shade recognized.

"No!"

Shade opened his eyes, escaping the nightmare. His heart was pounding inside his chest as he looked around, seeing three armed guards: two in the rear with guns aimed at the floor as they pulled the gurney, the third leading the way, his back turned. Shade recognized the guard to his left. He was always nervous, made rash decisions. The guard to his right, however, was a stranger, which meant he didn't know Shade either. That explained why he was standing so close.

Shade felt the straps around his body, as well as the straitjacket. So long as the straps were around him, he couldn't move a single part of his body, aside from his head.

That would have to be enough.

Shade moved his head as much as he could, slamming it into the unfamiliar guard on his right, temporarily sending him to the floor as the other two moved their guns on Shade.

The guard stood up, his entire mouth oozing blood, one of his teeth now missing. "You little—" he said, ignoring the other guards' orders to stand down, instead removing a knife from his pocket and jamming it into Shade's rib cage.

Shade grunted, but he had been expecting it. He shifted his weight on the knife, causing it to slide slightly higher, as much as the bone would allow, ripping more of his skin, as well as the straps holding him to the gurney.

The straps having loosened, Shade headbutted the already bleeding man again, this time knocking him out. In an instant he was off the gurney, but the guard in front was too far to reach without getting shot, especially while still confined to the straitjacket. But the other guard was visibly nervous, fumbling his weapon in his hands, so Shade moved on him instead.

"No!" the guard in charge screamed, but it was too late.

The nervous guard began squeezing the trigger as Shade rammed into him, causing the gun to move to the left, firing on the guard in charge, bringing him down to the floor.

Nervousness became complete terror as the only guard still standing was shoved into the wall, and now his body slid down it before being kicked in the face by Shade, making his vision blurry.

Shade groaned as he felt the knife still lodged in his rib cage. With his hands confined, his only hope of escape was to slide his arms up, using the buried knife to cut the fabric, freeing his arms. But it was too loose. The second he applied pressure, the knife would fall out of his side and onto the floor. So instead, he took a deep breath and pressed

his body against the wall, digging the knife further into his side, wincing as he held back a scream. Finally, he stopped and slid his white sleeves over it, cutting them but digging the knife even deeper, the blade grinding against his bones. Finally, he had one hand free, and he used it to pull the knife out, dropping it to the floor as he knelt down, grunting as blood poured from him.

He was losing a lot of blood. He knew he had to keep pressure on the wound, so he reached for the latch on his straitjacket and pulled it as tight as he could, the straps cutting off almost all circulation to his stomach, putting enough pressure on the wound that he was able to stand. He then picked the knife back up and cut his second arm free, leaving ripped white cloth hanging down from both of his hands.

The nervous guard, still on the floor but having regained his bearings, grabbed his gun and was about to move when Shade's foot hit his throat. He gagged, trying to fight it, but the pressure was too intense.

"Shoot the camera," Shade instructed.

"He's free," a voice said over the coms.

"What?" Jack asked.

"Shade. He's free," the voice repeated, and Jack took off out the door, motioning for Sara to follow him. He led her down the hallway to a room filled with computer monitors and a large control console. The security room. Director Williams was already there.

"Where is he?" Jack asked.

"We don't know," the director said, never looking away from the monitors. "The camera that was on him has been shot, and so far none of the other cameras have picked him up.

"He's avoiding them," Jack whispered to himself. "What about the guns?"

"What?" the agent at the computer asked.

"The guns," Jack repeated. "You have trackers on your guards' guns, right?"

"Yes."

"Then track them. There's no way Shade left without taking a weapon."

The agent nodded and pulled up a virtual map of the prison. Two stationary red dots blinked in the position where Shade had taken out the guards and shot the camera, with a third red dot pinging as it moved further into the east wing.

"He's going for the east exit," the director said.

"Take every guard from the hallways and put them on the exit," Jack said.

"Why?" the agent manning the computer asked. "Then we won't have anyone to stop him from getting there."

"Shade can take forty guards if they're spaced out three at a time in hallways. But forty in one spot, in the light, with guns on the only entrance— he can't get past it."

"Do as he says," the director instructed the agent as the little red dot inched closer and closer.

Guards from the entire prison began to move toward the east exit.

Shade kept running, grunting as his stomach left a trail of blood behind him. He entered hallway after hallway, trapped in a seemingly endless maze, desperate to make his way through it while he was still holding on. He knew if he started to lose it in here, he would never be able to leave.

The hallways began to merge together as he took countless rights and lefts, trying to make his way through the maze, each turn leading to another endless stretch of white walls and dim lighting.

But still he ran.

Jack and Sara watched the red dot move closer to the exit as dozens upon dozens of guards lined up in front of it, their guns aimed at the single hallway that led there.

"How does he know where to go?" Sara asked.

"He's been here before."

Shade took a wrong turn as he began running beside the walls, leaning on them to keep himself upright. His side continued to bleed, staining the white straitjacket red. He could feel the visions wanting to come back, but he tried to hold them off. Just had to make it a little bit farther.

"Why did you let us die?"

Sara and Jack watched the monitor as a virtual army piled up at the entrance.

"He has to know there will be guards waiting for him, right?"

"Yes," Jack responded. "I'm sure he does."

Sara wrinkled her forehead. "Then why is he still headed that way? Certainly he doesn't think he can get through that many guards in one spot." She watched Jack's reaction, curious that he didn't necessarily protest the idea. "You don't think he can, do you?"

Jack just watched the red dot moving along the monitor, heading straight for the guards. "I don't know anymore."

"Shut up," Shade said as he ran down the hallway.

"You let us die."

"Shut up," Shade repeated as he started to pass the prisoners, kept locked up inside black metal bars, the cells spaced ten feet apart, on either side. But the more he ran, the more he stopped seeing cells as his hallucinations began to take over once again, transforming the cells of the prison into the doors of the hospital.

White, endless, each with a small window in it, allowing him to glimpse the horrors hidden inside, rooms soaked red with blood, victims screaming inside as the sound of a surgical saw cut through the air like an ax, its blade spinning as it was brought closer to their flesh.

"It's not real," Shade said as he ran past the door. "It's not real, it's not real!"

An operating table rolled across the hallway in front of him.

The guards stood ready, dozens of lasers pointed at the entrance, virtually covering the entire room in green light. As they waited, holding their breath, they heard screaming in the distance.

"He's moving too fast," Sara said.

Jack didn't hear her. "Get ready," he told the guards over the coms. "He's almost there."

Shade ran after the operating table, but as he crossed into the next hallway, it had vanished. But it had caused him to make a wrong turn. He turned, looking for ways out, forced to look at all the cells around him, all of the hospital doors that contained the horrors of his past, the horrors he couldn't stop. They were everywhere.

"Why did you do this to us?"

The guards stood frozen as the screaming got closer, its sound echoing off the walls like the sound of rabid bats swarming through a cave in a panic, trying to escape something darker. It was almost there.

"He's close," Jack told them over the coms as he noticed Sara, who was watching the monitor, confused. "What is it?"

"He's moving too fast."

"What do you mean?"

"You said he's been here before, but this place is still a maze, and he isn't exactly stable. But he

hasn't made a single misstep, hasn't had to slow down. It's like he's running through his own house."

Jack looked back at the monitor, seeing that she was right. "Oh my–"

The screaming reached the guards, and at the end of the hallway a man entered, seemingly growing luminescent as he was completely covered in green lasers.

"He's coming!" the man yelled.

"Hold your fire," the guard in charge instructed as he stepped closer to see who the man was. As he approached him, he saw a fellow guard, holding a rifle.

"He's coming!" the man repeated, pleading with the guard to listen to him.

"Who's coming?"

"Shade. He took out the others, but I managed to get away. He's coming for me; he's coming for the exit."

The guard in charge grabbed him by the vest in anger. "You don't just get away from Shade."

Jack looked at the monitors. "Find him."

"But we already–" the agent started to say.

"We've been checking the east wing," Jack finished. "But Shade isn't in the east wing anymore. He's going for the exit on the west side."

The agent scrolled between cameras until finally, he selected one. "I got him," he said. "He's just behind cell block 117. He's only a few hallways away from the exit." He looked away from the monitors and up toward Jack, in shock. "He's going to get out."

Where was he? He could barely remember. The sound of victims screaming filled his head as he ran through the maze, no longer trying to escape the prison but trying to escape the nightmares. The victims.

He ran into another hallway and saw bodies lined up on the floor, covered in blood. He turned back and saw shelves lining the wall, with jars sitting on them. Jars filled with–

He ran into another hallway, filled with surgical equipment scattered across the floor, sparks flying from a spinning sawblade.

"It's not real," Shade reminded himself as he tried to make the visions fade, tried to remember why he was here. For a brief moment, he regained enough clarity to continue through the prison.

"He's back on track," the agent said.

"How many guards are left there?" Jack asked.

"Just three, all covering the door."

The director sighed. "That's not enough."

"I know," Jack said, staring at the monitor until he got an idea. "How many prisoners are there between Shade and the exit?"

The agent checked the screen. "Twenty-five."

"Let them out."

"Wait. This isn't like at the field office where our agents were only incapacitated," the director protested. "These men are in here for a reason. Shade will kill them without hesitation."

"Do you have a better idea, sir?" Jack said, not wavering.

Grinding his teeth, the director tried to think. But Jack was right. They were out of options. He nodded toward Jack, who once again instructed the agent to open up the cells.

The agent's hands moved over the buttons, unlocking the cells one by one, until finally his hand hovered over the last button, when Jack stopped him. "Not that one."

On the monitor, they saw the inmates step out of their cells, all dressed in black prison jumpsuits. Jack spoke to them over the intercom. "There's a man headed your way. An escaped prisoner

wearing a straitjacket. Anyone who helps get him in a cell will get time off their sentence."

Jack wasn't lying. He would get them time off their sentence. However, after he added the extra time for "attempting a breakout," he figured it would about even out.

They watched over the cameras as the prisoners began chanting in the hallways.

Shade reached the end of a hallway and turned to his right, where seven prisoners stood lined up on either side, outside their cells, waiting for him. Most were about his size, but one was massive, to the point that a single blow could probably break a bone, and mere inches from him was a smaller inmate, shadowing the giant. Shade knew there were three more hallways past this one, and that each would be filled with its own row of prisoners. With one hand, he felt his side, still bleeding through the straitjacket. In his other hand he held the knife that had been shoved into his ribs. He took one last deep breath, trying to stay calm so that the visions wouldn't come back, and then waited.

The inmates charged him.

The giant took two stab wounds to the chest and was on the floor before he could even swing.

His shadow threw a punch, but Shade backed up, dodging it while cutting the man's wrist and shoving him backwards, leaving him to bleed out.

Twenty-three left.

The next two inmates swung at the same time. Shade took the punch from the first, falling to his knees before stabbing through the other's ankle, dropping him to the floor, where a knife was shoved into his chest. The inmate still standing kicked Shade, causing him to roll backwards before he could grab the knife back.

Before the inmate charged, Shade was already back on his feet, and he shoved the man's head into the wall, cracking his skull.

Another large prisoner, whose arm contained a tattoo of a cobra, swung at him, but Shade ducked, letting the arm miss him and go straight in between the bars of a cell. He then reached in through the bars, and grabbed the man's wrist, pulling the arm backwards against the metal, distorting the snake and snapping the bones like fiberglass.

Twenty.

Shade felt a knife pass through his back. He turned to see a man holding the knife he had left in the other man's chest. Shade swung his elbow backwards into the man's face, crushing his nose.

Only two more inmates remained in the hallway. The first, grinning like an idiot, charged screaming but was silenced by the knife that Shade suddenly impaled into his lungs. The last inmate, either a coward or the only sane man there, saw Shade approaching him and nervously backed up into his own cell, shutting the door.

Eighteen.

Shade removed the knife, still implanted in the man's chest, and walked through the hallway, now littered with bodies, and into the next one, whose bodies were still very much alive.

As soon as he stepped within sight, the prisoners charged. The fastest one was met with a knife to the skull, and his body flailed to the ground, tripping the inmates closest to him. The ones that remained standing went after Shade.

The first one had his neck broken before he knew what had happened. The second was knocked to the floor and then tried to get back up before Shade's foot struck his face, knocking him out completely. The third tried to swing, but his wrist was caught midair, and his fingers snapped, the bones sticking out backwards through the skin. He fell to the floor, screaming in pain.

Fourteen.

The fifth and final inmate who hadn't tripped over the first's body had extreme facial scars, leading Shade to recognize him as a former mob enforcer,

and a good one. Unfortunately, the revelation came a moment too late, and the enforcer was already moving. He tackled Shade to the floor and pulled out a shiv, which he tried to bring down into Shade's chest, but Shade grabbed the enforcer's wrist with one hand, his elbow with the other, and broke his arm backwards, forcing him to shove the shiv into his own side. The enforcer screamed in pain before he was knocked out completely. Something Shade considered a favor.

Thirteen.

The remaining inmates who tripped had stood back up and were almost on Shade by the time he had the enforcer knocked out. The one in front saw the blood staining the side of his white straitjacket and went to kick it. His leg was caught midair and twisted sideways at the knee, splintering the bone inside into dozens of fragments. Another inmate stepped over him but was punched in the throat so hard that he lost his breath. As he gagged, Shade grabbed his shoulders and launched him against the side of a cell, the bars ringing as he hit. A third was kicked in the knee, causing him to trip, before a fourth landed a hit on Shade's jaw.

Shade spat blood from his mouth as he felt pain like needles digging into his jaw, reaching the bone beneath. Before Shade could register his surroundings again, the inmate landed another blow. He was fast, probably had martial arts training. Another strike to Shade's stomach, right in the wound. Shade's mouth opened to scream in pain, but no sound came out. The martial artist cocked his hand back to throw another punch, but as his arm moved forward, Shade caught it, holding him in place for a moment. Shade's head was dizzy, making it hard to move quickly. Might as well even it up.

Shade rammed his head into the martial artist's face, causing him to stagger backwards, dazed and losing his footing. He was about to fall back when Shade's hand grabbed his shirt, keeping him upright long enough for a strike to the head, knocking him back so far it almost broke his neck.

Ten.

The second hallway now cleared, Shade leaned back against the bars of a cell, retightening the straitjacket around his side. Pain still left over from the strikes to his head surged through his body, keeping him dazed just long enough for the voices to return.

"Why are you doing this?"

'No,' Shade thought. 'Not now. Please don't come back now.' Shade tried to focus, to make them go away, as he felt fingers creep around his ankle.

They belonged to one of the inmates, but when Shade looked down, he saw the mangled corpse of a victim, begging him to save her. He jumped back from her, watching her crawl towards him. The further he moved, the quicker she crawled, leaving blood and flesh on the ground behind her.

"Why did you let him do this to me? Why did you want me to die?"

"I didn't," Shade said, backing up further, stuttering, "I-I-I tried to save you."

The corpse picked up a shiv and stood up, lunging at Shade. Shade closed his eyes and let the shiv push into his stomach before grabbing the man he felt in front of him and shoving his head against the wall. Shade opened his eyes back up to see the corpse of the girl, now lying on the floor, not moving, surrounded by blood.

Nine.

As Shade walked toward the next hallway, the voices in his head grew louder, all chanting the same question, until eventually it became the only sound that he could hear.

"Why did you let us die?"

"Why did you let us die?"

"Why did you let us die?"

In the next hallway, the corpses waited for him. One charged. Shade tried to take him down, but he

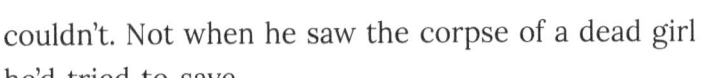
couldn't. Not when he saw the corpse of a dead girl he'd tried to save.

Shade was tackled to the floor by the inmate, and within seconds the others arrived. They began to beat Shade, kicking his ribs, stomping on his chest, until finally one of them stopped.

"Let's get him into a cell."

'No,' Shade thought as they began dragging him towards an open cell door. 'If they lock me in here, it's over. It can't be over.' He forced himself to fight back, trying not to look at the corpses he was fighting. He thrust his elbow into the inmate dragging him by the shoulder, breaking his jaw. He then twisted over and rammed the other inmate dragging him into the inner brick wall of the cell before grabbing the man by the hair and slamming his head into the bricks once more.

Seven.

A stoic inmate with a blind left eye, probably a snitch who'd been tortured by his gang, tried to shut the cell door but was shoved backwards by Shade. Three more inmates dove in at him, knocking him back into the cell. He was pushed back against the wall but managed to strike one of the inmates in the eye hard enough to knock him out. One of the other two, grinning psychotically, saw his opportunity and brought his foot down on Shade's right knee, twisting it sideways.

Shade fell to the ground screaming.

The half-blind snitch who had been shoved outside tried to shut the cell door with the other inmates still inside, but Shade grabbed the grinning psychopath's leg, tripping him and causing him to fall in the way of the cell door, and knocking the snitch outside back down.

Having to lean against the wall for support, Shade tried to stand back up as the other inmate still inside the cell, built like a boxer, attacked him, landing blow after blow. Blood poured from Shade's face as he deflected one of the punches and pushed the man back, giving him enough time to stand up completely.

He was holding his bleeding side, putting all of the pressure on his left leg, when the boxer charged again. Shade took the blow, grabbed the boxer's shirt collar, and used the inmate's own weight to sling him sideways across the cell, his face smashing into the small metal toilet in the corner, breaking it.

Five.

Shade grunted as he walked out of the cell, limping on his right knee. Once outside, he grabbed the cell bars and looked down at the man who had broken his leg, now lying in between the cell and the hallway, no longer grinning. Shade slid the bars of the door open farther before bringing them back against

the psychopath, pinning him between the wall and the cell bars and cracking his rib cage. Shade slid the bars back and did it again. And again. And again.

Four.

The snitch who had been shoved into the hallway was now on the floor, crawling towards a shiv. Shade limped over to him and bent down, reaching his arm around the man's neck, choking him. As he felt the man's breath start to leave him, the voices came back.

"Don't do this."

Shade closed his eyes so he couldn't see whatever hallucinations would be watching him in the hallway, but his grip didn't loosen.

"Please don't kill me," the corpse he was choking begged.

Shade opened his eyes for a moment and saw that he was surrounded by the trees from the forest, and the partially blind inmate he was choking appeared as the woman who had been gutted there.

"Why are you killing me?" she asked him.

He said nothing, closing his eyes and keeping his grip, until finally he felt the life go out from the inmate's body. He then let go, the body falling to the floor.

Three.

Shade stood up, his knee exploding in pain, limping toward the last hallway. Once he reached it, he dropped to the floor, horrified.

It was the hallway of the hospital. The one from his memories. White tile floor, flickering lights, doors lining the walls, hiding the horrors within. And a small operating table at the end of it. And her on it, bleeding.

"No," Shade said, trying to look away. "Please don't make me watch it."

Sara watched over the cameras, seeing Shade break down on the floor. Two inmates were in the hall, and they began walking closer to him.

"I think he's scared of us," the first inmate said, cracking his knuckles as they stepped closer.

"I think so too," his friend said, laughing as he pulled a jagged shiv from his pocket. "Maybe we should him give a reason to be."

Shade screamed on the floor, not seeing the inmates, not seeing the shiv, not seeing anything except the girl getting operated on in front of him.

Until he heard someone clapping.

"Crap," Jack said, looking at the camera's footage.

Sara looked at it too and saw the man clapping at the far end of the hallway, still in his cell, which was closed with reinforced glass rather than bars. "Is that—?"

"Yeah," Jack said. "That's him."

The clapping cut through Shade's hallucination, causing him to look up and see the man at the end of the hallway. The man who wasn't a part of his hallucination. The Surgeon.

Shade regained all clarity as he stood up and walked closer to him. The knuckle cracker tried to swing on him, but Shade broke his arm, never letting his eyes leave the Surgeon.

Two.

The laugher tried to stab him with the shiv, but it was ripped from his hands and used to slit his own throat.

One.

"Well, well," the Surgeon said, smiling. "If it isn't Special Agent Shade." He looked directly at him. "I see the madness has not yet left your eyes."

Shade said nothing as he walked up to the edge of the cell, coming face-to-face with him.

"It's been a long time." the Surgeon said, giggling to himself. "I hear that you finally snapped, killed a woman in the woods. Tragic," he said, emphasizing each word he spoke like it was a profound truth. "I wonder, if it hadn't been for me, do you think you would have eventually killed her anyway? I think you would have," he said, nodding. "When I saw you, I knew—this was a man so close to the brink of insanity, he just needed someone to tip him over the edge. One final laceration to the heart, allowing the cancerous guilt to grow into something new."

Shade remained silent.

The Surgeon continued speaking. "Does it bother you, that her death was for you? To make you into what you are now? That had it not been for your attempts to stop the inevitable, she would have been left alive, unharmed?"

Shade's grip tightened on the knife.

"And look at what I created," the Surgeon said, beaming with pride. "A man free from hesitation, healed from the sickness of a guilty, conflicted conscience. An archangel of death." The Surgeon smiled again, knowing full well it was impossible for Shade to get through the glass, before pointing to the end of the hallway that led to the exit. "Run

along now. I hear you have people to kill. May our paths cross again."

Shade didn't move an inch. Instead, he looked up at the camera. He knew Jack could see him.

Jack looked at the Surgeon, standing in his cell with such pride. All the hate Jack had ever carried for him came back, causing his blood to boil at the mere sight. Then he saw Shade, looking directly to him, asking him without words, and knew what he had to do.

"Don't do it," the director said. "I know what you're thinking, but don't do it."

Jack's mind ran back over all the pain the man standing in the cell had caused. Killing those girls, breaking his partner. Killing her.

Jack unlocked the cell.

Shade reached out and grabbed the Surgeon, dragging him out of the cell and throwing him to the floor and into the camera's line of sight. Jack should get to see this too.

As Shade knelt over him, tightening his grip on the shiv, the Surgeon's smile faded. "Do you want to know what she said as she died?"

Shade didn't answer, instead shoving the blade into the Surgeon's chest, doing to him what he had done to so many victims before.

Sara had to look away. Everyone in the room did, except Jack, who stared at the monitor, watching Shade do what he wished he had done himself the moment he had found him.

When he was done, Shade left the knife in the Surgeon's chest, and for a single, fleeting moment, he felt relief.

It was gone in an instant, and he walked out of the hallway, towards the exit.

A few moments, later, the agent at the computer looked up at Jack. "The guards at the door aren't responding. Shade is gone."

Jack didn't hear him, his attention still focused on the Surgeon, who was now reduced to little more than a lifeless corpse.

A corpse that was missing its heart.

Chapter Thirteen

The fifth victim's name was Erika Stevens. She was seventeen years old.

While she was alive, she had never had any surgeries done. She had never even set foot in a hospital since the day her parents had first carried her out into the world. Her appearance was nothing at all like that of the other four victims; she went to a different school, favored a different subject. All in all, her death didn't provide a single shred of new information.

Shade stood at the crime scene, looking down at the body, trying to keep the hallucinations at bay, but still, they clawed their way in.

"This is your fault."

He sighed as they replaced the sheet over the girl's body. Jack began to question the detective, trying to find out any new details whatsoever. But Shade couldn't get the voices out of his head.

"You know what will make us go away."

"Is there any new information at all?" Jack asked Washington. "Anything different about the girl, the crime scene, anything?"

"No. I'm sorry, but there just isn't."

"What about the girl's contacts? Did she know any of the other victims? Did any of her friends know any of the other victims?"

"I'm afraid not," Washington said, eyes weary. "I'm sorry, but we don't have any more leads than you do."

Right outside the warehouse, in clear sight, sat Jack's car, with Nora inside of it. They needed her close to keep her safe, but they couldn't let her near the crime scene. A kid didn't need to see that.

"I got something!" a CSI yelled from across the warehouse.

Jack and Shade ran over to him. In the CSI's hand was a small piece of paper, so old it looked like parchment. "It's a note."

Shade took it. The paper was coarse in his hands, and he inspected the words inscribed on it. Words written in thick cursive, with dark blotchy ink.

Nora sat in Jack's chair, spinning herself around in circles.

"Who was the man at the crime scene?" she asked. "The one who hit you."

"Dr. Benjamin Carter," Shade answered. "He's the father of one of the victims."

"Why did he hit you?" Nora asked as she stopped the chair from spinning before it could make her dizzy.

"He's upset for his daughter and needed someone to take the anger out on, someone to blame for it," Jack stated instantly.

"Oh." Her tone was sad. "That's not fair."

Shade nodded his thanks before pointing at a photo. "What about him?"

"Nope," Jack said. "No medical experience, no motive, nothing to tie him to the victim's death in any way."

Shade took the picture off the wall, letting it fall.

"He's got to be picking them somehow," Jack said, more to himself than anyone else in the room.

"What?" Shade asked.

"The victims," Jack said. "They're too random. If he's just going out and grabbing the first girl he sees, there's no way they wouldn't have a single connection between them. There's also no way he could tell what age they were ahead of time. There's

got to be something we're missing. Some connection that ties them together."

Shade nodded. He thought the same thing, but so far, they couldn't find anything. They didn't go to the same hospital, didn't go to the same school, didn't look alike, didn't know each other. Nothing.

Nora took a blue pen from Jack's desk and began spinning it in her hands. Shade noticed and knew what she was trying to do, because he had done it himself so many times. Get her mind off her sister, get focused on something else. Something to stop the memories.

She then asked Jack a question. "Why did your parents name you after Jack the Ripper?"

"What?" he said, taken aback. "They didn't. Why would you assume that?"

"That's just what people think of when they hear Jack."

"No, it's not," Jack said, unsure of why he was protesting. "You're telling me Jack the Ripper was the first thing you thought of when I said my name was Jack? You're thirteen, why do you even know who that is?"

"Thirteen and a half," Nora corrected.

"Sorry, thirteen and a half," he said, half mockingly. "But to answer your question, they named me Jack because my last name is Diamond. The jack of diamonds is a playing card. And Queen Diamond just didn't have the same ring to it."

That answer seemed to satisfy her question, and she grew quiet once again.

Shade and Jack looked back to the pictures, again discarding suspects one by one before turning their focus to the note. The handwriting was unnatural, the letters jutting off in distorted angles. The killer was probably making sure the handwriting couldn't be traced back to him.

Then there was the wording. "How many more are you going to let me kill?" That bothered Shade. Up until this point, the killings seemed to be only about hurting the victims; there was nothing hinting at the killer having a desire to toy with the cops, or the FBI. But now there was the note, and the fact that the body had been found in the same spot as the first victim. It all screamed the same fact. The killer's motive had changed. It was no longer about killing the girls; it was now about getting away with it. Playing a game with them.

Lastly, there was the name signed. John Buck. The same name used to reserve the room the third victim was found in. Everything about that name seemed off. "Why John Buck?"

"I don't know," Jack said. "We did a search just in case, and no one in the city is named that. More *than likely it's just the killer making a play on John Doe, making it seem like an anonymous killer."*

"But then why not just write John Doe?"

"Maybe our guy wanted to be more creative," Jack said. "He's a psycho, why do they do anything?"

"I know, but still, something seems off about—"

"KILLER!" the corpse screamed at his face, causing him to fall back against the wall, terrified as it moved closer to him. "You let this happen. You let all of this happen."

"Shut up," Shade said, opening the door and walking out of it, holding his head in his hands. "Shut up."

Outside, there were more of them. Corpses scattered in the darkness, their brittle bones cracking as they moved towards him, chanting the same message.

"You killed us! You let us die!"

"No," he said, falling to the ground, his head on fire. "No, I didn't. I tried to save you."

"No, you didn't!" the corpses screamed. "You didn't do what it took to save us. Why didn't you do it?"

"I can't," he pleaded with them.

"Shade," Jack said, shaking his shoulder. "Shade, what's happening? What are they telling you?"

Losing his grip on reality, Shade grabbed Jack by the throat and slammed him against the wall. Two agents in the hallway drew their guns out of shock, but Jack held out his hand, shaking his head.

The grip on his throat tightened as he waited for Shade to stop hallucinating.

One of the agents got nervous. "Drop him, or we shoot!"

Eyes never leaving Shade, Jack drew his pistol and pointed it at the agent. "You shoot him, and I shoot you."

The agent relented.

"C'mon, Shade," Jack said, struggling to get the words out as the grip on his throat grew even tighter. "You don't have to do this." The more seconds that passed, the more Jack became afraid. Not of dying; Jack hadn't been afraid to die since he was thirteen. If anything, dying because of a friend would be the best way he could think of to go. No, he was afraid of what Shade would do if he killed him. Shade had lost so much—one more body on his conscience might be too much for him. And Jack had promised him it wouldn't end like the military had done, with more blood on his hands.

But eventually, Shade saw clearly again and released his grip on Jack before backing up against the wall in horror at what he had almost done.

"I'm sorry," he said. "I didn't mean—"

"Hey," Jack said, cutting him off. "I'm fine. It's okay."

Shade looked down at the floor, remembering the soldiers buried six feet underground. Remembering what had happened the last time he'd lost control. Now he had again, all because he couldn't stop hallucinating.

Finally, he looked back up and saw Jack staring back at him, concerned. "What are they telling you?"

"They're telling me it's my fault they're dead. That I killed them."

"You didn't," Jack said, sympathetic.

"I may as well have. I let them die, because I can't think straight enough to catch this guy. I'm too afraid of losing control to help find him."

"That's not your fault," Jack said.

"Yes, it is. After the first victim, it became my fault. Erika Stevens is dead because I couldn't find him. Carter's daughter is dead because I couldn't find him. Nora's sister is lying in a coffin in the ground, missing her heart, because I'm too distracted by horrors that aren't real to catch the killer."

"I can't catch him either," Jack growled. "You think you're the only one who sees the victims' faces? Every night, I see them in my dreams. Every time I close my eyes, they're there. Every time I blink, they're there!"

Jack stopped for a moment, trying to calm down. "So, yeah, maybe it is your fault for being distracted. Maybe it's mine too. But sitting here blaming ourselves for everything isn't going to catch this guy. Feeling guilty won't save the next victim. And we have. To save. The next. Victim," Jack said, breaking his words up, almost in tears. "We have to save her."

After that, they both remained on the floor, silent as they took in all that had been said. Finally, Jack smiled.

"Do you remember that guy we interrogated a few years back? The rapist who'd been stalking all those women?"

"Yeah," Shade said, grinning himself. "I remember. We had nothing on him."

"I know. All that planning we did for the interrogation, so worried that he wouldn't slip up. Wouldn't give us the confession." Jack was beginning to laugh now. "And then we asked him one question and he just started sobbing, begging us not to give him the chair. For a second I thought he was gonna wet his pants."

"I think he did," Shade said, causing them both to laugh until their eyes watered. It felt so good to laugh again, even if just for a moment. A small reminder of the time before the war, before the scars that wouldn't heal.

Finally, after the laughter died down, Jack spoke again. "We'll get this guy, you and me. We always do."

Shade nodded, and for the first time since the case had started, he felt genuine hope that they could do this. Then Nora screamed.

They rushed back into the room, seeing Nora sitting in the corner, covering her eyes, sobbing.

"What's wrong?" Jack asked, running to her.

She didn't answer, instead crying even more.

Shade stood back a few feet, realizing what had happened. "Jack. Look."

Jack's desk drawer was open. The one that contained the photos of the crime scenes. The photos Nora must've found.

"Why didn't you move those?"

"How was I supposed to know she'd go through my drawer?" Jack asked defensively.

Shade glared at him. "She's a kid, that's what they do."

Nora's continued crying caused them to stop bickering. Shade walked over to her and knelt down. "It's okay," he said, trying to sound comforting but not really knowing how. "That's not going to happen to you."

Nora's voice broke between sobs. "It happened to Susie."

Shade had no idea what to say to her after that. After the war, countless well-meaning people had tried to console him, all with their own unique little anecdotes about life and death. But none of it helped. Because in the first moments, when it feels like you're drowning from inside, you don't want to be consoled. Don't want to be told it's okay, don't want someone to pull you out. Because that makes it real, makes the loss permanent. In those first moments, all you want to do is think of who you lost, focus on not forgetting their face.

So instead of telling her it was okay, he took off his dog tags and held them in front of her. When she looked up at him, crying and confused, he found the words.

"You asked me why I wore these. I lost a lot of friends while I was in the military. Sometimes I'm afraid I'll forget them, forget what they looked like." He tapped the dog tags. "These remind me." He then pulled up her hair and hung them around her neck. "Now they can remind you of your sister."

She hugged him.

Shade looked to Jack at first, not knowing what to do, but eventually, he hugged her back.

Chapter Fourteen

Sara moved through the hallways, following Jack through the maze as they examined the aftermath: twenty-five bodies lying motionless on the cold floor. Some of them were just unconscious. Most weren't. Blood covered the floor, the walls, the bars, everything. As Sara walked through it, she accidentally brushed against the wall, and blood crept onto her jacket, staining it.

As they looked at the carnage, no one said a word, not even the guards who were checking the bodies for pulses. The silence dug its way into Sara's ears, causing chills to drip down her spine, because in the silence, she couldn't escape her own thoughts. All this bloodshed was because of her. These men might have deserved to die, but that didn't matter. She was tired of people dying so she could live.

She caught herself looking down, away from the sight of the hallways, and the horrors within. Jack noticed.

"You asked me what his hallucinations are like," he said, pointing down the hallway, forcing her to look at the horrific scene of blood and bodies. "They look like that."

Later that day, after the hallways had been cleared, they returned to the FBI base. Before the door to his office had even clicked into place, Jack started speaking.

"Do you want to tell me what that was back there?"

Sara groaned. "Not really."

"Well, too bad."

She knew he deserved an explanation, but she didn't have one for him, so instead she deflected. "How do we know Shade isn't going to attack here again?"

Jack glared at her. "He was wounded pretty bad in the prison escape. He's going to at least have to wait for the bleeding to stop before he tries again."

She nodded her head, hoping that was the end of it.

Jack smirked at her. "You do realize I work for the FBI, right? You think no one has ever tried to deflect a question before?"

She held up her hand, trying to protest.

"I'm sorry," he said, not relenting, "but when I'm trying to protect someone from a killer, and that someone then tries to get herself killed, it makes my job significantly harder. So I need to know what exactly was going through your head to make you think that was a good idea."

Sara started to speak but hesitated. What could she say? She didn't even know why she'd thought it was a good idea herself. It probably hadn't been, but she hadn't cared. She was just tired of reliving the memory. However, it was clear that Jack wasn't going to let it go without an answer.

"The other morning, when you knocked on my door, I had a gun to my head. I was about to end it anyway."

"I'm sorry," he said, eyes wide and voice sympathetic. "I didn't know. But that still—"

"No, you don't understand." Her voice was starting to crack. "It wasn't the first time I had tried. Every morning I hear her voice in my head. Every night, when I go to sleep, I dream about that day. The day someone else died because I was too scared of losing my own life. The day I chose myself over someone else."

"You said you were in shock."

"So? I was a medic. It was my job to save people, whether I was in shock or not. I watched my friend

 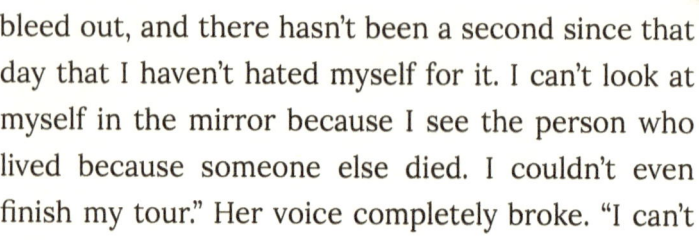
bleed out, and there hasn't been a second since that day that I haven't hated myself for it. I can't look at myself in the mirror because I see the person who lived because someone else died. I couldn't even finish my tour." Her voice completely broke. "I can't even look at my medical kit anymore, because I see the face of who I didn't save with it."

Tears began to fall down her face as she continued. "I wake up every morning and put that gun to my head. Every. Single. Day. Wanting it to be over, wanting to forget, but I can't pull the trigger, because I still can't bring myself to finish what the sniper should have. I still can't let myself die." Sara closed her eyes, her mouth quivering. "So, yes, I wanted Shade to kill me, because I can't do it myself."

After a few moments of consideration, Jack responded. "What will you dying change?"

She looked back up at him, confused. "What?"

"What will you dying change? Will it bring her back? Will it make what you did okay?"

"No," she said. What she had done would never be okay.

"Then what does killing yourself do? If it doesn't save her, then what's the point?"

Sara shook her head. "You don't understand."

"I don't understand?" Jack said, stepping closer to her, his voice growing angry. "You think I don't understand what it's like to look in the mirror and hate the reflection you see? You think I don't understand what it's like to wake up every day, wanting to put a bullet in your head, thinking that you deserve one?" He nodded slowly. "Believe me, I understand. But killing yourself solves nothing. If you kill yourself, it makes her death meaningless." His voice grew louder as Sara thought she saw tears forming in his own eyes. "If you kill yourself, it means she died for nothing, you understand me? If you end it, if you give up, Nora died for nothing!"

Jack caught his mistake as soon as he said it, but it was too late to take it back. Sara saw the pain in his eyes as he stopped speaking, and then he turned to face the wall, not daring to look at her. Sara now knew what he had left out of the story he had told her earlier.

"Who's Nora?"

He sighed, rubbing his eyes with his hands. She waited silently, giving him time to answer.

"She was a thirteen-year-old girl," Jack said, struggling to get the words out. "Actually, no, she was thirteen and a half," he said, giving a small grin, which Sara returned. "Her sister was the fourth victim of the Surgeon. We thought she might be a target too, so we kept her with us at all times so that he couldn't get to her. So that we could

keep her safe." His grin began to fade, and his voice began to quiver. "We were supposed to keep her safe."

Sara stepped closer to Jack, putting her hand on his shoulder. She was better at being comforting than he was. "What happened?"

A tear fell down Jack's face. "I made a mistake. I knew it was a mistake when I made it, but I still did it."

"Why?" Sara asked.

Another tear fell. "Because Shade wasn't the only one who was having hallucinations."

"What?" she asked, taking a step back, shocked.

"It started off as nightmares, and I told myself that was all it would be, but the killings just kept getting worse, and it was taking us so long to find the killer, so many bodies were piling up. I started seeing them even when my eyes were open, just like Shade. I started hearing their cries, pleading with me to save them. Asking why I didn't. And I knew as long as the Surgeon was still out there, they wouldn't stop."

Jack completely broke down in front of Sara. "I just wanted it to be over. I just wanted to find the guy as quickly as possible. But I missed something," he said, crying. "I didn't mean for her to die, I just wanted it to be over. I swear that's all I wanted."

Sara stepped closer to him, trying her best to be consoling, as he continued.

"The day she died, I put a gun in my mouth, and I almost pulled the trigger, because I knew she was dead because of me. Because I wanted the hallucinations to be gone so bad, I lost my judgment." He took a deep breath before continuing. "But I stopped myself. Because I knew that, sooner or later, a twelve-year-old girl would die, and then that would be my fault too, for giving up. So I put the gun down, and I forced myself to let Nora go. To let the victims go, to move on, so I could save the next victim. And I did. I caught that psychopath before he could kill another one."

He sighed. "But it didn't matter. Nora was still dead, and my partner was already too far gone to come back. And it was all because of me, because I missed something. So I know how you feel. I *really* know how you feel. Not a moment goes by that I don't think about picking that gun back up. But if I kill myself, who stops them?" he said, pointing to the serial killers on his wall. "Who saves their next victim?"

Jack looked directly into Sara's eyes, trying to make her understand. "Killing yourself doesn't save anyone. Being consumed by guilt like Shade doesn't save anyone. You have to find a way to move on," Jack said. "You have to."

After that, the room grew quiet, and Sara took in all that had been said, the voice still ringing in her head.

"Help me."

Was Jack right? Would killing herself make her friend's death meaningless? She didn't know anymore. But if he was right, it would mean killing herself wouldn't be helping anyone but her. It wouldn't be to save anyone, to atone for her sins. It would be for her, to make the memories go away. To finally forget what she had done.

She wasn't sure if she deserved to forget.

Chapter Fifteen

"How old was she?" Jack asked, looking down at the corpse of the sixth victim, already knowing the answer to the question.

The body had been found in another hotel room, once again reserved under the name John Buck. Everything about the victim's death remained the same: lying on a table, operated on, with defensive wounds on the girl's arms. The only thing different was the girl herself, once again bearing nothing in common with the previous victims.

Jack ground his teeth, frustrated. This victim had been found in another hotel room, just like the last one had been found in the same abandoned warehouse as the first victim. It meant the killer was either toying with them or was just too lazy to find another spot. Jack wasn't sure which theory irritated him more.

"Sixteen," Detective Washington answered.

"Please tell me you have something new. Anything at all."

"I'm afraid not. Sorry."

"Nothing?" Jack asked, desperate. "No new suspects, no jealous boyfriend, no creepy janitor at her high school?"

"It's still early. But, no, so far it doesn't look like there is."

Jack sighed. "Do you have any other leads, anything we might have missed?"

The detective shook his head.

"Of the suspects we do have, who do you like for it?"

"I was going to ask you the same question."

After a few moments, Jack noticed Shade hadn't said a word since they'd looked at the body, and his eyes were twitching.

"Can I speak to you for a moment?" Washington said, waving his hand toward Jack.

"I'm confused as to what we've been doing so far."

"Alone," he added for clarification, glancing over at Shade.

Shade stared him down for a moment before turning to Jack. "I'll go check on Nora."

Jack nodded, and then when Shade was out of earshot, he began speaking. "What's this about?"

"I'm concerned about your partner's stability," Washington said plainly. "I mean, I know we're all having problems with this case, you'd have to be a monster not to be struggling, but he seems particularly off."

"He's fine," Jack stated.

"Is he really? Because if he's not, it would be in everyone's best interest to take him off the case. Especially the victims."

"Why is that?"

"Because, I'm old enough that I've seen stuff like this before. People start getting too close to the case, and it starts messing with their heads. They start making mistakes. Mistakes that can cost lives."

In his heart, Jack knew the detective was probably right. Shade was being affected, and in all honesty he probably should be removed from the case. But Shade was also his partner, and behind the rough exterior, he was smart. Jack needed him to stay with him. He couldn't do this alone.

"I'll take it under consideration," Jack said, shaking Washington's hand. "And don't worry. We'll catch this guy before he takes another one."

The old detective sighed, a lifetime of regret in his face. "I used to tell myself that too."

Across the room, a CSI called out, "We got something."

It was another note. Once again written on old paper, in thick, blotchy ink, the letters distorted. And once again, it was signed.

WHY DIDN'T YOU STOP ME? WHY DIDN'T YOU TRY TO SAVE HER?
¬JOHN BUCK

"I'm gonna kill him," Jack said, staring at the note. "I'm gonna find him, and I'm going to kill him."

"Probably not wise to admit that in front of a cop, Special Agent Diamond," Washington said. "Although in this case," he whispered, winking at them, "call me if you need help disposing of the body."

"Will do."

Shade stared at the note. "Who is he writing these to?"

Jack squinted his eyes. "I don't know. The police, us. Who cares?"

"No," Shade said, pointing to the letter. "Why didn't 'you' stop me. Why didn't 'you' try to save her. He keeps saying 'you.' The killer is writing these to a specific person."

Jack's eyes widened. "You're right. Which means the killer must know at least one of us."

They all looked at each other for a moment. Finally, the detective spoke.

"Let's assume for a moment that it's not our wives or something stupid like that. That means it's probably a suspect one of us has already talked to."

"All our suspects checked out," Jack answered. "Have you spoken to anyone we haven't?"

"I'll get my suspect list, but it's probably gonna be the same as yours. I may have talked with a few more of them than you, though—although, like you said, they all checked out."

"Okay," Shade answered. "We'll give you ours too, just to make sure there isn't anyone we talked to that you haven't."

"Sounds like a deal," Washington said, shaking their hands before walking off.

Shade turned to Jack. "What are you thinking?"

Jack didn't hear him. Instead, he looked into the distance and tried to listen. Something was whispering to him. "Do you hear that?"

Later, in Jack's office, Nora had taken a seat on his desk, playing with his blue pen. Jack was sitting in his chair, and Shade had chosen to remain standing, looking at the detective's suspect list, which he had taped to the wall.

"It's the same," Shade said, frustrated. "It's the exact same."

"Well, glass half-full," Jack said. "We don't have any new suspects to look into."

"Glass half-empty. We don't have any new leads whatsoever." Shade looked back at the note attached to the wall. "Maybe I was wrong. Maybe he's not talking to someone specifically."

"No, I think you're right. We just have to figure out who it is."

"I think you're right too," Nora chimed in.

"See? Even the kid thinks you're onto something."

Then Jack got an idea. "You don't know anyone named John Buck, do you?"

Nora shook her head.

"No one at all?"

"No," Nora said, trying to think. "Why?"

Shade answered her. "It's what the killer signs his notes with. We thought maybe it might mean something."

"Maybe it means he's crazy," Nora suggested.

"Oh, it definitely means that," Jack said. "But usually crazy people still do things for a reason. The trick is finding out what that reason it."

Nora started to respond but then winced in pain.

"You okay?" Jack asked.

"Yeah," Nora said after a moment. "My stomach's just hurting."

"You need food or something?"

"No. I'm fine."

"Okay," Jack said, turning his attention back to Shade. "So, we have a killer who apparently knows us, who signs his notes with a name that appears to mean nothing, and every suspect that either we or the cops have looked into has been cleared."

"Yep," Shade said, sighing and looking at the suspects again.

"So," Jack said, looking at Nora, trying to keep her mind occupied so she wouldn't have to think of her sister. "What do you want to be when you grow up?"

"I want to join the Army."

"Really?" Jack said, surprised. "Why not go into the FBI instead?" He flashed his badge. "It's a much cooler job. Plus, you won't end up looking like the grim reaper over there," he said, pointing at Shade, who just ignored him.

Nora shook her head. "Military people are tougher."

"Whoa," Jack said, leaning back in his chair. "That's not true." He pointed to Shade. "I could take him right now."

Nora wrinkled her brow.

"I'm serious," Jack said before looking at Shade and faking a go at him.

"Don't make me kill you in front of the girl, Jack."

Jack winked at Nora, smiling. "You see how he talks to me."

Nora winced in pain again. This time, Shade and Jack both grew concerned.

"What is it?" Jack asked.

"I don't–aghh," she said, grabbing her side again.

"She had her kidney replaced," Shade said, picking her up. "It must be failing. Call her parents. We need to take her to the hospital."

Later that day, doctors and patients seemed to be swarming the hospital, far more than when they had come to question Urich. But even the extra display of people couldn't shake the feeling the hospital gave Jack. Something about it still seemed wrong. He couldn't quite place it, but ever since that day so many years ago, he could always tell when someone or something was hiding something darker. It was like a learned instinct, and normally it was subtle, just a small, almost unnoticeable discomfort in his stomach.

Right now, however, he felt like he could vomit.

But he couldn't focus on that, at least not now. They were with Nora and her parents, and Dr. Urich was informing them of what needed to be done regarding Nora's pain.

"If her kidney is failing, we need to look at her immediately," he said, already ordering nurses to get a room ready.

The parents nodded their permission, and Dr. Urich began to lead Nora through the hospital.

"Wait," Jack said, holding his hand up. "Is there anyone else who can look at her?"

"Why?" Nora's mother asked.

Dr. Urich just smiled. "Because I'm still a suspect," he said, looking at Jack. "Is that correct?"

"That's right."

"Well," Dr. Urich said, "I understand your concern. But unfortunately, no, there are only two other doctors trained in kidney surgery if the need arises, and they are both performing other surgeries at the moment. However, I assure you, nurses will be with me at all times. Even if I were the killer, there would be no opportunity for me to take advantage of the situation."

Jack looked at the nurses behind him, who nodded. "Okay."

"Thank you," the doctor said before leaving with Nora and the nurses.

"I don't like this," Shade said.

"Me either. But we've already proven he's not the killer, and even if he was, there's no way he'd be bold enough to do it here."

Shade nodded. "I guess you're right. Still."

"I know. It feels like we're missing something."

"You let us die," a corpse whispered in Jack's ear.

He flinched. Shade noticed. "You okay?"

"Yeah," Jack said, shrugging it off. "It's nothing."

That night, they waited in a hospital room for Nora to arrive. Dr. Urich had finished looking at her and found that while she should be fine, given her symptoms, there was a slight possibility of a kidney infection. It was determined by both him and her parents that Nora should stay there for a few nights to make sure that if it was an infection, she would be able to get help immediately.

Now, Nora stood across the hospital, saying goodbye to her parents. Hospital policy stated that they couldn't stay with her overnight.

The hospital room was small, containing only one bed, hidden by a white curtain that hung from the ceiling. By the bed was an IV drip, just in case, as well as a heart monitor. In the corner of the room sat two chairs, where Jack and Shade planned to spend the night, regardless of the hospital's policy.

Someone knocked on the door.

Shade opened it, expecting Nora and Dr. Urich, but instead he was greeted by Detective Washington.

The solemn look on his face told them all they needed to know.

They had found another body. A seventh victim. Photos taken from the crime scene lay scattered across the hospital bed as the cop explained what had happened. "We found her two hours ago. I called your office and didn't get an answer, so I called a contact at the FBI, and he told me you guys were here. I knew you wouldn't want to leave the girl alone, so I took these photos and came straight here."

"Tell us about the victim," Jack said.

"Age fifteen. Defensive wounds on her arms, found lying on a table, same as all the other victims. Toxicology has just started, but forensics on the scene doesn't think there are drugs in her system, which again matches the rest. The only difference—it looks like time of death was less than an hour before the body was found."

"So she was killed three hours ago," Jack said, checking his watch. "I guess that clears the good doctor."

"Dr. Kevin Urich? Was he still a suspect?" Washington asked. "I thought he already gave us an alibi."

"He did," Jack said. "Just never hurts to double-check."

"I hear you." He then pointed to a photo on the bed. *"We found another note too. Obviously, I can't bring it here, but that's what it looks like."*

I WONDER, WHEN YOU CLOSE YOUR EYES, DO YOU SEE THE GIRLS AS THEY WERE, OR AS I HAVE MADE THEM?

┐JOHN BUCK

"Well," Jack said, looking at Shade, *"at least now we know who he's talking to."*

"I figured that too," the detective said. *"It doesn't take a second glance at you to know something scary is going on behind those eyes of yours."*

Shade's eyes twitched even as the detective said it, and Jack saw him try to block out whatever horrors he was seeing.

"So," Washington said, *"I'll leave these pictures here for tonight, but I'll need them back sometime tomorrow."*

"Okay," Jack said.

The second the detective stepped out of the door, Shade spoke. *"Is this because of me?"*

"Is what because of you?"

"The killings. The killer apparently knows I'm seeing the victims. Is he doing all this just to get to me?"

"No," Jack said firmly. "It's not because of you. He's just trying to screw with your head, make you think it is. I mean, think about it—if these murders were just about making you go crazy, how would the killer have known about that beforehand? I mean, unless the killer turns out to be me, no one else knew about your hallucinations." Jack put his hand on Shade's shoulder. "Whoever's doing this is doing it because he wants to, and for no other reason. The note is just his attempt to make these killings look like they're about something more grand than his own sickness."

Shade nodded, realizing Jack was right. That made the voices in his head calm down, even if just for a moment.

As they waited for the doctor to arrive with Nora, Shade spoke up again. "Maybe you are the killer."

"Really?" Jack said, rolling his eyes.

"Sure. Anything's possible."

Jack smirked. "Well, then, maybe it's you."

They looked at each other for a moment before laughing softly together.

"If it does turn out to be me," Jack said, still joking, "I want you to kill me. I wouldn't survive in jail."

"Same goes for me," Shade said.

"So, it's a deal," Jack said. "If we turn out to be murderers, we kill each other." After a few moments, he added, "That is, if you'd even be able to kill me."

Shade pushed Jack's shoulder. "Don't tempt me."

The door opened, and Dr. Urich walked in with Nora, alongside two nurses. Nora immediately smiled before jumping onto the bed.

"I'm sure the parents already told you," Dr. Urich said, "but she's going to be fine. It's probably nothing at all, but if by chance it is an infection, it's safer for her to be here."

Jack nodded before commenting, "It seems pretty packed here."

"Preaching to the choir," Dr. Urich responded, giving a slight chuckle. "One of the floors upstairs is being restructured, so most of its patients and staff got moved down here temporarily."

"Ahh."

One of the nurses spoke up. "If you two can follow us, we can escort you out."

"Thanks," Jack said. "But we're good."

"You can't stay here."

"I disagree."

The nurse looked at him sternly. "It's hospital policy. I'm sorry, but no one can stay overnight."

Jack didn't back down. Neither did Shade.

"Oh," Dr. Urich said, waving his hand. "It's fine, you two can stay."

"But—" the nurse started.

Dr. Urich stopped her. "These men are here to protect this girl. If anything happens to her, it's on them, not us. Do you want to be the one to tell the parents that you made the two FBI agents leave the hospital?"

The nurse shook her head.

"Very well, then," Dr. Urich said. "It's decided. Feel free to spend the night." He checked his watch. "However, my shift ended an hour ago, so I'm going home. The desk at the front has my number if anything happens."

The nurses walked out of the door, followed by Dr. Urich, who waved goodbye to Nora as he left.

Later that night, Jack sat in the chair, awake. They had agreed to take turns sleeping while the other one watched out in case something happened.

Jack didn't think the Surgeon would be brave enough to attack Nora with both of them right there, even if they were asleep, but paranoia was always an advantage in this type of situation.

To combat the crushing boredom, Jack looked over at Shade. His eyes were closed, but the fact that he wasn't at least twitching slightly made Jack think he wasn't actually asleep. As bad as the hallucinations were, the nightmares were still worse.

But, regardless of whether or not Shade was asleep, Jack continued to stay awake, looking at the wall.

Until he heard something.

It was faint, but he thought he could make it out. It sounded like someone was crying in the distance. He stood up from his chair and walked to the edge of the room, looking out the small square window. He didn't see anything, but the crying had grown louder. Whatever it was, it was outside.

As he moved down the hall, the crying grew louder still, until eventually he thought he had found the source. He stopped outside of a small room with a closed door. The window on the door was too fogged up to see what was inside, but Jack could hear it. Crying.

He opened the door and stepped inside. At first, the room looked dark and empty, like a hollow cave. But after turning on the lights, Jack saw what was really there.

A girl, huddled in the corner, crying into her knees. Blood was creeping away from her on the floor, almost moving towards the surgical tools littering the floor. And then, in horror, Jack saw the shelves.

Shelves lining every wall, dozens of glass jars sitting on them. Glass jars filled with—

Something grabbed his shoulder.

Jack grabbed his weapon and turned in shock to see Shade standing behind him.

"What are you doing?"

"This room—" Jack said, not understanding at first why Shade wasn't horrified by the room and its contents. "It's, it's—" Jack looked around it, seeing it clearly for the first time.

"It's empty."

He lowered his gun and looked back and forth across the empty room. "No. No, it was just here. There was blood and a girl and—" He covered his mouth in horror.

"I'm hallucinating too."

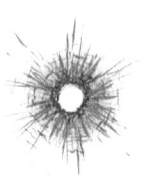

Chapter Sixteen

Sara sat in Jack's chair, staring off into the distance. She couldn't stop thinking about what Jack had told her. About how you only moved on by saving the next victim. If that was true, she had messed that up too, by getting herself discharged from the Army after it had happened. But then again, what could she have done if she had stayed, considering she could barely even stand to look at her med kit, much less give someone actual medical aid in the field?

The more Sara thought about it, however, the more she started to think Jack was right. Killing herself wouldn't help anyone. It wouldn't make up for her friend's death. It would only help herself, by making the voices go away.

Then she realized something. This was the first time since she could remember that she could think of a reason not to use the gun in her drawer. The first time she had ever seen a light at the end of the

tunnel, a potential way out. The only question now was whether she thought she deserved to take it.

Jack's phone rang. He had been standing in the corner of the room, presumably thinking about his own past mistakes. He answered it, and Sara could hear the agent on the other end of the line.

"Director Williams is on his way."

The director stepped inside Jack's office, closing the door behind him. The look on his face told Sara this wasn't going to be a friendly visit.

"Well, I'll get right to it," he said, talking mainly to Jack, clear pain in his voice. "We're out of options."

"What do you mean?"

"I mean exactly what I said. We're out of options to protect her. We have no safe houses to move her to that Shade doesn't know about, and after the previous two incidents, we don't have enough agents left that aren't in the hospital to defend against him even if we did."

"We're the FBI," Jack said, confused. "We've got hundreds of agents left."

"Yes," the director answered. "Hundreds of agents, scattered across the country, on their own assignments. I'm sorry." He looked at Jack, trying to help him understand. Sara could tell he was sincere.

"You know that if there was any way, I wouldn't hesitate to do it. But there simply isn't. We just don't have enough agents left here that he hasn't already put in the hospital. Unless you have an idea that I haven't thought of, in which case, I'm all ears."

Jack wanted to say something, but the director was right. Shade knew about their safe houses, and they wouldn't be nearly enough to hold if he attacked. They were out of options.

The director stepped toward Sara. "I'm sorry," he said, shaking her hand. "I truly am." As he stepped out, he turned back toward Jack. "You can use whatever safe house you think is best. I just can't guarantee anything working." On that somber note, the director left.

In that moment, for perhaps the first time she could remember, Sara saw the look of defeat in Jack's eyes too.

Jack rubbed his face in frustration as he went back over possible options. "We have three safe houses within a reasonable distance, but the director is right. Shade knows where they are, and we don't have enough men on site to risk it. And if we stay here, it's only a matter of time before he attacks again, and we won't get lucky a second time."

"Okay," Sara said. "So what other options are there?"

"None. At least none that are viable. We could go to a random place and hope Shade can't find us, but we would have to just stay hidden forever, and then"—he pointed to the crime scene photos the Hangman left behind—"who saves them?"

Sara nodded her head and sighed. He was right. She looked at the wall, seeing the grisly scenes left by the serial killer Jack was currently chasing, thinking about how every second Jack spent trying to save her was time he could be spending trying to save them. She then turned toward Jack and realized he knew what she was thinking.

"How many people did you save in the Army?"

"What?" she asked, confused.

Jack crossed his arms. "It's a simple question. How many did you save before your friend died? I know you know the number."

After a few moments, Sara answered, "Twenty-five."

"Okay," Jack said. "So, you saved twenty-five people and then lost one. You're still twenty-four up. That's twenty-four more than most people save in their lifetime. So right now, we're going to focus on saving you, whether you keep fighting me on it or not."

She realized Jack wasn't going to back down. "Okay. But that still doesn't give us any options."

"Actually, we do have one," he said, looking across the room to another picture hanging from the wall.

Sara recognized the picture from earlier. It was the photo of Frank Burrows, the crime lord, who couldn't be touched because people in the FBI owed him favors.

Jack sighed and whispered to himself, "Whatever it takes."

"What?"

"I used to say that to Shade. Whatever it takes to save the next victim." Jack walked over to his drawer and pulled out a file on Burrows, removing what looked like a business card from it.

"What's that?"

"Something Burrows sent me a long time ago."

Sara realized what he was talking about. "It's not worth this," she pleaded.

Jack began dialing the number. "Yes, it is."

The warehouse sat on the edge of the city, next to a dock that overlooked the ocean. The warehouse itself was massive, reminiscent of a military stronghold. Sara and Jack had been led through it,

passing more guards than she had ever seen, and were now walking through a hallway on the fourth and final floor, heading towards Burrows's office.

Finally, they walked into the room, where a man sat behind a large desk. Sara recognized the man from his photo. He looked younger than his picture, probably early sixties. He was larger in person, his shoulders seemingly stretching out three feet in either direction, giving him an imposing presence, even sitting down. He looked exactly like what Sara would expect from a crime lord.

As they walked in, Burrows greeted her without bothering to stand up. "Hello, Ms. Michaels. I understand you are in a bit of trouble." He spoke slowly and deliberately; his voice was deep and grandiose, but something about it still sent a chill down Sara's spine.

"Yeah, I guess you could say that," she said, not playing the scared victim that she knew he was expecting.

"Ah," he said, smiling. "I guess I should have expected such brazenness from one such as yourself, what with your military background and all." He stood up and walked closer, towering over her. He smirked again, and she noticed he hadn't yet acknowledged Jack's presence at all. She didn't know if that was out of spite or arrogance. "Death itself is coming for you, and yet you don't appear afraid. It has been my experience there are only two types of people who don't fear death. Those too foolish to know what it means, and those who welcome it as a release from this life. So tell me, Ms. Michaels," he said, looking down at her. "Which one are you?"

Sara glared up at him. Everything about him irritated her, but she also knew she had to be nice, at least to some extent. They were technically asking for his help. "It's Sara," she said before adding, trying not to sound snarky, "Which one do you think I am?"

"I think we will just have to wait and see."

Finally, he turned away from her and toward Jack. "I must say, when I heard that Special Agent Jack Diamond himself called needing a favor, I was surprised. I never imagined you'd actually use the card." He stepped closer to him. "You do realize the gravity of what you are doing?"

Jack nodded and pulled a file out of his jacket, the file with everything the FBI had on Burrows, and presented it to him.

Burrows waved his hand in the air. "Keep the file," he said. "I'll have one of my other agents steal it from your desk eventually."

"But—"

"You think I would waste a favor from Jack Diamond on a random file?" He laughed. Sara couldn't tell whether it was fake or not. "No, my friend, you won't be getting off that easy."

"Then what?" Jack asked, irritated.

Burrows simply shrugged. "I'm not sure yet. I prefer to have people indebted to me in advance. That way when situations arise, they can be swiftly taken care of. You understand, of course."

Jack bit his tongue and simply nodded his head.

"Good. Now that we have an understanding, what exactly is it that you need?"

"I already told you," Jack said, losing his patience. "We need a safe house from Shade. Isn't that why you had us meet you here, in your fortress?"

"Yes," Burrows said. "I suppose it is." He waved to the guards who had walked them in. "I know what Special Agent Shade is capable of, from when he slaughtered an entire warehouse of my men in the drug raid a few years ago. I would very much like to return the favor. That is why I have accepted your offer, Special Agent Diamond, and why you will have my best men here, guarding you and your new friend at all times. I know you want this matter finished as quickly as I do, so I've already sent out word that you are here. If Shade is looking, it won't take him long to find you."

"You're using us as bait?" Sara asked.

"Don't look so shocked," Burrows said. "Did you really think that one favor was enough for me to risk the lives of so many of my men?"

"Fine," Jack said. "You get your payback; you keep us safe."

Burrows was then handed an overcoat by one of his guards, which he put on. "Obviously I'm not going to stay here to witness the carnage, should Shade overtake my guards, but I do sincerely wish you the best of luck." He began to walk toward the door but stopped in front of Jack. "I heard about what happened with you and your partner. That must have been hard, knowing someone you trusted killed such an innocent woman."

Jack didn't give him the satisfaction of a response.

"You know," Burrows said, looking back and forth between Jack and Sara, "there is a story that I heard a long time ago."

"I'm dying of anticipation."

Burrows smiled, but it didn't deter him from telling the story. "There was a farmer who kept sheep. He was good at it, and eventually, he had grown a large herd, with which he made his living. But one day, the farmer went out to tend his sheep and saw one lying in the grass, bleeding, half-eaten.

The farmer thought maybe it was just a wandering animal, so he left it alone, until another turned up dead, and he saw the wolf fleeing the scene, blood dripping from its mouth.

"So, the farmer did the only thing he knew to do. He bought two sheepdogs, big enough to fight off any wolf that might come to take the sheep. And for a while, it worked. The wolf disappeared."

"Is there a point to this story?" Jack asked, growing impatient.

Burrows tilted his head slightly, not liking to be interrupted. "One day, one of the sheepdogs noticed a sheep was missing. He thought the wolf must have come back, so he scoured the entire field, finding nothing. But when he returned to the barn to tell the other sheepdog what had happened, he found him hunched over the missing sheep, blood dripping from his mouth.

"You see, the farmer had neglected to feed his sheepdogs. And the one dog knew that if the wolf returned, he wouldn't have enough strength to stop him, so he did the only thing he saw reasonable. He killed one sheep, so that he could protect the rest. And now he came face-to-face with his friend, who stood, realizing the horrors that he had committed."

"What did the other dog do?" Sara asked.

"No one knows," Burrows answered, looking directly at Jack. "Some say he left, knowing it was what had to be done but not being able to watch it himself. Others say he killed his friend to avenge the life of the innocent sheep." Burrows paused. "I wonder, Special Agent Diamond, if the time comes, will you find the strength to kill your friend, or will you simply stand by and watch what has to be done?"

Jack grimaced, not wanting to dignify the question with an answer. "Do you tell your kids that story before bedtime?"

"I don't have children, Special Agent Diamond."

"So you claim," Jack said, trying his best to irritate him.

Burrows simply smiled. "I look forward to finding out what choice you make," he said before walking to the door. Before he stepped through it, Sara asked him a question.

"What do you think the other dog did?"

Burrows cut his eyes toward her.

"I think he joined in the feast."

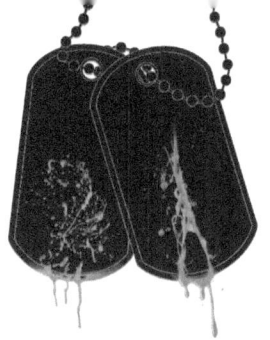

Chapter Seventeen

Nora screamed.

The scream alerted Shade. It was early in the morning, and Jack had left to get the crime scene photos back to the detective, leaving them alone in the hospital. "What's wrong?"

Nora didn't respond as she rose up in the bed, tears crawling down her face.

"You have a nightmare?"

She nodded her head.

"You want to talk about it?"

She shook her head.

"Okay," Shade said, turning to go back to his chair, when Nora started crying again. Shade closed his eyes and sighed to himself. He wished Jack had been here instead. He didn't know how to comfort a child. But Jack wasn't there, and he couldn't just let her cry.

"The nightmare was about your sister?"

A nod.

Shade nodded in return. He couldn't find the words, so instead, he remained quiet and sat on the bed beside her so she wouldn't have to cry alone.

After a few minutes, she stopped and wiped her eyes. "Jack said you have nightmares too."

"Jack talks too much," he said, hoping to brush it off, until he realized she was serious. "But, yes, I have nightmares."

"What are they about?"

Shade winced as he thought of them. "People I've lost."

"In the war?"

"Among others."

"Like my sister?"

"Yeah. She's there too."

Another tear fell down her face. "Will they ever go away?"

Shade realized now why she was asking him about his nightmares. He started to lie, to tell her that it would go away, that everything would be fine, but he couldn't. He was many things—soldier, agent, unstable—but a liar was not one of them.

"I don't know, kid."

"What if they don't?"

"If they don't, then I guess you just have to learn to live with it."

"How?"

Shade stared off into the distance. "I don't know."

Nora leaned back, resting against the head of the bed. Tears continued to stream down as she thought of her sister.

"That's the good thing."

"What?"

"You're thinking of your sister. That's the good part of the nightmares. They remind us of the people we lost. They remind us who they were, and why we cared about them." Shade looked her in the eyes. "As long as you have the nightmares, you'll never forget her."

She raised up suddenly and hugged him, still crying into his shoulder. "Thank you."

Shade said nothing, letting her cry.

"Why?" she said suddenly.

"Why what?"

Nora pushed away from him, and Shade saw she was covered in blood. "Why did you let me die?"

Shade woke up.

Out of breath and sweating, he reached up, trying to cover his mouth with his hand, but it was shaking too badly. He moved to the side of the bed, trying to make the memories go away.

He was in a motel. His side was still bleeding, and his knee was throbbing with pain from being broken, but he barely noticed it over the anguish of remembering. Tears fell from his face as he thought of her.

"Shade?"

He looked up, and across the room, a girl stood perfectly still, watching him.

"Nora?"

He tried to walk over to her, but she disappeared into the next room. As he followed her, everything turned to black around him, except for a small light that was shining over an operating table. And Nora was walking closer to it.

"Nora," he said, trying to go to her, but something stopped him. A hospital door, with a small rectangular window in the center. It was locked, forcing him to watch in horror as she walked closer to the table. "Nora!" he called out again, trying to get her attention. She turned, looking directly at him for a moment before walking right beside the table.

Shade cried out louder, beating on the door between them, looking at her through the small window. "Nora, come back." She didn't move. "Please! Come back."

She put her hands on the operating table.

"No! Please," he begged, beating on the door, tears falling from his face.

She raised herself up onto it.

"No!" Shade cried, continuing to beat on the door, trying to stop her. "Nora, please don't do this."

"You promised to protect me."

"I know I did. But please, just come back."

She lay down.

Shade screamed again, his hands growing bloody as he pounded on the door.

A man walked up beside Nora in a white surgeon's gown.

"No!" Shade screamed at the man. "Please don't do this. Please just let her go."

The man took out a scalpel.

"Nora, run!" Shade screamed, begging her as his legs gave out and he fell to the floor, listening to her begin to scream. "Please!" he cried, tears streaming down his face.

Shade collapsed completely, putting his hand on the door. "Nora," he cried.

"I'm sorry."

Chapter Eighteen

"Catch," Jack said from the corner of the room, throwing the pen from his desk towards Nora.

Nora, still sitting up in the bed, caught the pen and threw it to Shade, who was sitting in the chair across the room. He caught it and threw it back to Jack, and the cycle continued. The game was Jack's idea, an attempt to get Nora's mind off her sister, if only for a moment.

"So," Jack said as he tossed the pen back to Shade, trying to mix up the rhythm, "Doc says you'll be able to get out of here in a few days."

"Can't wait," Nora said. "This hospital is creepy."

"You got that right, kid," Shade said, tossing the pen to Nora, who in turn tossed it to Jack, purposely low so he'd miss it.

Jack still managed to catch the pen and cut his eyes toward her. "I feel like that's cheating."

She simply shrugged.

"Okay, I see how it is."

After a few more turns of throwing the pen around, someone knocked on the door.

Shade went to it. Right when he had his back turned, Jack looked at Nora and winked before throwing the pen as hard as he could right beside Shade's ear. He caught it without looking back and opened the door.

"That was disappointing," Jack whispered to Nora.

On the other side of the door stood Detective Washington.

"She was fourteen," he said as he laid the crime scene photos on the edge of Nora's bed. "We found her body in an alleyway, lying on another operating table."

"Is there anything different at all about the victim?"

"Nope," he said, shaking his head. "Same deal as the others. Nothing similar about her appearance, operated on, defensive wounds on her arm. Missing—" The word stuck in his throat. "Y'know."

Jack and Shade both moved away from the photos and closed their eyes, trying to lock the new crime scene images in their heads rather than letting them escape over into reality.

"You got it too?" Washington said, pointing toward Jack.

Jack nodded.

"Well, that's fantastic," he said, sighing and rubbing his forehead. "Look, guys, no one in my department, including me, is even close to having a lead, so you better pull it together. Alright?"

They both nodded.

"Good. And, hey, it's not all bad news. Since the killer has reached thirteen, the next victim should be her—"

Shade glared at him and motioned his head toward Nora.

"Oh," Washington said, realizing he shouldn't have said it in front of her. "Sorry."

Nora smiled. "It's okay. Two FBI agents are watching me twenty-four seven. I kinda put it together already that I was in danger."

The old detective smiled back at her. "Alright. Well, what I was saying is that since she should be next, as long as you two are watching her, the killer shouldn't be able to keep going down the list."

"Except we don't know for sure that she is next on the list. It's just a hunch."

"Well, either way, I don't figure you plan on leaving her anytime soon, so"—he pulled a large file from his jacket and set it on the bed—"I brought along all the information we have so far, including a new note left at the last crime scene." He winked at them. "Just don't tell anyone at my precinct."

"Deal," Jack said as the detective turned to leave.

As he left, he turned back and winked at Nora. "You stay safe now."

Jack and Shade stood back, looking at everything they had. They had pinned everything from the cop's file to the wall: crime scene photos, the suspect list, the notes left, all hidden behind Nora's bed curtain, away from her view. Jack looked at the newest addition to them.

SHE CALLED OUT FOR SOMEONE TO SAVE HER. I GUESS NO ONE CARED.

⌐ JOHN BUCK

The words made Jack's blood boil. He tried to focus, but he couldn't. He didn't know what was distracting him more—his hatred for the Surgeon, or the voices talking to him.

"You let this happen to us," the rotting corpse of Susan Doyle whispered into his ear.

Jack flinched as he tried to ignore it. So long as he was distracted by the hallucinations, he couldn't focus on finding this guy. He imagined what the victims must've felt, knowing they were next. How their skin must've crawled as they were trapped alone with a monster like this, knowing what he was about to do to them. Praying for someone to save them, but knowing no one was coming. His eye twitched slightly as the memory came back.

Rattling chains. Laughter. The butcher knife.

Jack shuddered as he looked to Shade and saw the same expression on his face, only worse. Jack knew if they didn't find this guy soon, it would be too late. They would both be too far gone.

Later that day, they stood in the same hospital room, looking over the evidence again.

"What do you think?" Shade asked.

"I don't know," Jack said. "The note is signed John Buck again, but we still don't know whether or not that actually means something."

"We have no new suspects," Shade added. "The new victim had never had any kind of surgery done and has no connections to the previous victims."

"There has to be something," Jack said, managing to block out the hallucinations for long enough to focus for at least a moment. "There's no way the killer could randomly pick out eight victims, each one younger than the previous one, without them having some connection."

"I agree," Shade said. "But still, we haven't found one."

"Let's look at it again. We have no new suspects, and the note tells us nothing, so it's all we got."

"Okay, where do we start?"

"Schools," Jack said. "All eight victims went to either different schools or colleges, except for two, who went to the same high school but were in different grades and, according to the families, never spoke. All of them also had different interests and majors."

"So, school's out. We've also talked to all of their families, and as far as we know, none of the girls, or even the friends of the girls, knew each other."

"So," Jack said, "personal relation is out. What if the killer was picking them all out randomly, but from the same location? Like a movie theater or something."

Shade shook his head and held up one of the cop's files. "Already looked into. None of them went to similar places, at least not often enough for the killer to select them from there."

"Okay," Jack said. "That just leaves us with the most obvious connection. Surgeons who have operated on more than one of the victims."

Shade nodded.

"But we don't have anything there either," Jack continued. "Most of them didn't have surgeries done, and the ones that did, the surgeon that operated is either out of state or Dr. Kevin Urich, who not only has an alibi for the one victim he has a connection to, he was also in the hospital with us when another victim died. Which leaves us with no surgeon suspects."

"The doctors don't match either," Shade said. "The first few victims went to different hospitals, and since then, none of them have matched up. Which leaves us with nothing. No possible connection between any of them." He sighed. "Something isn't right. It's not possible to pick so many victims without a connection. There would have to be something, some connection we're missing."

Jack sighed in frustration, leaning forward and resting his head against the wall, his eyes cutting left towards the evidence. But as he did, he noticed something. At this angle, the last victim appeared right in front of him, the youngest so far. To her left was the previous victim, one year older. The photos continued like that, a portrait of girls, each one appearing older than the last. It hit him in an instant. "They were growing up."

"What?" Shade asked.

"The girls." He pointed at the photos of the victims, suddenly anxious. "We've been looking at them in the order they were killed and eliminating suspects as we go. But what if we should be looking at the victims backwards?"

"You're saying try to match the last victims' doctors with the first ones."

"Yeah," Jack said before backtracking for a moment. "Only, they wouldn't have been to the same doctors yet, since the last victims were so young. They would have–" The last word caught in his mouth as the answers came all at once. "No," he said in frustration, pacing the floor, realizing his mistake. "No, no, I should have seen it."

"What?"

"It's not a surgeon. They aren't on the same hospital list because half of them haven't even been to a hospital yet." He slammed his hand on the photos of the younger victims. "It's not a surgeon. It's a pediatrician."

Shade looked at the evidence, eyes wide as he realized their mistake. "How did we not see this?"

Jack didn't answer him. This was it. He could feel it. This was the break they had waited for. Adrenaline surged through him as he pulled out his phone. Of course, they could have just run a check for pediatricians online, but that would take too long. They *needed to find this guy now, before his hallucinations got worse. Before he made another stupid mistake.*

He dialed the number of the first victim's parents. The mother picked up immediately. Jack put the phone on speaker, for Shade to hear, as he told her he was FBI and asked her the question.

"Who was your daughter's pediatrician?"

"Um," she said on the other end of the line, trying to think. "It's been a while. It's something with a C, I think. I have it written down, let me go check." They waited for her on the phone for what felt like an eternity until she finally spoke again. "Here it is. Her pediatrician was Dr. Carter."

They looked at each other in shock. "Dr. Benjamin Carter?"

"Yes," she said. "Why?"

"Thanks for your time," Jack said, hanging up the phone.

Jack started pacing in frustration. "We knew he had a motive. Why didn't we check out his background?"

"He had an alibi," Shade said, closing his eyes and trying to think.

"No," Jack said. "We should've still checked him out. It was a stupid mistake. And we both know why we made it."

Shade nodded. Jack was right. Had they not been hallucinating so badly, so disturbed by the victims, they would have seen it earlier. Much earlier. The victims' deaths were on them.

"Why didn't you save us?" a corpse whispered in his ear. "You could have saved us, if you'd only done what you had to."

Shade wondered if they weren't right. If he had done it and made the hallucinations go away, he might've seen it earlier, before more people had died. Maybe this was his fault.

Shade looked toward Jack and wondered if he was thinking the same thing.

Jack called the detective. As soon as he picked up, Jack spoke. "We got him."

"Who?" Washington asked immediately.

"Dr. Benjamin Carter, the fourth victim's father."

"You're sure?"

"Yes," Jack said. "He had a motive to kill his daughter, has surgical history, and was the pediatrician of the first victim, and probably all of them."

"Okay. I'll try and get a warrant, and we'll go search his house."

"No," Jack said immediately. "A warrant will take too long. We need to arrest him now."

"I'm sorry," the detective said. "But just being the pediatrician of one of the victims isn't enough to arrest him, especially since he already gave us an alibi. We have to find evidence on him, and we can't do that without a warrant."

Jack didn't say anything for a moment, trying to decide what to do. The detective was right—they couldn't arrest him without finding evidence in his house, and they needed a warrant for that. But Jack also knew that every second they waited, another victim could be dead. Another girl lying on an operating table, watching as an animal began to kill her, just because the cops were waiting for permission to stop it. He then remembered the promise he had made himself so many years ago. *Whatever it takes.*

"I understand," he said simply before hanging up the phone.

"What do we do?" Shade asked.

Jack began putting his jacket on. "You stay here with Nora, make sure she's safe in case we're wrong about this."

Shade nodded. "Where are you going?"

"To end this."

Jack knocked on the door, waiting for someone to answer. No one did. He knocked again, growing impatient.

The door finally opened, and Carter stood on the other side. Truth be told, Jack almost shot him on the spot.

"What do you want?"

"I'd like to speak with you about something. A new break in the case. May I come in?"

"You let my daughter die," Carter said as he began to shut the door. "I don't care what you have to tell me."

Jack reached out his hand, stopping the door. "Did you love your daughter?"

The question caught Carter off guard, causing him to release his grip on the door. "What right do you have to ask me that question?"

"I was just wondering if love was the last emotion you felt, when you began cutting into her."

Carter rolled his eyes. "This again. I thought we already went over this. I didn't murder my daughter. You're the one who said my alibi checked out."

"It did. But some new evidence has come to light."

"What new evidence?"

"I'm gonna need to search your house," Jack said, faking a smile at Carter.

Carter glared at him, and Jack saw in his eyes that he realized it was over. They had him. "Come back with a warrant," he growled before slamming the door in Jack's face.

Jack stood outside the door and chuckled to himself. Not out of amusement, or happiness, but the kind of agitated, sarcastic laugh that happens when you truly hate someone so much that anger isn't enough to describe it.

Jack knocked on the door. Again, Carter answered. "I thought I said—"

His sentence was cut off when Jack slammed his gun into Carter's face, knocking him back. Jack followed him into the house and shut the door behind him, locking it.

"You're crazy," Carter said, holding his bloodied nose.

"Certifiable," Jack said as he stood there, smiling. It felt good to see the look on Carter's face. So helpless, so surprised. Just like the victims he had taken.

"Get out of my house right now."

"Sure. Just tell me where you hid the evidence."

"Screw you. Leave before I make you."

"Do it, then," Jack said, holding his hands out slightly, provoking him. It worked.

Carter swung. Jack stepped back, watching him miss before shoving him back into the wall, shattering the glass of the picture frames behind him.

Shade wasn't the only one who knew how to fight.

Carter swung again, but Jack was faster. He caught him in the head with the butt of his gun again, knocking him to the floor. He then knelt over him, pressing the cold steel barrel against his temple.

"What's going on in here?" Carter's wife asked, annoyed as she walked into the room, carrying a cup of coffee. Her expression changed to terror as she saw Jack knelt down over her husband, her coffee cup dropping to the floor, shattering.

"What are you doing?" she finally screamed.

Jack ignored her, instead leaning down, close to Carter's ear. "I know what it's like, to feel helpless. To have someone standing over you, with complete control over whether you live or die. I know how your skin crawls all over your body as you start to realize that you are actually about to die, and that no one is coming to save you. I know how your stomach gets upset as you fight the urge to vomit—how something in your mind breaks, and you find yourself wishing you were already dead so that you didn't have to be here, in this moment, hoping beyond hope that the person standing over you shows you even the slightest bit of mercy."

Jack leaned even closer to Carter's ear, now whispering. "It's how your daughter felt when she realized her father was a monster for the first time. She probably begged you to stop, right. It's what we all do, all of us victims. We beg for our life, like a whimpering dog begging its master not to kill it. We hate ourselves for it, but we do it anyway, just on the faint hope that we get shown mercy." The hammer clicked back on the pistol. "I will show you the same amount of mercy that you showed her. So you can either tell me where you hid the evidence, or I put a bullet in your skull, right here in front of your wife, and then watch your faceless body bleed out onto the floor."

Carter remained silent. The wife started shaking nervously. Jack felt his grip tighten on the trigger as he waited for a response. None came. He took a deep breath. He wasn't going to let Carter walk. Wasn't going to let him hurt anyone else.

'Whatever it takes,' he thought as he started to pull the trigger.

"The basement," the wife said finally. "He goes to the basement a lot."

Jack looked over at her and then leaned down closer to Carter. "Is that true, Carter? Is that where you've been hiding it?"

A few seconds passed before Carter finally grunted a response, realizing Jack wasn't bluffing. "Yes."

"Well, then," Jack said, standing up and motioning towards the dark green basement door with his pistol. "Lead the way."

The steps creaked as they descended into the basement. The room was dark, the only light coming in from the door through which they'd entered, which only revealed blurry figures of what lay beneath them. Killers seemed to think the basement made it different, made it special. Almost as if being surrounded by the earth, already hidden below the dirt, below the world, somehow made the madness more normal, more freeing. Step by step, Jack's nerves only grew, remembering his last descent. Last time, all he'd wanted was to escape, to somehow crawl his way out of the living casket, to return to the world. This time, descending into this basement, he wanted to find the madness hidden within and bring it up, let the light of reality burn it to ash.

As they reached the final step, Jack reached over to the light switch, but the lights that came on were dim and flickering. His stomach turned as he smelled the air, filled with a sickly-sweet scent. The kind of sweet that most people wouldn't recognize but that made memories flood back into his mind. The pungent kind of sweet that signals death and decay.

The basement was crowded with shelves, like a twisted maze cutting through the darkness. As they walked through them, Jack still aiming his gun at Carter's head, he noticed the shelves were empty.

All except for one, which stood at the far end of the basement, covered in a white sheet.

Carter led him to it before stopping.

"Take the sheet off," Jack instructed.

"No," Carter said, shrugging.

Jack started to tell him again, but he knew it wouldn't do any good. Carter wanted him to do it, to be the one who saw. So he motioned for Carter to stand back against the wall, where he could watch him, and then walked up to the shelf.

The sheet's fabric felt smooth as he ran his hand against it. The light in the room was still dim, but it illuminated the room just enough to reveal figures hidden behind the sheet. Haunting shadows, lined up in a row.

A deep breath filled his lungs, an attempt to prepare himself for whatever was to come, when he pulled the sheet. It fell to the ground like a ghost, revealing what was hidden. Jack stepped back in horror as he saw it. Scalpels covered in blood, needles, tubes, a surgical saw that appeared rusted. And on the shelf above, lined up in a perfect row, sat eight jars, containing the mementos stolen from the victims.

Jack swallowed a lump in his throat as he pulled out his phone.

"Hello?" Shade answered.

Jack stared directly at Carter. "It's over. We got him."

In the interrogation room, Jack stood leaning against the wall, arms crossed, as he waited for Shade to arrive. He was also trying to figure out what to tell the police officers. Of course Carter wouldn't talk, Jack knew. That type of person would rather rot in jail than admit that someone had beaten him in a fight. Made him feel that helpless.

Jack also couldn't help feeling the slightest bit of guilt. Just like when he had stolen the security footage, he had once again crossed the line. But it was what he'd had to do to save the next victim. What he'd had to do to stop Carter, to stop the monster.

The door opened. Shade walked in.

Jack rested a congratulatory hand on his shoulder. "We did it, we got him."

Shade didn't speak, only nodding. But Jack knew how relieved he was. That this was over, that they had kept their promise and saved Nora. Now all that was left was to speak to the Surgeon one last time, and then they could be free of it forever—no more nightmares, no more hallucinations.

Washington walked in, cutting his eyes toward both of them.

"Evening, Officer," Jack said, in high spirits.

The detective spoke, his eyes still glaring at them. "You want to tell me how you managed to find the evidence in his basement, considering you didn't have a warrant, or even probable cause?"

"Strangest thing," Jack said, still smiling. "I went to his house to ask him a few questions, and he just invited me in."

"Really? And the broken coffee cup and picture glass?"

"Local earthquake."

"Earthquake?" he said, staring right at him.

For a brief moment, Jack tensed up, before he saw the detective crack a slight grin.

"Sounds about right to me," Washington said before winking at them. "Now, I guess the only question is..." He paused, turning towards the see-through glass. On the opposite side, Carter sat in a small metal chair, staying perfectly still, a small drop of blood coming down from his nose.

"Who's going to talk to him?"

"Hello, Detectives," Carter said, cutting his eyes toward them as they walked in.

They didn't respond. Jack sat down in the chair opposite Carter. Shade remained standing, arms crossed, a few feet away from the table.

"What's this about? Did you find out what happened to my daughter?"

"You killed her," Jack said calmly.

"I thought we already went down that road, Detective," Carter said, acting oblivious on purpose. "I have an alibi, remember?"

"Yeah, well, it wouldn't be the first time someone managed to fake an alibi." He put the confession paper in front of Carter. "How did you do that, by the way?"

Carter stayed quiet, not even acknowledging the paper slid over to him.

"Okay, if you're not going to talk, we might as well leave," Jack said, standing up.

"Stay," Carter said. "We have a lot to discuss."

"Fine," Jack said, sitting back down. "Then let's discuss."

Carter laughed a little to himself. "You come find me at the drop of a hat. You stay when I tell you to. You're really just a couple of lapdogs chasing your tails."

Jack's eye flinched, but he remained calm. People like Carter liked to provoke, but it was better not to let them. The more desperate they were to be noticed, the more often they slipped up. He placed some photos on the table—the photos of the victims.

"Did you kill these girls?"

"Is that what you really think? Or deep down, do you think that maybe you killed them, by taking so long to find me?"

"Just answer the question, Carter."

"Fair enough," he said, leaning forward, the chains of his handcuffs scraping the table. "Yes, I killed them. All eight of them."

"Why?"

"You already know why," Carter answered. "There is too much sickness in this world. Someone had to do something. Take my daughter, for instance. She thought she could move to another state for college. Thought she could get away, then go crazy, live her own life. She needed to be taught a lesson about respect. The rest of the girls were just necessary to cover it up. I thought if I played the part of a 'deranged serial killer' it would remove me from suspicion."

"Why the operations?" Jack asked. They already knew most of this information, but getting him to say it out loud would help make sure he couldn't backtrack in court. "Why not just shoot them?"

"I'm a doctor. I thought it would be a shame not to make good use of my profession."

"Why the hearts?"

"Well, you see, every sickness has to start somewhere, some weak link in the body that gives in, allowing the sickness to spread over a person like pestilence over a wheat field, destroying everything that was once beautiful and turning it into a withering meadow of blackness and decay.

"For physical ailments, the weak link can be anything from flesh to bone marrow, but for ailments of the spirit, aliments like my daughter had, the sickness begins in the heart. However, the treatment remains the same. Cut off the infected limb, the corrupted organ, before the rest of the body goes with it."

Chills ran down Jack's spine, seeing Carter like this. Still acting like he was in control, like this whole thing was some masterpiece he had put together. Like he wasn't just a stray dog that deserved to be put down.

But what was more disturbing was that in his own heart, something did seem wrong. Not so much that Carter was in control, but something else. The things he was saying, the way he was speaking. It was what Jack had expected to hear all along, but at the same time, he had never imagined Carter himself saying it.

"What about these?" Jack said, placing the four notes on the table. "Did you write them?"

"Yes."

"Why?"

Carter cracked his neck. "I have my reasons."

"Why John Buck? What does it mean?"

"Nothing," Carter said. "It's just a fake name I came up with. A play on John Doe."

"Then why not just write John Doe?"

Carter smiled. "That would have been a little on the nose, don't you think, Special Agent Diamond?"

"But the Surgeon isn't?"

He shrugged. "I didn't pick that name. The news just gave it to me after seeing what I had done. It does fit, though."

"What about the other victims? We checked, and you only had about half of them on your pediatric record. How did you find the others?"

"Coincidence. After all, it's not hard to find girls wandering the streets alone in this city. Especially at night."

"Okay," Jack said, leaning forward, coming within a foot of Carter. "Last question. Again, how'd you fake the alibi?"

"I didn't. I faked the time of death."

"What does that mean?"

"I'm a doctor. I grabbed her within minutes of her leaving my house and strapped her to the operating table, with a belt in her mouth to keep her from screaming. Then I pumped drugs into her system that would take a few days to kill her, so that I would be at *the hospital working at the time of death. Then, a day before you came to see me, I swung by on the way home and performed the operation rather quickly."*

A part of Jack almost felt disappointed. The speech about healing the sickness, teaching his daughter a lesson, the offhand way he referred to the other victims. It was clear that Carter had only really cared about killing his daughter and that everything else was just an act to him. Jack couldn't explain why, but somehow, he had expected more. Expected better. Carter was the surgeon, the self-proclaimed mastermind behind the hospital curtain, the one who'd killed more victims than anyone Jack had ever hunted, and yet here he was, retreating to the same higher purpose bullcrap as all the rest.

"Okay," Jack finally said, motioning his head toward the paper for Carter to sign it.

Carter still ignored it. "Don't you want to know why I kept going? Why I kept killing even after I had sliced my daughter apart and then been cleared of it?"

"Not really."

"I think you do. I think it's eating you both up inside, trying to figure out why I kept going. Why I left you those notes." Carter tilted his head, once again moving his hands, the cuffs dragging across the table. "I was going to stop, at least at first. My daughter was going to be the last one." He looked

up at Shade. "Until he showed up on my doorstep, and I saw the madness behind his eyes. I saw the potential he had, the infection of guilt within him. The opportunity for me to break an FBI agent, to heal him of his afflictions of grief. To create my own monster. Then I knew." He shook his head, smiling like a madman, an expression that didn't match his rough face. "I couldn't stop. That's why I left you those notes. That's why I asked you why you couldn't save my daughter, why I struck you at the crime scene. I knew you were so close to breaking completely, so prepped for a descent. I just had to push you over the edge, one final cut to heal your sickness completely.

"Do you understand me, Special Agent Shade?" Carter continued, leaning back in his chair. "The last four victims. They were just for you."

Shade didn't respond. There was nothing to say.

"Listen," Jack replied. "Just shut up and sign the paper."

Carter grinned and finally accepted the paper. "There's something off in your eyes too." He signed it and slid it back across the table before looking back at Shade. "I look forward to seeing you again someday, after you've been completely broken."

Jack took the paper from the table and stood up. "You do realize that you failed, right? You killed all those girls, you're going to go to jail and be executed, and you have nothing to show for it."

"Is that right?" Carter said as both Shade and Jack began to walk out of the room. "Well, maybe I'll just have to kill a ninth victim, then. I wonder who it will be? Oh, I know. What about that girl that I saw with you at the crime scene? I wonder how loud she'd scream."

The door shut behind them.

Carter continued to yell from the interrogation room. "I know you can hear me. When I get out of here, I'll find her, and I'll kill her slowly, just for you. You hear me, Special Agent Shade!

"Just for you!"

The hospital. For the longest time he had felt something was wrong with it, but standing in it now, saying goodbye to Nora, all he could feel was relief.

"Did you catch him?"

"Yep," Jack said. "We caught him."

Nora smiled, almost in tears. "Thank you."

"What for?"

"For finding the man who killed 'her.'" She still struggled with saying her sister's name out loud.

"Don't worry about it," Jack said, winking.

"So..." She stopped smiling, "Does this mean this is the last time I'll see you?" She lowered her head, suddenly sad.

"You never know," Jack said, trying to comfort her. "I'm sure we'll meet up again at some point."

Nora nodded. "I know. I'll just miss you." As she spoke, she outstretched her arm, attempting to give him back his blue pen.

He smiled. "You keep it. I got enough pens." With that, he stood up and walked to the door, passing Shade. Before he stepped out, he turned to wink at Nora one last time. "See you around, kid."

Once he was gone, the room grew quiet. Shade didn't know what to say to her. He had never said goodbye to anyone before. They had all died before he got the chance. So he just nodded and turned to leave, when she stopped him.

"Wait," she said, pulling his dog tags off her neck, "you forgot these."

Shade looked at the tags. He had always worn the dog tags as a reminder of what had happened overseas, a reminder of all the friends he couldn't save, a reminder that it wasn't worth surviving alone. And despite knowing that holding on would only make it worse, he had never been able to let it go. But now, looking at Nora, the girl who was going to live, the person he had saved, he felt he could finally move on.

He smiled. "You hold on to them for now. I'll get them from you when I see you again."

She smiled back at him.

Outside the door, Jack was leaning back against the wall, breathing a sigh of relief. They had caught him. They had finally ended it. No more corpses to see when he closed his eyes, no more crime scenes to have nightmares about, no more victims to be taken. They had ended it, they had caught him. This was it, Jack told himself. It was over.

It had to be over.

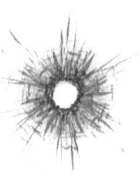

Chapter Nineteen

"So," Sara said, "I gotta ask. What's with the pen?"

Jack grinned, looking down at the blue pen in his hands, clicking it. "Nora found it in my desk one day. She liked it. I guess it just reminds me of her." His eyes watered for a brief moment.

"It's funny," he said, forcing a smile at Sara. "The memories you want desperately to forget are usually the ones you fight the hardest to keep."

Sara smiled back, not knowing what to say. She then turned and spoke to the guard in front of them. "What kind of security does this place have?"

They were sitting on the couch in Burrows's office. To their right was one of Burrows's personal guards, apparently named Lynns, who was keeping watch on the door and occasionally communicating with guards on the lower levels via coms. Lynns looked strong, but not quite as strong as he clearly believed himself to be, given the tough guy grimace in his chin. To their left, small glimmers of moonlight were slowly crawling their way to them, coming in from a single bulletproof window, which rested beside a rather large bookcase.

"Every kind," Lynns answered.

Sara sighed. Just once she would like to ask a question and not get a vague answer. "Specifically?"

"This place is a virtual fortress," he said, pointing out the window. "On the rooftop across from here, we have a sniper planted, so if Shade shows up, he'll be shot down before he reaches the front door."

Outside, by the door, a guard was talking over his coms. "Is everything still clear up there?" When he received no reply, he tried again, looking up at the building where the sniper was posted. "I said, is everything clear?"

The only answer he got was static.

"And then," Lynns continued, "even if he got past the sniper, there's only one way into the building— the front door, which is being guarded by a four-man team, all armed."

The guard tried his coms again. No reply. He turned to the man on his right. "I think something's wrong with our sniper."

A silent bullet took his partner's breath before he could answer.

The guard jumped back, raising his weapon. He turned back around to speak to the other guards on his left when he heard two more silenced gunshots and saw they had fallen too. Panicking, he started moving his weapon back and forth, trying to find the shooter's location. He finally did, seeing the outline of a man in the shadows, about fifty feet in front of him, holding a sniper rifle.

The guard fell to his knees before he could fire his own weapon.

"And let's say he manages to get past the guards outside," Lynns continued, moving his hands as he spoke as if he was telling a children's story. "The moment he steps inside, he'll be in the middle of a firing range of over twenty people, and that's just the first floor."

The guard outside was on his knees, clutching his leg, which now contained a bloody hole going

through the center. Before he could react, the man holding the rifle was next to him and raised him up by the throat, slamming him into the side of the building.

"How many are in there?"

"Screw you," the guard said, still wincing from the leg wound.

The man then put his hand over the guard's mouth before breaking his right index finger backwards. The man waited for him to stop trying to scream before asking again. "How many are in there?"

"There are four floors, and at least twenty men on the first," the guard said the second the man removed his hand from his mouth. "They're all watching the door."

"Do they have flashlights?"

"Don't need 'em. Room's already lit up in there."

"Where are the lights?"

"What?" the guard asked, almost crying from the pain of his finger.

"Where are the lights?" the man growled.

The guard pointed at the door to the warehouse. "Straight through, about twenty feet up. It's a row of fluorescent lights. They're all connected, but you won't have time to shoot them down once you step inside."

Shade knocked the guard out. He then walked right beside the door to the warehouse and lay on the ground with his head by the door. He raised the sniper rifle into the air and pointed it at the door, at an angle where the bullet would hit twenty feet up in the air. He fired, and once the bullet passed through the door, he heard the shattering of glass, and through the bullet hole now resting in the door, he saw the light was still on. He took a deep breath and adjusted the angle, firing a second time. The light grew dimmer. He fired a third, then a fourth shot, and finally, the bullet holes revealed only darkness. The lights were out.

The sniper rifle dropped out of his hands, and he leaned over to pick up the guard's AR-15 rifle and pistol, as well as an extra magazine. He then reached for the tactical flashlight at the end of the rifle, adjusting it to a three-second delay and a half-second flash. He did the same to the light at the end of the pistol and then holstered it in his jacket, where the light would be hidden. Finally, he kicked the door open and stepped in.

Flash.

Two guards dropped. The rest tried to fire on Shade but couldn't bring their guns to the light fast enough.

Flash.

Shade fired on three guards illuminated in the darkness. Before they could hit the floor, the light was gone. A few guards fired randomly but ended up hitting each other.

Flash.

A guard was illuminated, two feet from him, with his gun pointed right at him. Shade pulled the barrel down with his hand as the light went away. He then kicked the guard's knee, dropping him to the floor. He stood with his gun ready, waiting for the light to come back.

Flash.

Headshot. A guard behind Shade found the light before it could go away and fired on Shade, hitting him in the shoulder. Shade resisted the urge to scream and instead moved away from that spot, waiting for the light to come back on.

Flash.

The guard that had shot him took a bullet to the eye, as did the three beside him. The bolt clicked back on the rifle. Out of ammo. As the light went away, Shade grabbed the magazine from his jacket and reloaded, throwing the empty magazine across the room, hearing its thud. The sound caused four guards next to it to fire randomly, catching each other in the cross fire.

Flash.

Shade aimed his rifle. Headshot. Headshot. Headshot. Three bodies dropped. The light went away. From what he could tell, only a few guards remained.

Flash.

Three of the remaining four guards dropped as bullets passed through their skulls. The fourth, who was holding a shotgun in his hands, saw Shade in the light for a brief moment but was too terrified to pull the trigger.

Flash.

"What if he gets past the first floor?" Sara asked.

"Impossible."

Sara didn't let up. "Humor me."

Groaning, Lynns answered, "Well, if by some miracle he gets past the first floor, there are only two ways to get up to the second floor, and both are being guarded by a literal firing squad. He won't be getting past them."

The guards on the second floor waited in two groups, each having their backs to the other. They were watching both sides of the room, and both entrances to it. On one side was a stairwell, and

on the other was Burrows's private elevator. The gunshots fired below them had been suppressed, but they had still heard the sounds. They knew someone was coming.

The elevator light dinged on. It was headed up. One of them, wearing a bandana painted to look like a skull, went over to it and hit the button so it would stop on their floor. Lasers trained on the door, they waited as the light dinged again and the door opened. Standing inside was a man in a black overcoat with a rifle in one hand, the other hand leaning on the elevator's wall.

They fired. Blood stained the elevator's walls like an abstract painting as his body went limp. But still, his hand remained on the wall. The guards fired a few extra times, just to make sure he wouldn't be moving anytime soon.

"We got him," the man in the skull bandana called out to the guards still watching the staircase, who turned around to watch as he moved closer to inspect the body. It was now almost on the floor, riddled with bullet holes, lying in an ever-increasing pool of its own blood. But the hand was still on the wall, holding the body up. As the guard moved closer, he inspected the hand and saw the knife piercing it, holding it up.

"It's a trick!" he called out, but it was too late.

Shade raised his pistol and shot six men before they could turn around, then shot out the lights above him. Red lasers stayed bright in the darkness, searching for him.

His pistol light came on, and he fired three more rounds before he saw the corpses.

"You let us die."

'Not now,' Shade thought as the light came back on and he put bullets into the skulls of two more guards. In the darkness, he heard the voice again.

"Why didn't you try to save us?"

Flash.

Shade shot two more guards.

Flash.

Shade saw four guards, who now looked like the corpses of the girls he'd let die, their milky eyes rolled back in their heads, their rotting arms outstretched as they walked towards him like zombies, chanting in unison.

"You should have saved us."

Shade fired. All four dropped.

Flash.

Shade fired on five more corpses, but in the darkness, it looked like they had grown in number. He kept firing, even when the light was off, but for every corpse he shot down, five more arrived, all walking toward him.

Shade kept firing in terror, reloading his weapon again and again until finally he ran out of ammo, the hammer of the gun locking back as he continued trying to pull the trigger. They surrounded him now as he tripped and fell to the floor, his leg still broken from before. He tried to crawl away, but there were too many of them. They made horrific groaning noises as they closed in on him, like a group of spiders slowly inching closer to a bug caught in their web, waiting patiently to devour it.

"No," Shade begged, closing his eyes. "Please don't. Not now." He beat the floor as they grew closer. His mind began racing, going over all the victims he had let die. Going back to the woman in the forest. Going back to Nora, lying dead on the operating table. Another person he had promised to protect. Another innocent girl he had outlived.

He opened his eyes back and saw the room through the flashes of light. On the floor lay twelve guards, all dead. Shade remembered firing on at least three times that many corpses. He was losing focus on what was real. He had to hold it together a little longer. He only had one more floor to get through. Then he could finally do what he had come here to do; then he could finally let the memories go and be free of the horrors.

He walked over to the bloodstained elevator and took his bloodstained overcoat off the guard, now riddled with bullet holes, and put it back on. He then took the magazines out of his jacket and dropped them to the floor. Even suppressed, if he fired a gun on the third floor, it would be heard on the fourth.

And he couldn't let them know he was coming.

"What if he makes it past the second floor?" Jack asked.

Lynns grinned. "That's where things would get interesting. The first staircase stops after level two, and the elevator won't take him past three. The first two floors held armed guards, but the third is filled with professional hitmen—the kind who would rather kill you with knives and bare hands than firearms. Level three is a whole different ballgame."

"Why no firearms?"

"Because gunfire on the third floor would be heard here, and Mr. Burrows didn't want to ever be disturbed by nuances like gunfire while he was working."

Jack scoffed at the sheer arrogance of that statement.

Lynns just shrugged. "And then, if he somehow managed to get through them too, he'd still have to go through me."

Sara rolled her eyes.

"Hey," Lynns snapped, "I'm Mr. Burrows's personal bodyguard. I've gotten him out of warzones before, killed entire rival cartels. I once killed a man with a cigarette lighter. Trust me, no one is going to get through me."

With that, he stepped through the door, choosing to guard it from the outside, leaving Sara and Jack alone.

The elevator door opened, and Shade came face-to-face with six men. One held a butterfly knife, which he spun in his hands. The man was large, with a scar on his neck. Two more, both smaller, held throwing knives, and one had long hair, falling down past his eyes; the rest were weaponless, muscular and clearly brawlers, cracking their knuckles as they saw him. Within seconds, a long silver knife was thrown at Shade's eye. He caught it, spinning it in his hand, and threw it back, hitting the man in his own eye.

One down.

Not wanting to risk throwing another knife, the remaining men rushed him. Shade ducked under the butterfly knife swung at his head and struck the scarred man holding it, knocking him backwards. Long Hair tried to stab him from behind, but Shade shoved his elbow backwards into his throat, causing him to drop to the floor, gagging the whole way down.

Pain surged through Shade's skull as a brawler in front of him landed a blow directly to his eye. The strike caused his pulse to spike even higher than it already was, and in turn, he struck the man three times, the last strike so vicious it broke the man's jaw, causing it to hang down from his mouth, limp, as he too fell to the floor.

Two down.

Now that they were alone, Sara noticed the blood on her jacket. It must've gotten on her at the prison. She wiped it off on Burrows's couch, grinning as it stained the fabric, before looking at Jack and realizing he had some on him too.

She picked her hand up, tapping her wrist. "You've got some blood on your sleeve."

"Thanks," Jack answered immediately, looking at his right sleeve and wiping it off.

Sara raised her eyebrows at him before clarifying sarcastically, "It's on your other sleeve, genius."

"Oh," he said, seeing the blood on the other sleeve and wiping it off. "Guess it's been a long day."

Shade screamed as a knife grazed his ribs. The scarred man who had swung it tried again, but this time Shade countered it and swung for the head. Scar also countered, and they went back and forth for a few moments until another brawler tried to stab Shade from behind. Shade dodged left, grabbing the brawler's uncoordinated hand and forcing him to shove the knife forward into Scar's throat, right into the same scarred wound.

Three down.

The knife was then ripped out of the brawler's hand by Shade, who kicked him backwards and threw the knife. It flew through the air, missing the brawler's shaven head by about a foot, and stabbed into the wall behind him.

Confused, the brawler swung, but Shade caught his arm and spun him sideways, using the momentum to throw him backwards. His head stopped against the butt of the knife, but his back continued to the wall, breaking his neck.

Four down.

As Shade caught his breath for a moment, he realized his adrenaline had gotten too high and he

was having trouble telling what was real. His eyes were twitching rapidly as the sound of victims screaming clawed its way into his ears. The room went dark, but only for a moment, until suddenly Shade looked up and saw the two remaining men—both wearing long white lab coats and blue latex gloves, with stethoscopes hanging from their necks.

"So," Jack asked Sara, trying to be sympathetic, "how are you doing?"

How was she doing? She wasn't sure herself. She was in a crime lord's safe house, surrounded by criminals, with a crazy ex-agent coming after her, and yet she felt calm. Not in the way she had before, when she had wanted Shade to find her, but calm in the sense that she wasn't being haunted by the voice of her friend. She wasn't hoping for death, or thinking about the gun in her drawer back at her apartment. Instead, she was thinking about what Jack had said. About how the way to move on was to help the next person. For the first time since she could remember, she found herself hoping she lived through this, so she could save someone else. Make up for what she had done.

"Better," she answered. "I'm doing better."

The shock of seeing two Surgeons froze Shade for a moment as they charged him. It wasn't until he was struck in the face and staggering backwards that he found himself able to move. The first Surgeon swung a knife, but Shade ducked and returned a strike of his own, knocking him to the floor.

Five down.

The second Surgeon tried to strike him again, but Shade blocked the punch and brought his heel down on the Surgeon's knee, breaking his leg. As the Surgeon fell, Shade caught his head, holding on to his hair, and shoved his face into the wall, denting it and cracking the man's skull open.

Six down.

Shade knelt down on the floor, holding his side. The cut from the prison burned like fire, blood dripping from it. He tried to control his breathing as he got ready to move to the final floor. To face them. To finally end it.

But then he realized something. The first Surgeon on the floor was still alive. In an instant, all the hate Shade had ever held for him came back as he walked over and picked up the knife beside him. He could feel himself losing control completely as he began stabbing him.

"Please–" the man managed to get out. "Stop."

Shade didn't hear or see him. He just kept digging the knife in, over and over, as blood began to cover him. Shade kept doing it, not sure what was real anymore, when the Surgeon's face changed to his own. Shade jumped back in fear, landing on the floor, crawling away.

The Surgeon, now appearing as Shade in a white lab coat, looked over at him.

"You caused this," he said. *"You should have stopped him."*

Shade sat frozen in fear until he heard something beside him. Something that broke through the hallucination.

One man was still alive and had managed to crawl to the intercom system. "He's here."

Jack and Sara stood up off the couch, panicking, as Lynns stepped back into the room. "How do we get out of here?" Jack asked.

"Don't worry," Lynns said, pulling a long knife from his boot and twisting it in his hand before cracking his neck. "He still has to get through me."

Sara rolled her eyes as Jack repeated his question. "How do we get out?"

For a moment it looked as though Lynns wouldn't answer, but then finally he groaned and

pointed over toward the bookcase in the corner. "Behind that is a secret staircase that leads down to the ground floor. You can go through there if you want, but I'm staying."

Jack and Sara nodded at each other before moving the bookcase and running down the stairs behind it.

Lynns waited in the room for Shade to come. He could sense the anticipation in the air. He was about to kill Shade. The man the rest of the guards were scared of. He smirked. Now they would be scared of him.

The door opened, and Shade stepped in. Lynns, still grinning, swung a knife, trying to hit Shade's throat. Instead, Shade caught his hand, broke his wrist in an instant, and shoved the knife back into his clavicle. Shade looked around the room, seeing that no one else was there. "Where," he said, pushing the knife further against the man's bones, "did they go?"

Sara ran frantically down the steps, having already drawn her pistol. Jack ran beside her until finally they found the exit and ran out onto the first floor, right into the middle of the dead bodies—what seemed like dozens of them, scattered across the ground. Sara had never seen anything like it, even in the military.

"Come on," Jack said, grabbing her arm. "We have to keep moving."

They ran out of the warehouse into the night air. Rain was now falling from the sky, and the wind blew the cold air against them. In the distance, behind the warehouse, on the edge of the dock, Sara saw something, giving in to a faint glimmer of hope.

"There," she said, pointing. "The car."

Her mind was racing as she tried to run as fast as she could. She had to get there, she thought. She had to survive. She couldn't die like this. Not before she had made up for what she had done.

They had almost reached the car when a knife flew through the air behind them, knocking the gun out of Sara's hand. They both turned in horror to see who had thrown the knife.

Standing less than thirty feet away from them, limping, covered in blood, was the monster that war, guilt, death, and the Surgeon had created.

Shade.

Chapter Twenty

Shade stood in Jack's office, looking over the evidence still hanging on the wall. He knew he should be happy. After all these years, after seeing so many friends die, so many people that he couldn't save, he had finally helped save one. Nora was alive, because of what he and Jack had done. So why couldn't he relax?

"Something feels off."

Jack was sitting in the chair behind his desk. "Off how?"

"I don't know." He shook his head. "It just does."

Jack stood up and walked over to him, putting his hand on his shoulder. "It's over. We caught him."

"I know," Shade said, taking deep breaths. The hallucinations had quieted down since they had caught the Surgeon, but they hadn't gone away completely. He wasn't sure if they ever would. "But still, it doesn't add up."

"What doesn't?"

"I don't know. I just feel like there's something we're missing. Some detail we forgot." Shade sighed as he looked at the evidence again. Carter was a former pediatrician, currently a hospital doctor with surgical training, he'd treated most of the patients, and he'd confessed to the crimes. Jack was probably right. He was just seeing something that wasn't there. Still—

"Why did the daughter have defensive wounds?" Shade asked. "If it was her father, he should have been able to get close enough to knock her out without her having time to fight back."

"Maybe he wanted her to fight back. Maybe it gave him some kind of thrill or something."

"But what about John Buck? He said it didn't mean anything, but he signed all those letters with it. Why would he do that if it didn't have at least some significance? And then there's the way he got around the alibi. We checked for drugs in her system. It showed nothing."

"He could have used something that would be out of her system by the time we checked her. He is a doctor, after all."

"Okay, but if he really did what he says he did, his wife would have noticed."

"Maybe she lied to protect him," Jack suggested.

Shade shrugged. "She just didn't seem like the type."

"They never do."

Shade thought for a moment before nodding. "You're right. I guess I'm just having trouble accepting that it's finally over."

"I know," Jack said. "I am too. But we caught him. Me and you, we put an end to this, just like we always do."

Shade smiled, and after a moment of solemn silence, almost a mourning for all the victims they had lost, they both began reaching for the evidence on the wall, taking it down piece by piece. They took down the crime scene photos, the pictures of Carter's basement, and the photos of the suspects. As they did, Shade finally started allowing himself to calm down. It was still his fault that so many had died, but at least he had finally done what he couldn't do in the Army. What he'd joined the FBI to do. To save someone and then hopefully move on and leave the horrors in the past. To finally find peace.

But something wasn't right. He couldn't explain it, but somehow, he knew it wasn't over. Something was wrong, very wrong about all of this. "Carter didn't sound right in the interrogation."

"I was thinking that too," Jack said. "But they never talk like you expect them to. No matter who they are or what they've done, the motive always ends up being higher purpose crap."

"But it didn't sound like Carter. We spoke to him several times, and he never seemed like that. Even when he punched me, he was serious, almost distraught, and it didn't seem like an act. It seemed like he really only wanted to kill his own daughter. But the words he said in the interrogation, about curing a sickness, it sounded like someone else's words."

Jack sighed. "It sounded like Urich."

Suddenly it clicked. Shade saw the picture of Dr. Kevin Urich on the wall, seemingly staring back at him, and he remembered something. The detail they had forgotten.

"He said they worked together."

Jack turned, confused. "What?"

"How did we find out that Carter was a doctor?"

"He told us."

Shade shook his head. "No, he didn't. He didn't tell us he was a doctor. He told us he used to work with Dr. Urich, and we just put it together."

Jack was curious now. "So?"

"So, what if we focused on the wrong thing? We were so focused on Carter being a doctor that we didn't think to look into the connection between him and Urich."

Jack thought for a moment before responding, his voice now serious. "You're saying you think Urich might be in on it?"

Shade nodded.

"But—but he was only a suspect because of Nora's sister, and he has an alibi for when she died."

"Just like Carter had an alibi for when his daughter died," Shade said, moving the photos on the wall, aligning the victims underneath their respective killers, four below Carter, four below Urich. "They switched their intended victims, so they would both have alibis and we would dismiss them as suspects."

Jack took a step back from the evidence as everything started to come together. "The defensive wounds. That's why all the victims fought back. They didn't know who was killing them because they killed each other's targets."

"And that's why we could only find half of the victims in Carter's pediatric files. Urich must've treated the other ones."

Jack started to say something else when he looked at one of the notes the killer had left, which still hanging on the wall, and he was taken aback in shock, unable to speak.

"What?"

Jack took the note down and flipped it over, writing on the back of it. "Kevin Urich. Benjamin

Carter," he said out loud as he finished and placed it on the wall, directly in the center of the suspects. On it, he had written their names down, but out of order.

Benjamin. Urich. Carter. Kevin.

"Buck," Shade said as a chill went down his spine. It wasn't over. It had never been over. Then, all at once, he remembered. "Nora is still at the hospital."

They ran through the doors of the hospital, almost tripping as they frantically climbed the stairs, heading for Nora's room, expecting the worst. Shade could feel his heart stopping inside his chest, in complete and utter terror of what they might find if they were too late. But when they got there, they found it empty. Nora was gone.

They stood inside for a moment, confused, when Jack saw a nurse pass by the door. "Where's Nora?"

"What?" she asked, confused.

"The girl who was in this room. Where is she?"

"Um," the nurse said, trying to think. "Oh—Dr. Urich moved her upstairs this morning to run a few more tests."

Upstairs. Suddenly, a memory returned to Shade's head. Urich had said the next floor was about to be restructured. Which meant it wouldn't have patients, doctors, or security. Which meant—oh no!

"Which room!" Shade asked.

"I don't know."

They ran up the stairs to the next floor and looked down the hallways, dozens of them, each filled with countless rooms. Jack spoke up. "I'll check the hallways on the right, you check the left, and we'll meet back in the middle one."

Shade nodded, and they began searching.

She was still alive, Shade told himself as he opened the first door. Urich wouldn't be bold enough to kill her here. They would find her in one of the rooms, sitting on the bed, alive. She had to be.

The first room he checked was empty. His heart rate quickened as he opened the next door, still hoping to find her alive. But that room was empty too.

The voices came back.

"You let her die."

No, Shade thought. She wasn't dead yet. She was still alive. He could still save her. He had to save her. He couldn't take losing anyone else. He opened another door—another empty room. He turned into the next hallway, filled with a seemingly endless number of white doors, stretching down the sides.

"You can't save her."

He ignored the voice. It wasn't true. She couldn't be dead. He didn't know if he could take it if she was. He didn't know what it would make him become. He started checking the doors, seeing only empty rooms. Until–

"It's too late."

Shade heard something.

It was faint, but he could make it out. It sounded like someone crying. He began to walk down the hallway, searching for the origin of the sound, when at the edge, a silver operating table rolled across the hall, its wheels squeaking, into a room, out of sight.

Desperately, he followed it, and as he got closer, he noticed it left behind a faint trail of blood: small red specks that lay scattered across the floor, leading into a room. The door was shut. Shade could've sworn it had been open when the table had been wheeled into it a moment ago. He opened the door and stepped into the small hospital room.

Surgical equipment lay spread across the floor: scalpels, needles, saws. So many saws. All covered in blood. The whole floor was covered in blood.

The light above him started to flicker. The sound of electricity popping filled the room, echoing off the walls, growing too loud to hear anything else. And by each of the three walls that didn't hold the door was a small silver operating table resting against them.

Body bags covered the tables, black ones with long gray zippers down the middle. Shade stood motionless, not daring to open them up. He knew what would be inside. Who would be inside.

The one in front of him opened itself.

A girl rose up out of it, with black hair and deformed white skin. Her teeth had rotted out, leaving only fleshy gums in their place. "Why didn't you save me?"

Something grabbed his leg.

He jumped back, seeing the other two bags had been opened, their contents now spilled out and crawling on the ground, moving closer to him, repeating the same question. "Why did you let us die?"

Shade ran out of the room in terror, trying to escape them. He slammed into a door across the hallway, still unable to look away from the horrors inside that room. But then, he noticed something on the door behind him. He turned, coming face-to-face with the small window, seeing it was stained in blood so thick he couldn't see through it.

Shade grabbed the door handle, but it was locked. He looked at the window again before instantly looking away. No. It couldn't be what he thought he saw. This wasn't real. He was still hallucinating.

"Nora!" he cried out as he slammed into the door with his shoulder.

"You can't save her," a voice whispered behind him.

Shade continued to beat on the door, breaking it open inch by inch, until finally, it gave way and he stepped inside, seeing what had been left in the room, and dropping to his knees.

"Shade, where are you?" Jack called out as he searched the hallways. Finally, he saw an open door, and he went to it, not yet knowing just how much everything was about to change.

Blood was everywhere. Scalpels and needles lay scattered across the floor, and a surgical saw sat on the operating table in the corner. Shade was kneeling down in the middle, holding what was left of Nora's mangled body in his arms, his dog tags still hanging from her neck.

"It's not real," Shade said, tears falling down his face as he looked up at Jack. "Please tell me it's not real."

Jack couldn't. Because he saw it too. His legs buckled and he fell to the floor, staring at what was left of Nora, the girl they had promised to protect. It wasn't a hallucination.

It was real.

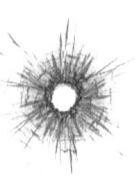

Chapter Twenty-One

Rain was pouring from the sky, soaking everything in sight. The wind was unforgiving, causing the water from the lake to crash violently into the side of the dock, as moonlight scarcely illuminated the night. Sara's palm was bleeding, the knife that had struck her still lying on the ground, next to the gun it had knocked from her hands. She watched in horror as Shade limped closer.

Jack raised his weapon. For a brief moment, he had a clean shot. But he couldn't pull the trigger.

"Jack?" she asked, seeing him hesitate. She saw the look on his face and knew what he was thinking. Now that the moment was here, he couldn't do it, couldn't shoot his friend. It was up to her.

She knelt down, picking her gun back up. She aimed it to fire, but another knife flew through the air, once again knocking it from her hand. It was too far away to reach for again; he was too close. She couldn't get to the gun in time. Out of options, she decided to fight.

She swung at him, but he deflected it effortlessly, grabbing her arm and throwing her to the side.

Jack still had his pistol pointed directly at Shade's head. "Please don't make me do this," he pleaded.

Shade said nothing as he continued to limp closer, now only a few feet away from Jack.

"Please," Jack begged. "You don't have to do this. We can still fix this, you and me. Please, don't make me do this. Not to you."

He received no reply, and he knew if he didn't fire now, it would be too late, but as he tried to pull the trigger, he realized it already was.

Shade grabbed the gun from his hand and threw it aside. Unarmed, and being backed closer to the edge of the dock, he decided to swing at Shade. The strike was dodged, and in return Shade struck him in the face, forcing him backwards. Jack swung a second time, and again, he was knocked backwards.

Now dangerously close to the edge of the dock, and the water below it, Jack made one final attempt. He aimed for Shade's stomach and punched suddenly. He knew that Shade wouldn't be able to block it if he was hallucinating.

He wasn't.

Shade blocked it and struck Jack one final time, knocking him to the ground, so close to the edge of the dock that his head was hanging over.

"You don't have to do this," Jack begged.

Shade took out his final knife.

"Please," Jack said. "This won't make the hallucinations go away. Don't do this. Let me help you. We can still fix this. Don't let the Surgeon win."

Shade raised the knife up in the air.

"This won't bring her back."

Shade didn't answer. He knew it wouldn't bring her back, but it didn't matter. He just wanted it to be over. He raised the knife up further, about to bring it down into Jack's heart, when he heard the gunshot.

He turned to see Sara, holding Jack's gun. His chest felt warm as he touched it, feeling the blood pouring out of it. Before he could speak, she shot him again, another chest shot.

He staggered back in shock, blood dripping from his mouth as he collapsed, falling backwards off the dock, landing in the cold, violent water beneath it.

Sara dropped the gun, in shock herself. She hadn't fired a weapon since the military, and now she had

shot someone. Killed someone. But he had been about to kill Jack. She'd had no choice.

Jack raised up and looked over the edge of the dock, where his friend had fallen. She walked up and knelt beside him.

"I'm sorry. But he was going to kill you."

"I know," Jack said, tears mixing with rain as they fell from his face. "It's just—I still thought I could save him."

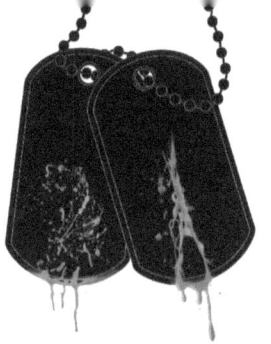

Chapter Twenty-Two

It was over.

In her apartment, alone, Sara allowed herself to calm down for the first time since Jack had knocked on her door. She now stood holding her dog tags right in front of her, looking directly at them but not really seeing them, her mind too focused on the memories they represented.

The FBI had shown up mere moments after she had shot Shade on the docks and had confiscated her 1911 pistol as evidence. She didn't understand the point—it wasn't the weapon she'd used to fire on him—but Jack had said it was protocol. A medical evaluation had also been done on her, despite her protests. Being around all the medical equipment brought back memories that she had tried to forget; brought back the voice of her friend.

"Help me."

But this time, the voice wasn't as loud. It no longer consumed her thoughts; instead, it was merely a reminder of the mistakes she had made. The mistakes she was now determined to spend the rest of her life trying to make up for.

Without realizing it, she found herself standing beside the drawer, the one containing the weapon that she had almost used just a few days ago. She pulled the revolver out and spun its cylinder, seeing it still had the one bullet she had placed in it. The weight of the gun felt heavy in her hands as she looked at the picture of her friend that rested above the drawer. The friend she had let die.

Sara remembered all the times she had been here before. Staring at the picture of her friend, remembering what she had let happen, holding a loaded gun in her hands. But this time was different. This time she didn't feel the need to raise the gun to her head. She didn't feel the need to escape the voice of her friend, to escape the memories. Instead, all she wanted to do was put the gun down and move on—make something of the rest of her life, find a way to help people.

But that meant facing another fear, something that used to be so simple but now caused terror in her very bones. She placed the revolver back in the drawer and took one last look at the picture.

Once inside her bedroom, she paused at her closet door, holding her breath. She wasn't sure if she wanted to see what was inside, wasn't sure she was ready. But if she couldn't get past it, she couldn't move on.

She opened the door.

Immediately after she stepped inside, fear made her walk back out. She tried again, but again fear took hold, and she stepped out immediately after seeing it. 'What's wrong with you?' she scolded herself as she continued pacing, trying to make up her mind. If she couldn't even do this, then how could she move forward? Finally, she tried one last time, closing her eyes at first at she stepped forward, not wanting to see, before finally forcing them open, staring right at the medical kit in front of her. With cautious hands, almost as if she was grabbing a snake that would strike at any moment, she reached out and lifted the kit, feeling the familiar weight in her hands. It was over two feet long, camouflage, with pouches on the outside and a zipper running down the middle. Relief washed over her as she placed it on her bed; she had made it this far. But she also knew that this was the easy part.

The voices grew louder again, causing her to hesitate, but only for a moment, before she found the strength again. She took deep breaths as her

fingers ran over it, feeling the texture in her hands. It had been so long. Chills ran through her fingers as they gently touched the cold metal of the zipper, and she was about to pull it when something stopped her. On the day her friend had died, she had frozen in fear, seeing everything through distorted vision, with her hand on the zipper just like this, her mind screaming at her to open it but her body unwilling, unable to move at all. Now, she found herself in the same position, trying to find the strength to finally do what she hadn't been able to before. She tightened her grip and was about to try when her doorbell rang.

Rolling her eyes, Sara stepped away from the med kit. 'Who rings someone's doorbell at midnight?' It rang again. "Hold your horses," she muttered under her breath as she approached the door and looked out the peephole, seeing Jack standing outside.

She opened the door. "What are you doing here?"

Jack smiled. "You don't get a lot of guests, do you?"

"At twelve o'clock at night?" She motioned for him to come in. "No, not really."

As Jack stepped in, he removed his hand from behind his back, holding up an evidence bag containing a 1911 pistol. "I come bearing gifts."

Sara took the bag from his hands and pulled out the 1911. It felt light. "Thanks. But I thought it was going to be a few days."

"I convinced the evidence guys to go ahead and look at it tonight. Figured you would want it back."

"You figured right." She waved her arm toward the couch, inviting him to sit with her. He did, and she placed the gun on the coffee table before leaning back on the couch opposite him, her elbow on the armrest, her cheek resting on her hand. "So, is there any other reason you're here?"

"Actually, there's two."

"Really?" she said, acting intrigued.

"Afraid so. Firstly, they haven't found his body yet."

That caught her by surprise. "You don't think he's still alive?"

"No, but based on where it looked like you hit him, it wouldn't have necessarily killed him immediately, so there is a very slight possibility. It is Shade, after all, and history's proven his ability to stay alive purely by adrenaline and rage. However, even if he did survive, he would be bleeding out, and"—Jack looked at his watch—"he would only have about another thirty minutes before he bled out entirely."

"And you wanted to come here, to make sure I was safe until then," she said, giving him a mocking smile. "How sweet. But what's the second reason?"

"Honestly, I can't sleep. I just keep thinking that there was something else I should have done, some way I could have helped him. I guess—" Jack paused before looking directly at her. "I just didn't want to be alone."

"I couldn't sleep either," she said, shrugging. "I guess we both just need a friend to talk to right now."

"I guess so."

"You killed her!" the voices screamed in Shade's head.

It was the night after he had found Nora in the hospital, dead, her chest cut open. Shade was in his office, pacing the floor, desperately trying to make the visions go away. But he couldn't.

"You let her die!"

"No," Shade said, despite knowing it was true. He had let her die. It was his fault. Hands shaking, eyes twitching, he began to break down completely. In the corner of his room, he saw a silver operating table.

"No," he said as he turned, but it was there too, only now Nora lay on top of it. He turned back

around again but still faced the same twisted sight, only now Nora's body was shrouded in a white sheet, blood soaking through. He twisted his head, trying to find a spot in the entire room where he couldn't see it, but there was none. And to his horror, he saw a man in a white doctor's gown walk in, carrying a surgical saw.

Shade hit the wall with his fist, bloodying up his knuckles. He closed his eyes, trying to escape it, but it was in his head too. It was everywhere.

"Please," he pleaded to a ghost as he fell down to the floor. "Don't make me watch. Please."

"So," Sara asked, "what are you going to do now, since all this is over?"

"I'm going to get back to it. Work on the Hangman case."

"Any new leads?"

"Not really," Jack answered before pointing to his head and making a spinning motion with his hand, the universal sign for going loony. "Been having trouble focusing. But I'll catch him."

"I have no doubt about that." She smiled, sincerely this time. "How did you get into this anyway?"

"Get into what?"

"The FBI. What made you join?"

"Oh." He raised his hand up, dismissing the question. "It's a long story."

"No, really, I want to know." When he still didn't answer, she pushed his shoulder. "C'mon, after everything that just happened, you owe me this."

"Ow," he groaned, moving his arm. "Old shoulder injury, remember?"

She just looked at him, rolling her eyes at his attempt to dodge the question.

After a few moments of silence, he finally relented. "Okay," he said, smiling at first as he began telling the story.

"When I was a kid, I always wanted to be an astronaut. You know, go up into space, play around in zero gravity"—Jack motioned with his hands as he spoke—"look down at the world. I always imagined how small it would look from up there, floating in space."

Grinning, she listened to him, genuinely interested. "What changed?"

In an instant, his expression altered. The look in his eye resembled that of a beaten dog whimpering on the ground. "He happened."

Jack said the word *he* with such disgust and horror that for a moment, Sara regretted asking the question and making him relive whatever he was about to tell her.

"The papers called him the Butcher." His teeth ground as he spoke that word. "I was about Nora's age when he grabbed me off the street and took me back to his house." His eyes squinted, trying to block out the memories as he spoke. "He locked me in his basement, with five other children. We tried so hard to escape, but there was no way out. He had chained our feet to the floor. And then..." Jack let out a small nervous laugh, the kind of laugh that was a defense mechanism, a way of downplaying the horrors he was reliving. "And then he started coming down into the basement with us. He would tell us how lucky we were to be chosen by him, how he was going to make us into something better. Something worthwhile. Every day, he would take one of us up, out of the basement."

A tear ran down Jack's face as he buried his head in his hands, hiding it from Sara's view. "I can still remember their screams as he earned his nickname."

The room was quiet for a moment, Jack having trouble going on, Sara too horrified to speak. Finally, Jack managed to compose himself again.

"One by one, I watched all of them get taken up the stairs, led to their deaths like lambs to the slaughter, knowing that eventually, it was going to be me. And then one day, it was. I had already been

escorted upstairs—strapped into a chair with rusted black chains and forced to watch as he sharpened his butcher knife. I knew what was about to happen, and I had accepted it.

"But then I heard the sound of a door breaking open and saw the cops rush in. They had him on the ground in seconds. He looked so helpless, lying there." Jack smiled for a brief moment. "And that was it. It was over."

Sara smiled, trying to put him more at ease. She felt guilty for making him relive that, but she was glad that she knew. "So that's why you joined. You wanted to be like the cops that saved you."

Jack chuckled as he ground his teeth again. "No. No, the cops aren't the heroes in that story."

"Why not?"

He sighed. "Because later I found out that they had known who the Butcher was for a week, and they didn't do anything about it."

"What?" she asked, confused. "Why?"

"Because they didn't have enough evidence to get a warrant. And none of the cops were willing to risk their jobs, were willing to bend the rules, even just a little, to stop that monster."

Jack tilted his head and looked off into the distance. "I don't blame the Butcher for the other kids' deaths. When a rabid dog bites someone, you don't

blame the dog—you blame the owners, who should've put the dog down before he got the chance."

He turned back to Sara. "So, no, I didn't join the FBI to follow in their footsteps. I became an agent because I realized they were half measures. The world was full of too many people, too many cops, who would rather let a monster like that kill a kid than do what it took to stop him. So on that day, I promised myself that as long as I was alive, I would do whatever it took to save the victims. That I wouldn't be afraid of crossing a line if it meant stopping the monsters in this world."

Sara felt her heart break for him when his voice grew remorseful.

"I just never thought that would mean stopping Shade."

She tried to find the words to say to him. It was clear that what had happened to Shade bothered him, that he thought it was his fault. She knew what that felt like. "I'm sorry."

Jack nodded before forcing a smile to return to his face. "What about you?" he asked, leaning back on the couch. "What are you going to do now?"

"I don't know. I want to do something to help people." She grinned for a moment and laughed to herself.

"What?"

She waved her hand in the air, dismissing it.

"No, seriously. What's funny?"

"Nothing," she said. "I did some training in investigations in the military. I thought for a second about joining the FBI."

Jack wrinkled his brow. "Why is that funny?"

"Because," she said, the grin coming back, "I pictured what I would look like in one of your fancy suits."

"Hey," he said, faking offense. They laughed for a moment.

"Are you really thinking about the FBI?"

"No." She shrugged. "Well—I don't know. Maybe."

"You'd be good at it."

"You think?"

"Sure," he said. "You're clever, you've had training. Why not?"

Sara thought about it for a moment, actually considering it. She imagined what it would sound like. Agent Sara Michaels.

"Plus," Jack said, "I suppose I do need a new partner."

Shade was on the ground as the corpses crawled towards him. One for every victim the Surgeons had taken. Every life Shade had let die. They crawled

across the ground like spiders, their deformed legs twisting under the weight of their hollow bones and rotting flesh. Behind them, still lying on the operating table, was Nora, now missing something. Something that had been taken from her.

They were closing in on him as Shade stood up and tried to run, but he found the door locked. Or was he even at the door? It was getting harder for him to tell what was real. Finally, the door opened, and he walked out into the hallway, only to see Nora standing at the end of it.

"Why didn't you do what it took to save me?"

Why hadn't he? He had known the visions were distracting him, keeping him from focusing on the case, saving Nora. But he hadn't done what he knew would make them go away. It wasn't worth that.

Or was it?

Shade wasn't sure anymore. Violently, his head twisted in every direction, trying to escape the visions, escape the horrors. But they wouldn't go away. He saw operating tables, dozens of them, stretched out across the hallways, each with a black body bag on top. He tried to run through them, but as he did, the bags opened and hands came out, clawing at his side. The bodies lying within rose up, pulling on his flesh, all chanting the same message.

"You could have saved us!"

Shade felt something touch his back, and he turned to see the Surgeon standing in front of him, grinning ear to ear. In an instant, Shade had him by the throat and backed him against the wall.

"Shade?" the Surgeon asked with fear in his voice.

Shade already had a knife drawn and had it against the Surgeon's throat.

"Shade, stop!" the Surgeon screamed.

That voice. Shade recognized it as he dropped the knife to the floor and stepped back, seeing clearly. In front of him stood a fellow agent, an innocent man he had almost killed.

He stepped back in horror at what he had almost done. But it wasn't him, he told himself. It was the hallucinations. They were doing this to him. He needed to stop them, to do what would make them go away.

No! How could he even consider it? He wasn't thinking clearly, couldn't trust himself. He needed to find Jack. Jack would know what to do—he would be able to help him.

He started towards Jack's office as the visions came back.

"So, do you mind if I ask you a question?"

"Go for it."

Sara chose her words carefully. "The man that Shade killed in the prison. Which one was that?"

"Urich."

"And he's the one who–" Sara paused, not knowing how to finish the question.

Jack knew what she was asking. "Yeah. He's the one who killed her."

"How long was it until you found him?"

Jack looked off into the distance. "Three weeks. At first it looked like he had dropped off the map completely, but after a few days I picked up on his trail and then had him running for a little while before finally bringing him in. It took longer than it should have, but I got him before he could hurt anyone else. That's what's important."

"What about Carter?"

"In prison, serving four life sentences. One for each of the girls he killed."

"Are you okay with that?"

"Personally, I had hoped for the death penalty, but at least he'll never be getting out."

"Did you ever find out how it started? How they both teamed up for it?"

"We could never get a straight explanation out of either of them. Neither one would tell us whose idea it was to kill in the first place, how they coordinated it, or who came up with the specific

plans. All we really know for sure is that they used to work at the same hospital."

Sara nodded, and then they sat in silence for a moment. For some reason, Jack seemed distracted, like he was just talking to keep himself busy, almost nervous about something. She brushed off the thought. It was probably just due to him reliving the Butcher story.

Because of this, she debated not asking her next question, but she wanted to know. Almost felt like she needed to. "What about Shade?"

"What about him?"

"Well. It's just—what exactly happened on that night? The night he killed the woman in the forest."

"Oh," Jack said, shifting uncomfortably on the couch.

"It's okay. You don't have to tell me."

"No, it's fine. You deserve to know." He leaned forward on the couch, resting his arms on his knees and staring into the distance. "Shade had already been having trouble. The visions were getting worse, and he was starting to lose his grip on what was real and what was a hallucination. And then after *she* died"—Jack paused for a moment as Sara saw him try to remain calm—"he just couldn't take it. He broke down completely. I found out later that he almost killed another agent on his way to my office."

"Why was he going to your office?"

"I don't know. I wasn't there. But I assume he was looking for me because he thought I could help him. And maybe I could have," Jack said, his voice cracking. "Maybe if I had been there for him, I could have helped the visions go away. Maybe I could've helped him understand it wasn't his fault, helped him move on, like I did."

Sara moved closer to him, putting her arm around his shoulder. They stayed quiet for a moment as she thought about how he had helped her move on. Helped her see that the way to move forward wasn't to give up but to save the next victim, as he had put it. She also felt sorry for him. He had helped her move on, but he had had no one. With Shade already too far gone, he had been forced to deal with it alone. She couldn't imagine herself being able to do that.

"How did you do it alone?"

"Do what?"

"Move on."

Shade tried to hold on just a little longer as he ran towards Jack's office. He looked at the floor, keeping the tables and body bags to the side of him, but the horrors were on the floor too: blood, scalpels, saws, broken jars. A voice came from one of the body bags.

"You let us die."

Just a little farther, Shade thought. Just a little farther, and he would be at Jack's office. Then he wouldn't be alone. Then Jack would be able to help him. Shade kept running, focusing on it as if it was a lighthouse in the distance, guiding him through the dark ocean, lest the waters overtake him and bring him back into their depths, drowning him forever.

Finally, he reached Jack's office and opened the door.

"How did you manage to put what happened behind you?" Sara asked, brushing a strand of her hair behind her head. "How did you get your hallucinations to finally go away?"

Shade stepped into the office, looking for Jack, but he wasn't there. Instead, case files lay sprawled across the room in a frenzied, chaotic nature, and a chair was partially lodged in the wall, as if thrown in anger.

Was he still hallucinating? He didn't think so. He stepped further in, papers crumpling under his feet. The case files, the chair—the room almost looked like a crime scene.

"You let them die," the voice repeated in his head, but he didn't listen, stepping further, now behind

Jack's desk. A single item rested on it: a case profile of someone. A woman.

Jack considered the question. She wanted to know how he had gotten the hallucinations to go away. She was still smiling at him, even as he glanced behind her, seeing the rotting corpse of Nora standing in the corner, blood dripping down her body, her eyes rolled back in her head.

Jack smiled back at Sara.

The woman in the file had dark red hair, blue eyes, and pale skin. The file described her as a potential victim of a serial killer several years before, but nothing had come of it. Shade's eyes cut to her address. She lived less than forty miles away.

Shade stared in confusion, not understanding why it was the only file left on Jack's desk, until he noticed something. The paper looked indented, like something had been written on it. Nothing was on the front, but as Shade turned it over, he saw it.

The file fell from his hands, landing upside down, still showing the words Jack had scribbled wildly on the back. A single phrase.

Whatever it takes

"Well," Jack said, "it's hard to explain."

Nora's rotting corpse whispered to him from across the room. *"You let me die."*

Jack continued smiling, completely ignoring it. "I guess I finally realized that the hallucinations were what was causing me to make mistakes. That it wasn't my fault Nora died, it was the hallucinations, the voices distracting me. Keeping me from catching the Surgeon, from ending it. Once I realized that, I knew that I had to find a way to move on, so that I could save the next victim."

"Simple as that?"

Jack grinned at her, not paying any attention to Nora's cries. "Simple as that."

Shade stood in absolute horror. It wasn't true. It couldn't be. Jack wouldn't do that; he was just hallucinating. But deep down, Shade knew it was real. He turned around and ran out the door. If he could get to Jack, maybe he could still stop him before he crossed that line.

Maybe it wasn't too late.

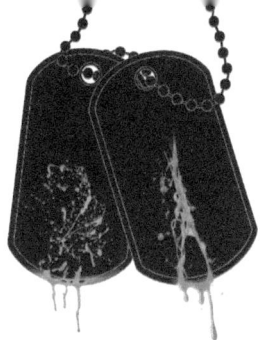

Chapter Twenty-Three

Jack walked up to the house. It was old, the wooden siding was chipping off, and the roof looked like it had seen better days. It was located a few miles off the highway, with a thin gravel road leading up to it.

It was also right on the edge of a forest.

Creaking softly screeched in the silence as his feet pushed down on the wooden steps of the porch, broken and rotting. He stopped for a moment, considering what he was about to do. It seemed wrong, unthinkable, but there was no other way. If he didn't make the hallucinations go away, he couldn't catch Urich before he killed another victim, next time a twelve-year-old girl. He hadn't saved Nora. He would save the next.

Whatever it took.

Jack knocked on the door. It opened, and he was greeted by a woman with dark red hair and blue eyes. "Can I help you?"

"Hi," he said, flashing his badge. "I'm Special Agent Jack Diamond with the FBI. We need to talk."

"I don't know about you," Sara said, standing up from the couch, "but I could use a drink."

"Sounds great," Jack said.

She walked over to her kitchen, which was practically in the same room due to the small size of the apartment, and pulled out two wineglasses. "So," she said, half-joking, "how's the pay at the FBI?"

"Could be better."

When she was finished, she handed Jack a glass and sat back down next to him.

Jack looked at the glass. Blood from his hands appeared to stain it, distorting the white wine behind it. In front of him, Sara sat on the couch, her throat slit, and blood dripping down from it, soaking her jacket. She raised her glass.

Jack smiled as he raised his, the glasses clinking together.

"What's this about?" the woman asked as she led Jack into her living room.

Jack hesitated before answering. He had left his gun behind and brought something else in its

place—something more personal. She, however, was unarmed. He could kill her right now, get it over with. But a part of him was still holding back. He knew what he had to do, but he wasn't ready to yet. Sometimes, he'd found, if the decision you have to make is horrifying enough, the only thing you can do is talk: tell fake stories, make pointless conversation, anything to delay the inevitable conclusion. In this case, anything to delay the blood from creeping onto his hands, to delay his own descent into the world of justification and madness that had turned so many once good men into savage killers.

So instead, he stalled, savoring the last few breaths before his corrupted fate took hold, changing his life forever.

"The FBI has reason to believe you're being targeted by a serial killer."

"What?" she asked in shock. "Why?"

Jack paused, trying to think. He needed a reason to be there. Then he noticed her blue eyes and red hair: a rare combination. It wouldn't make perfect sense, but enough to fool her for a little while.

"The killer is targeting victims with red hair and blue eyes. That's a one-in-a-million combination. Plus," he added, figuring he needed to add something to make it more believable, "we have reports that someone was stalking your property. The

eyewitnesses can't give a good description of his face, so we're not sure it's him, but it's not worth the risk of waiting if it is." He paused. *"I'm just here to keep you safe."*

"So," Jack said, trying to work up the nerve to do it, like he had all those months ago. "Tell me about your time in the military. You said you did some training in investigations."

"Yeah," Sara said, taking a sip of wine. "It was difficult, but I really liked it. Honestly, I kinda missed it after I became a medic." Behind her, Jack saw Nora being dragged onto an operating table, screaming out for help as she was tied down.

"Why did you end up picking medic over it?" Jack asked, ignoring Nora's pleas for help.

Sara shrugged. "I don't know. I guess medic was what I enlisted to be, so I didn't want to change. Plus, I felt more nervous in investigations. It's more about instinct, and problem solving, and I wasn't sure I could take it if I screwed up." She drank the rest of her wine before setting her glass down on the coffee table. "I guess that ended up happening anyway."

Jack nodded sympathetically, finishing his own glass of wine just as the Surgeon started the saw.

"Please," Nora screamed. *"Please help me."*

Blood hit Jack's face as he glanced over at it for a moment before sighing.

Sara turned around to look behind her. "What do you keep looking at?"

"What?"

"You keep glancing behind me. What are you looking at?"

No, Jack thought. It was too soon. He didn't want her to find out yet. He wasn't ready. Suddenly, the corpse of the woman from the forest grabbed onto his leg. *"Why did you kill me?"*

"I wasn't looking at anything."

"So," the woman said, *"what do we do now?"*

"The only thing we can do," Jack answered. *"We wait and see if the killer shows up. Based on the previous killings, it will probably be tonight."*

The woman cut her eyes towards him. "Why don't we go to a police station, or back to your base?"

Jack groaned. He hadn't been expecting her to ask so many questions. "We need to catch the killer in the act, so we have something to pin on him."

"Wait," the woman said. *"If you don't already have enough evidence, then how do you know for sure he's after me?"*

"I just do." He knew he could just kill her now, but he still wasn't ready. Still trying to stall, holding on to a cruel hope that he would talk himself out of it. *"All I'm saying is that I need to wait here to protect you until he shows up. Then I can arrest him, and be out of your hair."*

"I don't know if I feel comfortable letting a strange man stay the night, FBI or not."

"I understand that. But I need to be here to protect you in case he shows up."

"I can take care of myself," the woman said.

Jack sighed. He was out of time, and he hadn't managed to talk himself out of it. The voices were still in his head, and the hallucinations were still around him, corpses crawling towards him on the floor, voices in his head screaming, *"Guilty!"*

"Well, it's—" Jack started to say, trying to make up another excuse before giving up.

"Actually, I'm here to kill you."

He had looked at something. Sara was sure of it. Maybe he'd just noticed some paint cracking or something, she told herself, trying to shrug it off. But then why would he deny it?

She glanced behind her one last time. Nothing was there, and yet when she looked back at him,

for the briefest moment she saw his eyes cut once again. What was he looking at? There was nothing back there. Nothing to warrant looking at and then lying about it.

Unless he had seen something that wasn't really there.

The thought sent a chill down Sara's spine. What if he was still hallucinating? For a moment, her nerves flared up before immediately calming back down. Even if he was hallucinating, that didn't mean he was dangerous, like Shade was. She was just overreacting.

But if it wasn't a big deal, why wouldn't he have just told her? Why would he have lied about them going away? Suddenly, she remembered what he had done at the safe house, how he had wiped the blood off the wrong sleeve, almost as if he couldn't tell what was real blood and what was a hallucination.

"What were the hallucinations like?" she finally asked, watching as he tensed up at the question.

"They were"—he paused—"like a nightmare."

"When was the last time you had one?"

He squinted at her, apparently confused by the question. "I'm sorry, I don't know what you mean."

Sara saw it now. How uneasy he was. Just like when he had shown up at her door, the first

time, especially after the other agents had shown up. Then, she had just assumed it was for fear of Shade, but what if she had been wrong?

"I mean, how long was it after Nora died that you had your last hallucination?"

"A few weeks," Jack said, shaking his head. "Why?"

Sara held her breath for a moment, studying him. In his eyes she saw the same thing she always had. Fear. But now she recognized that it wasn't a fear of Shade, or even a fear of the hallucinations. It was a fear of getting caught.

"Because I think you're having one right now."

Jack's eyes widened with surprise, but he didn't say a word. Didn't try to convince her otherwise, or even deny it. Instead, they just stared at each other for a moment, feeling the shift of tension in the air as the truth set in. Now she knew, and there was no going back. Not after this.

As Sara maintained eye contact, she remembered the pistol she had laid on the coffee table. She thought she could get to it before he could, but as she looked into his eyes, she realized he was debating the same question.

She went for it.

"What?" the woman asked, taking a step backwards.

"I said I'm here to kill you." It felt so strange to say it out loud. Almost made it feel too real. But in a strange way it was a relief. The visions were about to be gone, and he could focus on catching Urich. And he could, he told himself. Without the hallucinations, he could catch him before he hurt anyone else.

Jack rushed her. He grabbed her arm and pulled her closer, drawing his knife. She tried to get away, but his grip was too strong. She was forced to stay helpless as he pushed the knife into her stomach.

As soon as he did, he regretted it. His grip loosened as he backed up, shaking his head. In a moment of shame, he almost dropped the knife and walked away. Until he realized something. The hallucinations were still there. But suddenly they didn't bother him as much. Weren't as distracting. It was actually working. He knew then that he had to finish it. He tightened his grip on the knife and looked back to where the woman had been, now seeing only a pool of blood on the ground.

She was gone.

The back door was open, and a trail of blood crossed right through it. He ran, following the trail, until it eventually brought him to the edge of the forest. It was vast, guarded by dying trees with brittle bark and broken branches, the spaces between them

revealing nothing except utter darkness, making it appear somehow disconnected from the world, as if once you stepped inside, into its heart, there would be no way out back out. At least none that didn't leave monstrous, distorted scars as deep as the forest itself.

She was in there, Jack knew. He had to find her. He had to finish this.

Sara got to the gun first, lining up the sights with his chest and backing away slowly. "Why?" she asked, her entire body shaking.

"It's not what you think," Jack said, holding his hands up.

"Really?" Anger growled in her voice. "You weren't just about to kill me?"

Jack didn't answer.

"Why?" Sara asked again. "Why are you doing this? Is it just to make the hallucinations go away?"

"No."

"Then why? Tell me why!"

"It's not about making them go away. It's about making yourself numb to them. Doing whatever it takes to make yourself such a monster that you no longer care about the victims you've let die."

A tear ran down her face. "You were going to kill me, just so you can sleep better at night."

"No," Jack said, trying to keep his voice calm. He wanted her to understand. "No, that's not what this is about. This isn't about whether or not I have hallucinations, it's about whether or not I can stop the monsters out there, killing innocent people. I killed the woman in the forest so that I could catch the Surgeon before he could kill his next victim, which would have been a twelve-year-old girl—and I did. I saved her. And for a while, I was able to focus on catching more serial killers, saving more victims. But now," he said, anger creeping back into his voice, "the Hangman is out there, and he's already killed three women. He tied a noose around their necks and hung them up on light posts like some kind of animal. And I can't catch him, because I can't focus. The hallucinations are starting to bother me again, and the longer I wait to deal with it, the more women he's going to murder. So it's either kill you or watch that madman kill countless more just like you."

She watched him in horror, a tear streaming down her cheek as she realized how far gone he really was. "So that's how you justify it."

"I'm not justifying it!" Jack screamed suddenly, taking her off guard. "I know what I am, what I've become. But if I do nothing, the next victim dies. If I kill myself to escape my hallucinations, the

next victim dies. So maybe I am the monster you probably think I am." He took a step closer to her. "But if that's what it takes to save the next victim, then that's what I'll be."

Sara's hands began shaking. "Why not kill me earlier?"

"There was never an opportunity. I was about to when the other agents showed up, thinking Shade was after us. The FBI field office and prison had too much surveillance, and whenever we were alone, you always had that 1911 in your hands, and I wasn't sure that I could outdraw you. Couldn't risk it."

Suddenly, she remembered the holster Jack had given her, how it was broken and had caught when she'd tried to draw. Terror crept into her mind as she realized that if she hadn't fixed it, he probably would have murdered her already.

He took another step closer.

"Stop," she begged, but he didn't, instead moving even closer. "Stop!" she screamed again, but it didn't deter him, and she knew if she didn't fire now, it would be too late. She pulled the trigger and listened as the hammer clicked down on an empty chamber. For a moment she was confused, until she remembered how the gun had felt light in her hand when Jack had given it back. He must've unloaded it.

"Sorry," Jack said as he moved on her, trying to grab her arm. She ducked and pushed him back, trying to think. She couldn't risk a full-on fight; he would overpower her. But there had to be something.

Before she had time to think, Jack moved on her again, striking her in the head and knocking her to the floor.

"Please don't make this any harder."

As she tried to lift herself off the floor, she remembered the drawer, and the revolver inside it. She crawled over to it as fast as she could and reached up, pulling out the revolver. She looked back, seeing Jack was right in front of her. Out of time, she aimed for his chest, forgetting that it only had one round inside of it, from when she had almost played roulette with her life. She had time to click it twice, going through two empty chambers, before Jack swung on her, knocking her out.

Jack ran through the forest, looking for the woman. The trail of blood was getting harder to follow, now barely visible in the little glimpse of moonlight that escaped through the clouds. The trees were growing thicker, their bark such a light brown that they almost appeared white, and Jack observed the red stains that had been left on them. He was close.

Then, finally, he heard something fall. He ran farther up, seeing a small section of the forest where the trees were less dense. In the middle was the woman, collapsed on the ground, leaving a trail of blood as she tried to crawl away.

Jack walked up to her slowly, listening to the sound of his own breathing, goose bumps cascading over his skin as he twisted the knife in his hands. This was it, he thought. The hallucinations, the voices—they were about to not matter. After this, he would be able to catch Urich and put an end to the horror, the suffering. It would finally be over.

He reached the woman and knelt down beside her, watching her try to crawl away from him. "No! No, please!" she begged as she saw him. "Please don't kill me."

Jack closed his eyes, tears falling down from them. "I'm sorry." He took one last deep breath, thinking of Nora, and how he had let her die because he wasn't willing to cross that line. "Whatever it takes," he whispered to himself as he began stabbing her.

Sara woke up. Sharp, aching pain coursed through her skull as she tried to remember where she was. Something had happened. Her eyes tried to scan the room, but the images were too blurry

due to the burning sensation that seemed to be spreading over her head. Had something hit her? For some reason, she wasn't able to move her arms. She tried to think, tried to reassemble the foggy pieces of her memory. She had been crawling, afraid of something, and had pulled a revolver. And then—

Her breath left her as she remembered. Jack.

Finally, her vision returned to her, and she realized she was sitting in a chair, her hands handcuffed to it behind her back. And standing in front of her, holding a knife, was Jack.

"If you want to kill me, just do it already." She said the words calmly, not wanting to give him the satisfaction of knowing how scared she really was. After all the days of wanting to die, of staring down the barrel of her own gun, she now found herself scared. For the first time since that day in the military, she was afraid to die.

"I don't want to kill you," Jack said. "But I have to. Someone has to stop the Hangman, just like someone had to stop the Surgeon."

"And it's got to be you? You don't think anyone else can stop them."

"No. I don't."

"What about Shade?" Sara asked. "If you care so much about him, why did you frame him?"

Jack's head twitched slightly. "I never wanted to frame him. I wanted to help him. Show him that there was a way out, a way to move on. He just wouldn't take it. He broke down instead. And I thought I could still help him. I thought maybe after all this time, he would be able to move on if I gave him no other option." Jack sighed, truly sorrowful. "But I guess he couldn't."

The pain in her head was overshadowed by the crawling of her skin as she realized how much Jack believed what he was saying. He really thought that killing her was what he had to do. That he wasn't doing it for himself, but for the next victim.

"What did it feel like?"

"What?"

"After you killed her," Sara said, with spite in her voice. "You say you only did it because you had to. Which means after you killed her, you should have felt remorse. Did you?"

Jack's eyes began to water. "Yes."

Jack knelt over the woman's mangled body. Her blood covered him as he dropped the knife from his hands and looked up at the moon, crying. What had he done?

Clouds gathered in the sky, rain beginning to pour from them, washing over Jack, cleansing the blood

from his face. He screamed out in anguish, wishing he could take it back. Until he saw it. Nora, standing by a tree, blood pouring down her body. Only this time, he didn't recoil in fear. It didn't consume his every thought, didn't distract him like it had before. He was finally free. Now he could focus, and stop the Surgeon before he killed anyone else.

"You let me die," Nora cried.

"I know. I'm sorry I didn't do what it took to save you." His remorse turned to conviction as he remembered the promise he had made so many years ago. "But that will never happen again."

Suddenly branches cracked behind him. Someone else was there.

"You don't have to do this," Sara pleaded as he moved closer to her with the knife. "Please. This won't help you catch the Hangman."

"Yes, it will," Jack said as he put the knife to her stomach.

She shifted in the chair, causing it to tip over sideways, her cheek colliding with the floor. "Please!" she screamed out, hoping someone would hear her. "Help me!"

"No one's coming," Jack said as he remembered the note the Surgeon had left for them. "Because

no one cares." He knelt down beside her, running the blade over her cheek, cutting it.

Sara continued to scream on the floor, calling out for help. But she knew no one was coming. Only one person had been trying to help her, and she had shot him. Killed him. Maybe she did deserve this.

Jack was about to push the knife into her stomach when the door crashed open.

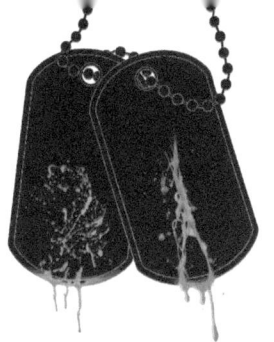

Chapter Twenty-Four

Blood dripping from his mouth, a man limped through the door, clutching his chest where he had been shot, trying to keep pressure on the wound, to give himself a little more time.

Jack stared in disbelief. "Shade?"

"Shade?" Jack said in shock as he turned towards the sound of the crackling leaves.

Shade stepped out from the trees, seeing Jack kneeling on the ground, knife in hand. Blood looked like it was dripping from his face, mixing with the rain. But even then, Shade held out hope that it wasn't too late—that maybe Jack hadn't crossed that line. That was until he saw the mangled body that Jack was kneeling over.

"What did you do?" he asked in horror, stepping closer to the body. Her eyes were glazed over, and

her skin was pale. Her blue dress now appeared purple, and blood dripped from the hole that used to be her stomach.

"There was no other way," Jack said. "I had to make the visions go away."

Shade couldn't speak.

"It's okay," Jack said, walking up to him. "I can focus now." He put his hand on Shade's shoulder. "I can catch him now. Urich. Now that I can see clearly, I can find him, and we can end this."

Still staring at the woman's body in horror, Shade barely heard him. It felt like a dream, a hallucination. This couldn't be real. Jack wouldn't do this.

Shade limped into the house, desperately leaning against the wall for support. As Sara watched him, she knew he was on death's doorstep. That much blood loss, that many injuries; the adrenaline from the hallucinations was the only thing keeping him standing up, and it was barely doing that.

"You're alive," Jack said, genuinely happy. "That's good. We—we can fix this."

Shade's head was twitching back and forth. One moment he would look directly at them; the next he would look off into the distance, staring at something only he saw.

"You've gotten worse," Jack said. "You see them all the time now, don't you?"

Shade didn't answer.

"Please," Jack said. "Let me help you." He glanced down at Sara. "I can wait a little longer. You can kill her. You can make the horrors finally stop."

Still, Shade said nothing.

"Please, just let me help you. You can make the hallucinations go away."

Blood dripped from Shade's mouth as he spoke, his lungs evoking the pain of suffocating as he struggled to breathe. "I don't want them to go away."

"What?"

"If they go away," he answered, finally cutting his eyes directly to Jack, "I become you."

"Nora died," Jack said, "because we were too distracted to save her. But now I can save the next one. I can stop this."

Shade still remained frozen in shock as he slowly realized he wasn't hallucinating, that all of this was real. Jack had murdered a woman. Killed her in the woods, like the animals they were after, and now he was trying to justify it. Trying to say that this was what it took to save the next victim.

Was Jack right? The voices in Shade's head were telling him the same thing. The hallucinations had stopped them from saving Nora. They would stop them from saving the next girl Urich decided to kill, a twelve-year-old. Maybe this was how they would save the next victim. For the briefest moment, Shade considered it. But deep down he knew. This couldn't be the answer.

"It's not worth it," he whispered.

"What?"

"It's not worth this. If this is what we have to do to stop him, then maybe we shouldn't."

"What?" Jack said again, anger creeping into his voice. "How can you say that? He killed Nora!"

"And if we don't stop this now, then we're no different than he is."

Jack's head twitched in frustration. "You think I care if I'm like him? You think I care about being better than him?" Jack got right in Shade's face. "I care about stopping him. About not letting anyone else die. And if I have to kill one person, become a monster to save the rest, if that's what it takes, then that's what I'll become."

They focused on each other's eyes for a moment, neither one backing down. Everything had changed now. Their partnership, their friendship, it was gone, and in their hearts, they already knew it but couldn't bring themselves to admit it just yet.

Finally, Jack started to walk away. "I'm going to catch the Surgeon. I'm going to stop this with or without you."

Should he let him walk away? There was no going back now, and Jack was right, the hallucinations were what had caused Nora's death. Maybe, even if he couldn't do it himself, Jack was right—maybe this was what had to happen. What would be gained from stopping Jack now? It would only end one way, with Shade losing control like he had in the military, and then there being no one left to stop Urich.

But then, as he considered it, he once again looked to the corpse on the ground. An innocent victim. The truth forced itself to be revealed, no matter how hard he wanted to ignore it. He couldn't let this happen any longer. He had let this go on for too long because he was afraid of losing control. Afraid of what he might do. But now, that didn't matter.

"I can't let you leave."

Jack turned around. "What?"

Shade didn't repeat himself. He knew Jack had heard him.

"You can't let me leave?" Jack said, almost mockingly. "You're going to stop me from catching the Surgeon? You're going to stop me from saving more lives—lives of girls like Nora?"

Shade just looked at him, begging him without words to stop this now.

Jack twisted the knife in his hand. "To stop me, you're going to have to kill me."

"Don't do this," Shade begged.

"Whatever it takes," Jack said, repeating it like scripture as he made up his mind and rushed Shade.

"You become me?" Jack asked in anger, still standing over Sara, knife in hand, eyes becoming bloodshot. "Who stopped the Surgeon? Who kept him from killing anyone else?" Jack's voice began to crack. "Who did you save by fighting me in the forest? By hiding for eight months? How many killers did you stop by being the better person?" Jack twisted the knife in his hands, moving it closer to Sara. "I caught him. The animal who killed Nora. I caught him. Not you, me!"

"Please don't do this," Shade pleaded.

The knife pressed against her throat. "I have to."

Shade almost fell as he removed his hands from the wall and rushed Jack.

Rain was now flooding from the night sky, soaking everything in sight, as Jack swung his knife at Shade,

who effortlessly sidestepped it before striking Jack in the jaw, knocking him backwards.

Agonizing pain spread through Jack's jaw. He tried to shake it off and attack again. This time he aimed the knife for Shade's chest, looking to sink it into his rib cage. But again, Shade sidestepped it, this time grabbing Jack's hand and pulling him closer before slamming his elbow into Jack's nose, almost crushing it. He then shoved Jack's chest with one hand, making him fall onto his back in the mud.

"Just stay down."

Rain and blood streamed down his face, shimmering in the moonlight, as Jack found his footing and tightened the grip on his knife. He couldn't stay down. Couldn't stop. Not after he'd come this far. Taking a deep breath, he rushed again, swinging the knife

at Shade's head. Shade dodged it, but just barely. Blood was still pouring out of his chest, and it was all he could do to stand up, but he had to. Had to fight, had to save Sara. Then he could stop.

He swung at Jack, but Jack backed up, almost causing Shade to trip from the momentum as his broken leg buckled under the weight. Jack took advantage of the opportunity and punched Shade

in the face, causing him to stagger backwards.

Blood dripped from his mouth, and he rushed Jack once again, but the injuries had made him too slow, and Jack dodged before shoving his knife into Shade's stomach and then pushing him backwards into the wall.

Barely noticing the new pain in his stomach, Shade stayed at the wall, having to lean on it to even remain standing as his vision started to blur.

"Look at yourself," Jack said. "Look what the hallucinations have done to you. You can't even fight me."

Shade tried to focus, even as he felt himself slipping. At this point he knew he couldn't win, not when he was this injured, but maybe he could last long enough to save Sara. He had to try, and he swung

at Jack once again, slamming him into the ground. For a moment Jack rested in the wet mud, trying to figure out what to do. He couldn't stop, but he also knew he couldn't fight Shade, at least not like this. And what terrified him even more was he still got the sense that Shade was holding back.

In a burst of anger, he ran at Shade again. Shade dodged and used Jack's own momentum to throw him backwards, his back lighting up in pain as he crashed into a tree. Before he had time to think,

Shade rushed him, but he managed to dodge to the side just in time before slipping into the thicket of trees, trying to hide, trying to run.

But he knew he couldn't. If he got away, Shade would just find him later, and stop him before he could catch the Surgeon. Before he could make the woman's death worth something. He peeked his head around a tree and saw Shade walking in the darkness, head moving, eyes twitching. He was hallucinating, Jack thought. And maybe that would be enough.

Jack slipped out from behind the tree and swung

his knife, burying it into Shade's shoulder. Shade screamed as Jack ripped it back out and kicked him backwards, into the large mirror that sat in the room.

Glass shattered everywhere, cutting into Shade's back. He winced from the pain, the sound drowned out by that of the glass cracking as it hit the floor.

"You don't have to do this," Jack said. "Getting yourself killed isn't going to save anybody. You can just walk away now and let me do what has to be done."

The words rang in his head as Shade moved his hands down the broken mirror behind him. He looked up to his friend, pain filling his voice with

every word. "Ignoring the horrors doesn't make them go away."

Jack's eyes flinched, and for the briefest second it looked like regret suddenly marked his face. But it was gone the moment it came, and he erupted in anger, wildly swinging his knife at Shade's head.

The sound of glass cracking echoed through the house as Shade broke off shards of the mirror, one in each hand. He then raised his left arm up, blocking Jack's knife before using his other hand to slice Jack's chest, the jagged shard drawing blood.

It took Jack by surprise, and before he could react, Shade was on him again, shoving one of the shards into his stomach and leaving it there. Shade wanted to move on him again, but he once again felt the pain of his own wounds as more blood dripped from his chest, and he had to lean back on the wall for support.

Jack reached down, grunting as he pulled the bloody shard from his stomach before dropping it and watching it shatter.

They exchanged glances for a moment, each realizing that the other one wasn't backing down. Jack sighed before swinging

at Shade from behind a tree, striking him in the face. Shade tried to swing

back, but Jack was gone before he could, and in the darkness, the hallucinations returned.

Dozens of bodies began to crawl out of the mud around him, with twisted, contorted necks and pale, withered skin. Their eyes were merely hollow holes as they moved closer toward him.

"You let this happen to us," they moaned in the moonlight.

They started moving faster, running at him with their backs bent down and their knees twisted sideways. Desperate, Shade spun in a circle, trying to figure out where he could escape to, but it was too late. In his hallucinations, he didn't see Jack coming.

A knife pressed into his side, raking against his ribs. He struck Jack, knocking him backwards, pulling out the knife as Jack was disoriented. But as he started to move on Jack, he saw more bodies, circling him, crying out. He didn't know which one to fight.

Jack took advantage of it by striking him over and over, each time moving back behind a tree to blend back in with the corpses.

"You can't fight me like this," Jack said. "You can't save anyone if you keep hallucinating."

Shade's head twisted back and forth, trying to find the origin of the voice.

"I'm begging you. Please just let me do what I have to."

Shade thought he found the origin and stepped behind a tree, swinging the knife he had pulled out at the corpse in front of him, hoping it was Jack.

The knife's blade passed through the hollow corpse, scraping across the bark of the tree. Before he could react, the real Jack tackled him, causing both of them to crash into the wall, denting it as they did. Shade swung the shard of glass at Jack's head, but Jack dodged it, watching the shard stick into the wall. He then swung his own knife, but Shade caught his hand and landed a headbutt, disorienting him long enough for Shade to shove him backwards.

Shade took the opportunity and grabbed the chair Sara was sitting in, slamming it against the wall and breaking it into pieces, allowing the handcuffs to slide off. She looked up at him for a moment, not knowing what to do, before Jack stood back up, gripping his knife tighter.

"Run," Shade said as he blocked the knife from hitting her.

She did. She ran away, out of the apartment as fast as she could. She had to get away. She didn't want to die. She reached the hallway outside, and she

kept running. Down the hallway, down the steps, away from the danger, as fast as her legs would take her. But then, suddenly, she stopped herself.

What was she doing? How could she run away, leaving Shade alone in the room? In his condition, Jack would kill him. She was sure of that. How could she let him die for her?

But he had told her to run. Maybe that made it okay. She looked down the steps, wanting so badly to keep running, every instinct telling her to. But if she did, that meant that another person would die because she wanted to live. She looked back up the stairs, trying to make herself go back but knowing that if she did, she probably wouldn't survive the night. She wouldn't have the opportunity to make up for what she had done.

She stood frozen, trying to make up her mind, when the voice in her head came back.

"Help me!"

"Why did you do that!?" Jack screamed in anger as he struck Shade, blood flying from his mouth. Jack swung again

striking Shade in the eye and causing him to stumble backwards in the mud, leaning against a tree to steady himself.

"You're seeing them right now, aren't you?" Jack took another swing at Shade, landing it. He then grabbed him by his coat and threw him backwards, into another tree.

"I see them too," Jack said as he watched Shade try to figure out what corpse was real. "But now I can see past it. Now it doesn't bother me as much."

"It should," Shade said, slicing his knife through the air. He swung at the wrong hallucinations as Jack kicked his legs, knocking him to the ground.

"You can't win like this," Jack said as he began kicking him until he heard his ribs start to crack. But still, he kept going,

kicking Shade's broken knee to throw him off-balance before grabbing Shade's head and slamming it into the wall. Shade tried to swing back, but he missed.

The blood loss was making his mind foggy, and the hallucinations began to creep back in. The sound of an operating table, its wheels squeaking as they rolled across the floor. The image of a saw turning on, knowing what it was going to be used for.

He swung at Jack one last time, but Jack caught his hand and kicked him backwards, knocking him over onto the glass coffee table, shattering it.

Shade lay there, surrounded by bloodied glass, defeated, as Jack knelt down over him. But it didn't

matter. Sara was gone now, and Jack couldn't get her. That was all that mattered.

"I'm sorry," Jack said. "I didn't want it to end this way."

With that, he raised the knife in his hand and started to bring it down into Shade's chest when something stopped him. His shoulder twitched in pain as something stabbed him from behind.

He turned to see Sara, holding the shard of glass that had stuck in the wall, now covered in his blood. He smiled.

"You came back."

She glanced over at Shade, the man who was trying to save her now on the floor, about to die himself. The voice of her friend, begging for help that Sara hadn't given her, rang in her head as she spoke.

"No one else dies because of me."

Jack sighed, nodding. He knew this was what she had to do. Just like he was doing what he had to. For a brief moment, they looked at each other in silence before he went at her with his knife.

She moved back, but the knife still caught her forearm, slicing through the skin. In pain, she tried

to punch him, but he was too quick, dodging it before shoving her back into the wall and moving closer to her with the knife.

He raised it, about to swing it at her neck, when he felt a hand grab his elbow. He turned to see Shade, now standing back up, throwing a punch.

Jack leaned back to dodge it, but it gave Sara a window of opportunity, and she used it to slice his back open with the shard of glass. Jack grunted as he turned and backhanded her, sending her back against the wall before Shade struck his jaw, causing Jack to stagger backwards as a tooth fell to the floor.

They both began to move on him, and Jack realized he couldn't win this. He couldn't fight them both, not at the same time. He had to think of something, like he had in the forest. Then he saw Shade's eye twitch, and that gave him an idea.

He swung the knife at Shade, who caught it and ripped it from his hand, just like Jack had known he would.

While Sara thought he was distracted, she moved to slice Jack's arm with her shard of glass. He stepped into her swing, getting closer as he let her slice his arm. Before she knew what had happened, he shoved her backwards towards Shade and watched it happen.

Shade was hallucinating so badly he was having trouble knowing what was real. So when Sara suddenly moved closer, instinct made him catch her, holding one arm around her shoulders so she couldn't escape his grip and using the other to hold a knife to her throat.

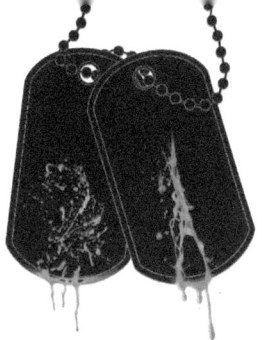

Chapter Twenty-Five

Shade stood, holding the knife to Sara's throat. He could hear her breathing in his arms. She wasn't struggling to get away, wasn't trying to fight his grip. He took a step away from Jack, moving closer to the door of the apartment, as Jack began speaking.

"Do it."

"No," Shade said, his head twitching back and forth slightly. He wasn't going to do it, he told himself. He couldn't. But then why hadn't he dropped the knife? His head twisted again as he started hearing the voices.

"You could have saved us!"

Shade closed his eyes and tried to focus.

"You're hearing them, aren't you?" Jack said. "The voices telling you that you let them die. The victims who knew that we could have saved them had we only done this sooner."

"That's not true," Shade said, trying to fight it.

"Yes, it is. In the forest, you attacked me because you didn't think it was worth this. But it is—we know that now. I stopped him, Shade. I stopped him before he could hurt anyone else. And then I kept going. After the Surgeon, I caught two more serial killers in a matter of months. Do you know what they were doing?" Jack stepped closer to Shade. "They were raping and torturing their victims for days before killing them. They killed two people within a week's time. But because I killed the woman in the forest, I could see clearly enough to stop them. How many more do you think they would have tortured if it had taken months like the Surgeon did? Four? Seven? Twenty? Would her life have been worth that many more victims?"

"He's right," a corpse beside Shade whispered into his ear. *"You could have saved us."*

Shade tried not to listen to them. Tried to block them out. But they wouldn't go away. His grip tightened on the knife as the hallucinations began to worsen.

"The Hangman is out there," Jack said. "He's already killed three people. How many more are we going to let him kill? Are we going to let him get to nine, like the Surgeon? Or are we going to do what it takes to stop him, together?"

'Don't listen to him,' Shade told himself. It wasn't worth this. But what if it was? Jack was right—he had stopped the Surgeon. He couldn't bring himself to drop the knife as he looked up and saw Nora standing in the corner.

"You see her, don't you?"

Nora raised her hand and waved at Shade before being dragged backwards by a man in a white doctor's gown. Shade started to cry out "no" but found himself unable to speak.

"We could have saved her."

Nora was raised up on an operating table as she began begging Shade to help her. He wanted to, but he knew this wasn't real. He couldn't help her; she was already dead, because of him. He looked down at the knife in his hands, trying to think.

"It's too late for her," Jack pleaded. "We can't save Nora. But together, we can stop the Hangman." He hesitated for a moment, an expression of shock spreading across his face as he looked at Shade, seemingly discovering a long-buried secret for the first time. "You know I'm right, don't you? You've always known. That's why you never contacted the director, isn't it? You never turned me in because you knew I was the only one left who could catch Urich. That's why, all those times I felt you watching me at my house,

you never attacked. You were willing to hide for eight months, let the real killer go, because deep down, you knew that I did what had to be done to stop the real monsters."

Jack stepped closer, speaking to him as a friend. "So help me do it again. Together we can still fix this. We can save the next victim."

Shade took a deep breath as he saw Nora one last time before looking back at Sara, still in his arms, with a knife to her throat, and in that moment, he knew what he had to do. Shade threw her backwards out the door before slamming it shut, breaking the handle off so she couldn't get back in.

"She is the next victim, Jack."

They stared at each other for a moment, realizing what each of them had to do. They didn't want to, but they had no choice. This only ended one way.

"I'm sorry," Shade said as he flipped the knife backwards in his hand.

Jack sighed and picked up a piece of broken glass. "I'm sorry too."

They stayed motionless for a moment longer before Jack swung.

Shade moved left, dodging the glass shard before crashing his elbow into Jack's nose and shoving him back against the wall. The sound

of the wall cracking filled the room as Jack went after Shade again with no hesitation. He swung the glass overhead, but Shade caught his arm. He then released his grip on the glass, letting it fall before catching it midair with his other hand and thrusting it into Shade's stomach.

In pain, Shade swung his knife again, but Jack just barely ducked under it, the blade slicing through the edge of his hair before he kicked

Shade in the ribs, violently lashing out as rain continued to drench everything in sight, Jack not relenting.

Shade lay there on the ground, taking it. Feeling his ribs crack with every kick. And every time another blow came, he could feel himself losing control. Could feel the memories of war coming back. Until finally, the day he was afraid of came.

Jack went for another kick, but Shade caught his leg and dragged him down to the ground with him. Before Jack could react, Shade was on him and pulled him back up, slamming him against a tree.

Suddenly, after seeing the look in Shade's eyes, Jack was afraid.

The knife was still in Shade's hand as he swung

at Jack, who parried the strike and returned one of his own. Shade dodged left and

swung again at Jack, who backed up just enough to miss it before pushing Shade against the wall and raising his shard of glass up, trying to bring it down towards Shade's eye.

Shade caught his hand just in time, the edge of the glass a hairsbreadth away from his pupil. They both struggled, Jack trying to shove the shard further and Shade resisting.

Finally, Shade managed to shift Jack's hand right, letting the shard fly forward, into the wall beside his head. He then dragged Jack's hand down the wall, the glass carving a line into it before the pressure finally cracked it and Jack was left defenseless.

Shade shoved him backwards and then swung his knife, forcing Jack back. He swung

again, forcing him back farther, until finally, he was backed against a tree with nowhere to go as Shade swung the knife again. Jack dodged, causing the knife to stab in the tree behind him. He swung once at Shade and landed it, but Shade barely flinched as he threw him back against another tree and grabbed his arm, twisting it backwards against the trunk, dislocating Jack's shoulder.

An agonizing scream filled the air as Jack was then thrown across the forest, through the trees, landing back in the open space, only a few feet away from the woman's body.

To Jack's horror, he looked up from the wet mud and saw Shade rip the knife from the tree and move closer to him.

Jack tried to stand, but his feet slipped on the mud and he fell back down into the wet ground. In an instant Shade was there, like a wild animal after its next kill, bringing its claws down full force

burying the knife into Jack's shoulder. Jack screamed as he kicked Shade backwards, buying himself a few more seconds. Shade had a knife, but he had nothing. He scanned the ground for more glass, but it was all either broken or too far away, and Shade was moving closer.

Finally, Jack did the only thing he could think of and took the pen from his pocket, the one he had thrown to Nora that day.

When Shade went at him with the knife, he blocked it and shoved the pen into the open cavity made by the bullet wounds. Shade screamed as Jack ripped the pen out and shoved it in again. And again.

He went for one last strike, shoving the pen forward. But to his horror, Shade caught his hand, and he saw the same look in his eyes that he had in the forest.

Horrific screaming filled the room as Shade twisted Jack's wrist backwards, breaking it, before

striking him in the jaw, blood spilling from his mouth as he tried to remain standing.

Before Jack could react, Shade's hand was on his throat,

shoving him back against a hollow tree at the edge of the open area, still in view of the body.

"Please," Jack begged as he felt the grip tighten. "I can stop him," he said, his voice breaking against the pressure on his throat. "I can make this worth it."

Shade didn't let up, and Jack knew he couldn't get through to him. Couldn't convince him that this was what had to be done. So, he did the only thing he had left to do as he saw how much Shade's eyes were flinching.

"Why didn't you save me?" Jack said, knowing Shade would see him as Nora, the girl they couldn't save. The girl he couldn't hurt.

It worked. Shade released his grip, and he backed away, confused, as Jack continued.

"You let me die."

Shade started shaking his head, trying to block out the visions, but it was too late. Jack tackled him to the ground, landing next to the corpse, and began beating him.

Over and over again, he struck him in the face, until finally, he wasn't sure what he was fighting for anymore. Was he beating Shade to death because

he'd tried to stop him from leaving, or because he didn't want anyone to know what he had become?

The thought sent chills down Jack's spine, and he suddenly stopped. He'd killed the woman because he had to, but he couldn't kill Shade. Not when he didn't know what the reason was for killing him.

He stepped away. He couldn't kill him, but he also couldn't let Shade turn him in. He still had to stop Urich. Make it worth something.

So as he walked away, leaving tracks in the mud, he pulled out his phone and began dialing the FBI to report Shade for murder.

"I'm sorry," he said as he walked away, seeing Shade still lying there, bleeding, looking at the corpse of the woman beside him in horror.

"I'm sorry."

Jack struggled to escape Shade's grip as his lungs erupted like fire from a volcano, trying desperately to get oxygen. But none came. Jack knew if he didn't do it now, he wouldn't get another chance.

"You could have saved me."

Shade's head twisted sideways as he backed up, suddenly back in the hospital room, surrounded by

blood-soaked walls, Nora's corpse standing right in front of him.

"You let me die," Jack continued.

Shade knew what he was doing, but he couldn't fight it. He stepped back in horror as Jack swung on him, knocking him backwards. Shade could hear the body bags around him being unzipped as he tried to swing at Jack with the knife, but he missed, and Jack knocked him back farther, this time into the wall, the pain loosening the knife from his hands, which Jack picked up.

Screams echoed in his head as he tried to think. He couldn't fight Jack like this, not while he was hallucinating. But he couldn't stop it.

Jack moved closer to him, twisting the knife in his hands.

Shade remembered something. Jack had something that bothered him too. Something that made him unstable.

The knife rose up as Jack readied himself to swing.

In one last desperate attempt, Shade reached up and ripped the dog tags from his neck, the ones still coated in Nora's blood, and swung them against the wall. The chain that held them raked against itself as it hit the wall, mimicking the sound of the chains from Jack's past.

Jack's head twisted sideways at the sound of it, which brought back the memory of feeling helpless.

As he looked up, he saw Shade as the Butcher, a monster heading straight for him. He was too afraid to move.

Shade tackled him to the ground. They both landed hard, feeling the extent of their injuries as they lay there still for a moment until Jack began desperately trying to reach the knife

"Stop," Shade begged.

Remorse filled Jack's voice as he spoke. "I've done too much to stop."

Shade found enough strength to reach over, and he lifted the knife up before Jack could reach it. Voices rang in his head as he began crawling closer.

"You couldn't save us."

He reached him, placing one hand on Jack's chest, keeping him down.

"You let us die."

Shade sighed as he raised the knife.

Jack knew it was over. Unless...

"You let me die."

Shade looked down, seeing Nora below him. He knew what Jack was doing, but it didn't matter. It looked so real to him, seeing Nora on the ground, him holding a knife on her. Tears fell from his face as he watched, knowing what he had to do, what he couldn't do before.

"You could have saved me."

"I know," Shade said, looking down at Nora. "I'm sorry."

Jack smiled for a brief moment before he saw the look in Shade's eyes.

"But I can still save her."

Shade brought the knife down into Jack's heart.

Then, once the unthinkable was done, Shade backed away from him, leaning his back on the wall closest to him, still on the floor. Shade sat there, not saying anything, as Jack began to fade.

"After everything," Jack said, his voice sad and broken, coughing up blood as he spoke his last words, "I thought you'd understand."

A tear fell from Shade's face as he watched his friend die.

Soon it was over, and as blood continued to leave his chest, Shade closed his eyes, knowing he didn't have much longer. He rested his head back on the wall and felt himself drifting off.

The memories, the horrors—they were finally over.

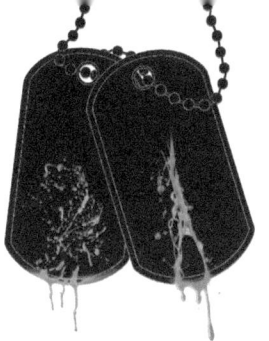

Chapter Twenty-Six

Sara slammed into the door with her shoulder. She had to get inside, had to try to help. She couldn't run again. Couldn't leave someone else to die. She had already gone to the next apartment and called the cops and an ambulance, but she wasn't sure Shade could wait that long. She slammed into the door again, cracking the wood as it finally burst open.

Inside, Jack was lying on the floor with glassed-over eyes, staring at the ceiling, a knife lodged in his heart. Beside him, Shade was on the floor, leaning back against the wall, his eyes closed.

"No," she said as she ran up to him. He couldn't be dead. She couldn't handle someone else dying to save her. She checked his pulse, hoping to find something, some trace of life, as the words of her friend echoed in her head.

"Help me."

There it was. She felt it: a pulse. He was still alive. She looked at the bullet holes in his shirt and inspected the wound behind them. The wound was too deep. She couldn't risk pulling the bullets out. But if she didn't do something, he would bleed out before the ambulance could get there.

Running to the bedroom, she looked in fear at the med kit lying on her bed. Chills ran down her spine as she realized what she had to do. What she hadn't done last time.

She grabbed the kit and ran back to Shade. From it, she pulled out the needles and tubes she needed and began setting up a blood transfusion.

She connected a needle to a tube and inserted it into her own vein right below her wrist. She then wrapped white cloth around it tight to make sure it didn't come out before raising the tube up and clamping one side down to stop the flow and force the blood down the other side. She watched as O negative blood, the universal donor, left her wrist and flowed through the small hollow opening, up to the clamp, and back down.

"Come on, stay with me," she said as the blood reached the other end of the needle. She couldn't lose him. Couldn't let another one die.

She waited for a drop of blood to push out of the needle before placing it in his vein. Then all she

could do was wait and listen to the voice of her friend.

"Please," she begged, a tear falling from her face. "Please don't die."

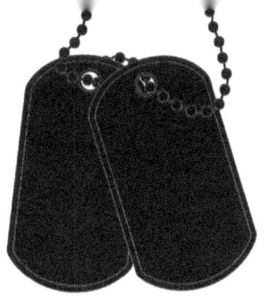

Chapter Twenty-Seven

Where was he? Underneath his feet was soft green grass, and all around him stood tombstones, each one a monument to someone who had faced down the horrors of war and hadn't made it back, each one a reminder of friends not forgotten. But behind the tombstones, watching him like a shadow, stood Nora.

He looked at her in shock, still trying to figure out what was happening. She was wearing his dog tags, and she was smiling. Not a single drop of blood was on her.

She said nothing as she walked over to him and took the dog tags off, handing them back to him. They were pristine silver, just like when he had given them to her. He tried to speak to her, but he couldn't find the words.

She smiled before running off, leaving him alone, holding the dog tags in his hand.

Shade woke up. He opened his eyes and saw that he was in a hospital bed. A sharp pain stung in his chest, and it hurt to breathe, but he was alive. Beside him, Sara was sitting in a chair, watching him.

Immediately, he knew what she had done. He couldn't have made it to the hospital without getting blood first. She had saved him. But that meant it wasn't over.

He closed his eyes as he spoke to her, pain filling his voice. "Why didn't you just let me die?"

She raised up in her chair. "I could ask you the same question."

He didn't respond, instead sighing. He wasn't dead. It wasn't over.

"For what it's worth, I'm sorry I shot you." Her eyes turned soft and sympathetic. "Why didn't you say something in the prison? Why didn't you try to tell me?"

Shade glanced towards her, eyes full of sorrow and pain. "Would you have believed me if I had?"

Sara gave him a warm smile. "No, I guess not."

For a few minutes they just sat there, each one not knowing what to say, not knowing what to do, now that it was over, now that they had survived.

Finally, Sara was ready. "So, I told Director Williams what happened. Evidently, he had to call

in a lifetime of favors, but the incident at the field office is being overlooked, and the blame for the bodies you left at the prison is being placed on Jack for opening the cells, with the official record stating that you acted purely in self-defense, which is more or less true anyway. You've also been reinstated. Williams says when you've recovered, you can get back to it, so you better rest up. Plus"– she smiled–"you'll have a new partner to train."

Shade cut his eyes to her, surprised.

"I talked to Williams about that too," she said. "He approved it. You're stuck with me."

"Are you sure that's the best idea?" Shade said, groaning from the pain in his chest. "After all, I did just kill my last partner."

"True." Sara shrugged. "But he kind of had it coming." Her tone then grew serious. "He was right about one thing, though."

"What's that?" Shade asked, staring off into the distance, not wanting to accept it. He was supposed to die at the apartment. It was supposed to be over.

"That you can't move on by standing still. You've got to focus on moving forward, saving as many people as you can. Besides, you seemed to be sleeping okay. No hallucinations?"

"They'll come back." His voice was, tired, weary. "They always do."

Sara thought about that for a moment before leaning closer to him. "You know, in the interrogation room, when I asked you to kill me, I meant it. I couldn't take the memories anymore—the voices in my head. But still, you saved me. You gave me a second chance. So maybe the hallucinations will come back. But if they do, this time you won't only have to see the people who died. This time, you'll also be looking at the one you saved."

Shade considered that. For his entire life, he had only known bloodshed, only been able to kill the enemy, not save his friends. But now, looking at Sara, the one person he had managed to save, maybe she was right. Maybe he could move on. He looked down, seeing dog tags in his hand. They were a bright silver. She must've cleaned Nora's blood off them. He had never been able to do it, but now, it felt right.

"So," Sara said, holding up a file marked Hangman, "shall we?"

Agents Shade and Sara will return in

ACE OF ████

Acknowledgments

Firstly, I would like to thank my family: my mother, my father, and my older brothers for their continued support, as well as for being the best beta readers a writer could ask for. I couldn't do it without y'all.

Thanks also to MiblArt, who did the cover art and the formatting for this book. I couldn't have asked for a better company to work with. They not only designed an amazing cover but also did fantastic interior artwork, and formatting as well.

Thanks to my editor, Eliza Dee, who did the copyediting and proofread.

Also, I would like to thank all the amazing booktubers, Instagrammers, and bloggers who reviewed my debut novel, Nightmare, last year, including but certainly not limited to:

- Lezlie: The Nerdy Narrative
- Allen: Library of Allenxandria
- Alex: Alex Nieves
- Jessie: Jessie Mae
- Erin: Erin Megan
- Kayla: Kayla Lenzen
- Richard: Are You Into Horror
- Mark: Slowly Red
- Mindy: Mindy's Book Journey
- Cristal: Reading and Retail
- Linda: Linda's World of Books

- Joshua: Working Man Reads
- Jane: Lady Jane Books
- David: David's Book Reviews
- Ali: Book Binge
- Andrew: Get Write On In
- Ariel: Reading and Whatnot
- Merphy: Merphy Napier
- Erika: The Perks of Books
- Regina's Haunted Library
- Nichi: Dark Between Pages
- John: Books of Blood
- Sara: Sara MG Reads
- Carla: Carla's Book Bits
- Kim: Native Book Warrior
- Stormi: Storm Reads
- Gloria: Gloria McNeely
- QandTG: QandTG
- Manda: Bear Pig Loves Books
- Carol: Carol Marie Reads
- Sharon: In Love With Books
- Irene: Well Worth a Read
- Marie: Marie McWilliams
- Nakia: Nakia's Hideaway
- Steve: Talks About Books
- JJ: The Bearded Bookworm
- Devin: DevK Thrillz
- Brad: Brad Proctor
- Kristi: Reader of the Written Word

Lastly, thank you, for reading this book.

Author Bio

CHAD NICHOLAS is a horror, mystery, and thriller author who particularly loves writing foreshadowing and plot twists, which can all be seen in his debut novel, *Nightmare*.

When he's not writing, Chad spends his time studying for his mechanical engineering degree, watching movies, and reading comic books. Chad was also ranked #1 in the world on the Teen Titan challenge map from *Batman: Arkham Knight*, a fact he is very proud of.

If you are reading this, it means Chad has finished writing his first crime thriller, *Shade*, and is now working on his third book, a slasher novel that he's very excited about.

Keep in touch with Chad via the web:

Instagram: @thechadnicholas

YouTube: Chad Nicholas

Website: thechadnicholas.com

P.S. If you are someone in charge of DC Comics, please let Chad write a graphic novel about Scarecrow's origin story, so he can finally shut up about it. Like, seriously, it's all he talks about. How awesome the idea is, how terrifying Scarecrow would be. Please just help make it stop.

I'm begging you.

Books by the Author

NIGHTMARE

SYNOPSIS

Had it come back? No, it couldn't have. He had buried it for good. Or at least that's what Scott told himself. But what if it had? Was that why the scarecrow now watched him?

But the more Scott tries to ignore it, the more the evidence begins to pile up. So do the bodies. Because sometimes, the dead don't stay buried. Sometimes the monster survives.

As the bodies mount, and the secrets of his past grow more haunting, Scott must do whatever it takes to save his family. But what if by doing so, they find out what happened all those years ago? What if they realize what he did?

Scott learns that there is no escape from his own past, or the crows that have crawled out of it. He can only watch, as his life is turned into a living nightmare.

REVIEW QUOTES

"A Jekyll and Hyde for the modern age."
—John Mountain, Books of Blood

"Nightmare is a psychological horror at its best!"
—Nichi, Dark Between Pages

"This book was a page turner – the story was so interesting and fast paced that I almost read the whole book in one sitting. I thought I had it figured out so many times as far as where this story was going and I was wrong at almost every turn."
—Lezlie Smith, The Nerdy Narrative

"Chad might just be the plot twist master! Perfect pacing, great characters, extremely believable yet terrifying circumstances and amazing plot twists. This is now on my favorite Horror novels list for sure!"
—Ariel, Reading and Whatnot

It's the one you just read.